ONE DEAD HEAD

by Ian McCollum

Published in 2019 by FeedARead.com Publishing

Copyright © Ian McCollum

The author or authors assert their moral right under the Copyright, Designs and Patents Act, 1988, to be identified as the author or authors of this work.

All Rights reserved. No part of this publication may be reproduced, copied, stored in a retrieval system, or transmitted, in any form or by any means, without the prior written consent of the copyright holder, nor be otherwise circulated in any form of binding or cover other than that in which it is published and without a similar condition being imposed on the subsequent purchaser.

A CIP catalogue record for this title is available from the British Library.

Somersgill is a fictional village but most of the other places named in this book exist in and around Chesterfield, Derbyshire. All characters and events in this publication are fictitious and any resemblance to real persons (especially the author), living or dead, is purely coincidental.
Any mistakes in police procedures or equipment are mine alone – it's just a story and I hope you enjoy it.

Guidance for Headteachers from the author:
'Those who can – do'
'Those who can't – write about it'

Best wishes,
Ian

ONE DEAD HEAD
by Ian McCollum

Prologue

A few people saw the police car pull up. Sunday night in Somersgill rarely provided distractions so some even stayed around to see what would happen next. A black sports car arrived and a man fiddling with a large bunch of keys stepped out. He approached the police officers, spoke a couple of sentences and then unlocked the gate. The three men walked up the drive into the school. A light came on. Silence. Ten minutes later the two police officers emerged and returned to their car. The small group of onlookers had already dispersed so the shout surprised both policemen. They looked up. A woman was leaning out of the window of one of the flats opposite the school entrance.

"Thank you for coming, gentlemen. It was me that phoned. There were some boys climbing on the school roof. Your arrival scared them off. I hope I haven't caused you any trouble?"

"No madam, none at all. There were several calls, thank you. Did you recognise any of the little so and sos?" replied the younger officer.

"I'm sorry but I didn't; too dark. They sounded like teenagers, I think."

"Not to worry. Could I have your name, just for the report?"

"Oh yes, my name is Margaret Mallender – I'm a School Governor, you know."

"Goodnight, Mrs Mallender," stated the older PC.

"Miss," she replied with a cheeky grin as she closed the window.

"Goodnight, miss," he repeated to himself. "Well, that was yet another waste of time," he grumbled to his colleague.

"Oh, I don't know, Miss Mallender looked a bit of alright to me – I have a thing about the attractive older woman. I think I might have to go around and conduct a further interview sometime!"

"The youngsters of today!" grumbled the older guy. As they drove away, they looked at each other and simultaneously burst out laughing. It didn't last long; they were sent on another job seconds later.

The third man reappeared at the gate – but he didn't lock it. Instead, he walked to his car, started it up and drove into the schoolyard.

The office light stayed on.

When all the lights in the surrounding residences were extinguished, dark figures arrived at the gates from several directions. They studied each other in silence before disappearing into the school grounds.

-

Like many of the villages on the northern edge of the Borough of Chesterfield, Somersgill had all the potential to have become a real dump. That it didn't fall into that trap was due to the resilience of its inhabitants. 'Poor but decent' was a description that could accurately be thrown at the people of many abandoned mining areas in North-East Derbyshire.

Somersgill was luckier than some; it still had a good pub, a Miners' Welfare, a Spar, a well-used charity shop and now the inevitable TESCO Express. Unemployment was high but crime was low. Some small companies had opened units in the new industrial estate close to the main road and there was cause for optimism; the village had a future.

What really kept Somersgill going was the popularity of its two schools. Since the arrival of Headteacher George Carmichael, the primary school had gone from strength to strength. At around the same time, the secondary school had been re-born as an academy and was also making phoenix-like progress. For the first time in a generation, children from outside Somersgill were being transported in to share the quality of education on offer.

So, Somersgill wasn't a bad place to live – most of the villagers were good people. Most – but not all.

Chapter One

Monday July First, 6:30am

Despite the time of year, it was dull and grey but then you can't expect too much this early in the morning.

Pete Barker was still drowsy as he approached the school's main gate and he fumbled through his overall pockets to find the right bunch of keys. "Three more bloody weeks," he thought, "then the bloody kids'll be going on their bloody holidays and I'll be left in bloody peace."

This often-repeated soliloquy calmed him and he was able to insert the appropriate key in the oversized padlock.

As he swung half the gate open, he hesitated. "What the hell's that?" He stood still and looked around for a few moments before setting off in the direction of the surprise.

On the bare tarmac of the playground was a bunch of keys. He recognised it immediately. "Careless – not like him!" he thought as he looked around again. Nothing else was out of the ordinary so he pocketed the keys and returned to the entrance to complete the job. Having secured the heavy iron gates, he drove his old Vauxhall inside and parked it in the usual place outside Boiler House No.1.

Still mystified by the appearance of the Head's keys, he immobilised the alarm and wandered over to the School Office. His curiosity turned to concern when he spotted the Head's old sportscar parked in the middle of the junior playground. Pete's pace quickened as he approached the office door and he patted his pocket to make sure his mobile was in the right place.

The outer door was locked but that presented no obstacle; he walked into the office and noticed nothing out of the ordinary. The door to the Headteacher's office was closed so he tapped briefly and tried the handle. Now that was strange – it was very rare for this door to be locked.

Pete's capacity for imagination had always been limited but the hairs on the back of his neck were certainly doing a dance now.

Another set of keys was produced and he opened the door very slowly.

For an old guy, he was surprisingly spritely – he just made it outside before he threw up his breakfast.

The young constable who was first on the scene did too. However, to his credit, he did have the nerve to go back inside to check for vital signs.

Fortunately for the two unhappy blokes, someone made of sterner stuff was soon to arrive.

With a quite unnecessary squeal of brakes, a blue Mondeo pulled up behind the response car and out stepped Detective Sergeant Amanda Sharp. Within seconds the aptly named detective was equipped with overshoes and gloves.

"Where?" she asked the constable.

The youngster began to lead the way inside.

"No! Just point!"

He did – and, five seconds later, he heard from within, "Fuck me!"

Even in his weakened state the constable was able to think, "Yes, please!"

Like almost every male at the station, he would have given his right arm to spend the night with the unattainable Ms Sharp.

The detective swept out into the open, phone in hand. "Yes, everyone – the whole murder team," she demanded down the line. She turned her attention to the caretaker. "Name?" she asked.

"Barker, Pete Barker."

"You're the school caretaker? You found the body? You phoned in? Is that the only open gate?" DS Sharp knew the answers to her first three questions but the fourth demanded a response.

The still stunned Mr Barker nodded – and immediately received a barrage of instructions. "Check the locks on the other buildings then let whoever needs to know at the Local Authority the school is closed for today. When you've done that come back here – do not leave the premises – do not make any other calls – do not use your mobile."

"I can't close the school, I'm only the bloody caretaker – that's the boss' job!"

"If that's him in there, I don't think he's in any condition to do that. You've got my authority – do it!"

"Is it okay if I phone Mrs Jennings, the Office Manager, she can send out texts to tell parents the school's closed?"

"Yes, do that – but say it's a police incident – police instruction – only that - understood?"

"Local radio station?"

"No!" On a couple of previous cases, Sharp had had positive dealings with the News Team at Peak FM but it was way too early for unnecessary publicity.

Barker nodded and ambled away.

The sergeant turned to the constable, "Dawson isn't it?"

"Yes, sarge."

"You've obviously been inside – what did you touch?"

"Only his wrist, sarge. I needed to see if there were any signs of life."

DS Sharp almost chuckled. She'd seen quite a few dead people during her career but this one was by far the most dead. "Go to the gate and stay there. Don't let anyone in except our lot." She looked at her watch. "It's seven o'clock; the keen teachers will be here soon. Get their names and phone numbers and send 'em home. Tell them to stay at home until they're contacted. Don't tell them what's happened – it's a 'police incident' – nothing more. If appropriate, make a note of how each one reacts to the closure; they're all suspects."

As Constable Dawson jogged off to his allotted place, Amanda hit speed dial on her mobile.

Day's DAY 1
7.00am
DCI Derek Day was having a well-earned lie-in. It was to be his first full day off for weeks and he'd only been vaguely aware of his wife, Jess, creeping out of bed to get the kids up for school. She'd promised he could sleep until 9.30 – and then they were going clothes shopping. He didn't mind shopping on his one day off because he needed stuff – and shopping for stuff he actually needed gave him a logical pleasure.

He'd just dropped back into a good sleep when his mobile rang. He rolled over, cursed silently and sat up to examine the caller ID. After a few seconds his eyes focused on an instantly recognisable number. "Oh, come off it, Mandy, it's my day off – I was fast asleep in bed - call some other poor s…"

"I'm certain you'll want to see this one yourself, boss," she interrupted as she tried hard to picture her DCI lying in bed. She needed a distraction from the hideousness she'd just viewed. Pyjamas or buff? Buff - now that would be a sight worth seeing.

Day reached over and took a sip from last night's glass of water. "Go on, what is it?" he sighed.

"The Headmaster at Somersgill Primary – dead as a doornail!"

"A Headteacher? It'll be a suicide!" Day's apparently flippant comment was only a half-joke; Jess worked part-time in a school and the detective understood some of the pressures.

It was in bad taste but DS Sharp was all business. "Good theory, boss – but I've never heard of anyone killing themselves by bashing in their own face fifty or sixty times!"

"Wait a minute! Somersgill? It's not George Carmichael is it?"

"Yep, that's the name on the office door. Do you know him?"

"I've met him; he used to work with Jess. I'm on my way. Have you sent for the cavalry?"

"Of course." The detective's flat tone suggested she was slightly insulted by the question. They both cut the call at precisely the same moment.

A shout downstairs was required. "Jess, shopping's off. Sorry, love!" That wasn't the only thing that was off, he had promised his recently widowed mother she would be involved in the trip to Meadowhall. He hated to let her down; she was one of those rare older people who gave everything and demanded nothing in return except, perhaps, the occasional shopping trip.

DCI Day was a fast mover. Within twenty minutes he had washed, shaved and dressed in his number one work suit. (It had been due to be demoted to number three that very day.) During that time, he'd also phoned the station and asked for a response car to swing by and pick him up – only to be told there were only two on duty in the whole district and both were fully occupied. One was already at the murder scene and the other was attending a breakfast domestic in Boythorpe.

Cursing budget cuts under his breath, he yelled downstairs once more. "Love, I'm going to need the car; can you get a cab to take the kids in? Sorry!" He wondered what percentage of sentences he exchanged with his wife ended with the 'sorry' word.

Jessica Day was unusual amongst police wives; she totally understood the irregularities of her husband's chosen career. Besides, he was such a considerate man, she found it almost impossible to fall out with him.

"No probs," she replied. As he entered the kitchen she added, in a passable impersonation of Bugs Bunny, "What's up, Doc?" Alice and Sophie laughed.

Day didn't. He shook his head, kissed three foreheads and walked out without another word.

As he climbed into the car, his wife came out of the house and called, "Dee, if you can get the car back here by lunchtime, I'll take your mum out for an hour or two." She thrust a Thermos Flask and a slice of toast in his hand. Jessica Day was the only person on the planet allowed to call Derek, Dee. Anyone else would be risking life and limb.

"Thanks, love. Will do!" he replied through toast crumbs as he started the engine. She was a definite candidate for the 'best wife in the world' award but, later on, he would ruin her day; she had always spoken fondly of the ambitious Deputy Headteacher in the classroom next door to hers in her previous school. This would hit her hard.

-

Arthur Ross lied about his age and enlisted in the army at the outbreak of war in 1939. After a tough time in basic training, Arthur was a changed lad. He'd learned to use his brain more – and his mouth less.

Fighting in North Africa and Italy, he proved himself to be clever, capable and, above all, steady under pressure. Senior officers spotted his qualities and he rose quickly through the ranks. No one else knew that

Arthur had to concentrate very hard on being steady – as a young teenager, he'd had a strong tendency to go crazy when things didn't go his way. It was a good job he had the tendency under control – sort of.

6th June 1944, Gold Beach, Normandy
22-year-old Captain Arthur Ross was lying in a shallow shell crater in the bloodstained sand. Like all the men around him, living and dead, he was pinned down by a single machine gunner in a concrete bunker built into the sea wall about fifty yards ahead. The German was good. Almost every movement on the beach attracted a short burst of accurate fire.

As he lifted his head to glance around, a bullet ricocheted off the very top of the captain's helmet. He fell back into his refuge, head pounding and his vision blurred. He had no idea how many seconds had passed before his sight returned almost to normal but he knew more of his men had died while he was doing nothing.

For the first time since he'd left training, he began to feel a little crazy. "Oh, bollocks!" he said to himself before cocking his Thomson sub-machine gun. Somewhat louder, he yelled, "Covering fire!" and jumped up, screaming like a maniac, to run zig-zag at the enemy post. He was hit four times during the desperate charge but impetus carried him on to collapse at the base of the bunker. For almost a minute he didn't move but then his comrades saw him twist his body so that his back was against the rough concrete. Agonisingly slowly he straightened his legs until his head was only a couple of feet below the exposed machine-gun's smoking barrel. Again, a terrible pause - but there was no reaction from above - the German had seen his bullets strike home so anticipated no trouble from the imagined corpse collapsed below his gun slit.

Captain Ross unclipped a Mills grenade from his webbing and pulled the pin. In his agony, he almost dropped the damn thing but, after a moment's juggling, he managed to lift his arm and toss the grenade backhand through the slit. It exploded before the German could even register surprise.

The craziness subsided and everything went black for the captain. His knees buckled and he slid, in graceful slow motion, down the rough concrete wall leaving a wide, bloody smear across its surface.

No orders were given, but all the survivors of Captain Ross' Company leapt to their feet and charged up the beach and onto the road behind. The stalemate was ended.

That was the end of Arthur's war; he was in hospital until late in 1945 - when he limped into Buckingham Palace to receive his country's highest award for gallantry.

A year later he was strong enough to take over management of his father's farm in Derbyshire. Arthur proved to be a clever chap and the business grew. A Victoria Cross hero with a limp and plenty of money was never short of girlfriends, but Arthur had a problem; his doctors had told him that one of his wounds meant he would never be a father. Despite this, the love of his life, Diane agreed to his honest proposal and they were married in 1951.

Five years later, the miracle happened – Diane gave birth to a baby girl. Inevitably, Arthur insisted the child be named Victoria Charlotte.

Arthur Ross wasn't at all typical of those bravest of the brave; he was proud of his achievement and was happy to tell the story, if asked. This talkative hero, now well on the way to becoming a rich gentleman farmer, couldn't believe his luck when his daughter Victoria chose to fall in love with a chap called Alan Day.

Arthur wasn't over impressed with the man his daughter had chosen but he loved the name. "You'll have my blessing, not to mention some financial support, if you allow me to choose the names of your children!" he declared when Alan asked for Victoria's hand. Since the couple were committed to their careers and had more or less decided they had no intention of ever having any children, both readily agreed.

Arthur was delighted and built them a lovely little house close to the edge of his largest farm.

It was no second miracle – but accidents happen! Victoria gave birth to a fine, healthy boy ten years later. Despite their surprise, Alan and Victoria were delighted with their beautiful baby - but alarmed when Arthur reminded them of his right to name the child. In fairness, he gave them choices for his grandson's given name: David, Donald, Damien and Derek were all acceptable but there was to be no negotiation on the child's official first name.

Thus, our detective came into being. Overlord Derek Day would soon begin his own long-term battle with that unusual name - and his inherited tendency to go quite crazy.

Chapter Two

At just thirty-three years of age, Derek Day had achieved the limit of his ambition in the police. He had no desire to progress beyond DCI; sitting behind a desk and becoming overburdened by paperwork held no attraction. Interacting with the worst kind of criminals was his forte. He was, however, a gentle man who hated violence – it was a paradox that he was so terribly good at it.

7.40am

By the time Day arrived at Somersgill Primary School there was quite a traffic jam in the street that led to the main gate. He parked behind a new cream Mini Cooper. In the driver's seat, an attractive but obviously irritated young woman was tapping the steering wheel. He made no comment as he walked past but laughed inwardly, "And teachers complain about low pay almost as much as coppers!"

Three cars further on, he reached the head of the queue where a young constable was bent into the window of an SUV, apparently in some sort of argument with the woman driver.

"Good morning, Mr Dawson. Having trouble?"

The constable looked up. "Oh, morning, sir." Like all his lowly colleagues, Dawson was amazed that the DCI knew everyone's name and always addressed the PCs, 'Mr' or 'Ms' – never by their rank. "This is Ms McAllister, sir. She's the Deputy Headteacher and she wants to know what's going on and why I won't admit her."

Day twisted his head to indicate Dawson should stand back and he bent to the open window. "Good morning, Ms McAllister. I'm Detective Chief Inspector Day. If you'd be kind enough to drive in through the gate and park just inside, I'd be grateful. Please wait in your car and I'll come and talk to you in just a while."

Ms McAllister looked up into the vivid blue eyes of an otherwise rather non-descript man and recognised a calm authority. "Thank you, Inspector," she said and, with a well-practised withering look at the constable, engaged gear and moved forward.

"Don't let anyone else in, Mr Dawson. I expect you've been told to collect info. and send them home?"

"Yes, sir. By DS Sharp."

"Quite right!" He threw his car keys to Dawson. "As soon as help arrives and this jam has cleared, go and get my car and bring it inside, will you?"

"Of course, sir," he replied – while thinking, "I wish all senior officers were as polite as you."

It didn't take a genius to work out where the action was; there were cars, vans and several white suits next to the big sign that read 'SCHOOL OFFICE'. Day approached the shapeliest white suit and said, "This had better be good, Mandy. It was supposed to be new suit day today."

Recognising an attempt to make everyone relax a little, the detective sergeant raised a half-hearted smile. "I couldn't risk the dire consequences of you not being one of the first on the scene. This is a proper job; very dirty!" She handed him the protective gear. As he struggled into it, she filled him in with scant details. "Photographer's done a preliminary and the doc's in there now. We think it's the Headmaster, George Carmichael – although he hasn't been identified yet. My guess is he's only been in there a few hours but we'll know more soon."

Day looked around. White-suited technicians were crawling over a black Honda S2000 abandoned in the middle of a playground. "Who found him?"

"Caretaker – he opened up as usual at around 6:30am. He says he saw a few things out of the ordinary so he came over to the main office straight away."

Day looked at his watch. 8.05am. "Well done, Mandy – getting everything moving so quickly at this ungodly hour." He moved towards the office door. "Doc!" he shouted, "Make a space, the crimefighters are moving in!"

DS Sharp had already been in the office so she stood aside to let her boss go in first. DCI Day stepped into the doorway and surveyed the scene, taking in every detail. His team thought he had a photographic memory – he hadn't, he was just extremely good at looking.

Doctor Smythe was kneeling next to the body, temporarily obscuring much of the view. Without looking round, he exclaimed, "Ah, the Chief Inspector and his right-hand woman have arrived – all will be well with the world!"

The victim was on his back strapped into a fallen office swivel chair. Each forearm was fastened to the chair's armrest with three black cable ties. His ankles were strapped together and another longer cable tie secured them to the chair's base.

Doctor Smythe lifted himself up and stretched. "He really upset someone, didn't he?" he said with the nonchalance of long experience. He turned to the Detective Sergeant. "I concur with your initial assessment, Sharpy – midnight to 2am." DS Sharp rolled her eyes. Any other bloke calling her 'Sharpy' would probably have received a sharp jab on the nose, but Dr Smythe was a family friend – almost as ancient as her granddad.

"Just a quick look, Doc, then we'll let the techs in," said Day.

Day flinched at the sight of the body. The man was completely naked. Around his neck hung a bloodstained cardboard sign. But it was the face that caused the most horror – it wasn't there! It was pulverised beyond recognition. The front of the skull was completely caved in. Splintered bone and broken teeth mixed with brain where eye jelly had oozed through dried blood.

"Crikey, he really upset somebody!" whispered Day as he used a gloved hand to turn the sign around. It read, 'Sexual Predator – not fit to be near children'.

Given the savagery of the beating, there wasn't a lot of blood around but damage to the office was extensive. Cupboards, drawers and filing cabinets were all open and their contents spread around. An empty wallet stood open on the desk. An empty Cadbury's Milk Tray tin labelled 'Petty Cash' was discarded in one corner. However, the closed Venetian blinds were undamaged.

"Why so little blood around, given the facial injuries, doc?" He paused but the doctor didn't respond. "Oh, I get it!" Day had noticed the edge of a much larger spread of blood underneath the body.

Doc Smythe laughed. "I'm thinking of changing careers. I'll train as a detective and hope one day to be as bright as you two. Yes, Chief Inspector, he was probably dead before the facial attack. Looking around the room for clues, I would say he was pushed back very violently. The chair toppled and his head struck the edge of the filing cabinet drawer. Dead in seconds, I'd say. You've already noticed part of the pool of blood and there's a lot more underneath."

"Yes, thanks Doc – I need a new Detective Constable so I'll put your name forward. Any other ideas?" Day knew the doctor's first impressions were often right and he always took them very seriously. "What about the weapon used on his face?"

"Almost certainly a hammer – or similar."

"Why bash his face in? The thief lost his temper when he couldn't find much money? Doesn't make sense." DS Sharp was answering her own questions. "There's real personal hatred in the hammer work. It's possible someone thinks their child's been abused and Carmichael's got away with it – until now!"

"Any of those scenarios are possible," added Day. "They'll be our first lines of attack but this was a carefully planned assault by at least two people. My first guess is this was intended to be a photoshoot, Mandy – a total career-wrecking humiliation. That sign suggests to me there's a chance they might not have meant to kill him."

"You think the robbery angle might be a cover for blackmail then, boss?"

"Possibly – but obviously, something went dramatically wrong. Perhaps he denied or admitted something that sent them off the rails. The facial thing seems pretty hysterical – perhaps when they realised they'd killed him they just went berserk?"

"Crime of revenge then?" asked DS Sharp.

Day nodded. "Or a deranged, cold-blooded killer! Whichever – we need to find him pretty quickly."

"Him?" asked Sharp.

"Good point, Mandy. This is far from the type of wounding I would expect from a woman, but we have to keep open minds. How sure are we this is Carmichael?"

"95%. The Caretaker only got a glimpse before he puked but he didn't seem to be in any doubt."

There was a bit of commotion outside. "Sir, sir! Important information, sir!" Day recognised Dawson's voice; had reinforcements arrived?

The two detectives left the crime scene to the specialists and went to see what Dawson was so excited about. "I've found witnesses, sir!" The young PC beamed enthusiasticly as he handed over Day's car keys. "A lady in the flats opposite says she called our lot last night to complain about youths on the school roof. A car came by and two of our lads met the Headmaster and went inside for a look around. She says the police left a little later, she spoke to them, sir. She didn't see the Headmaster leave."

Day turned to DS Sharp. "Call in, find out which officers and the time of the call."

"Sorry, sir. I've already done that while I was listening to the witness. It was PCs Rouse and Adams; the call came in at 10.44pm," interrupted Dawson.

"Good lad. Get them in here!"

"They're already on the way, sir."

Day looked at the young PC. 'Potential!' he thought. The scene in the playground was beginning to look much more organised and then Day realised why. Old 'Pug' Davies, a veteran detective from Ripley HQ, had arrived and was warming to the task of Crime Scene Coordinator. Day nodded to his oldest friend and then turned to his DS. "Mandy, go with Mr Dawson and get everything you can out of this woman."

Three Detective Constables had also arrived and they were despatched to do interviews, check if the CCTV was working and organise a search for the murder weapon and the victim's apparently missing mobile phone.

As he crossed the playground towards Ms McAllister's parked SUV, Day called his boss, Detective Superintendent Halfpenny. She was all business. "Hello, Derek. What have we got at Somersgill?"

"A proper nasty one, ma'am. Gruesome death – could be murder or manslaughter. My guess is it was personal but witnesses say there were vandals in the school grounds."

"Victim?"

"95% sure it's the headteacher, a George Carmichael."

"Only 95%? Proper brutal, then?"

"Certainly is!"

"You got all the help you need?"

"Yes ma'am, they're arriving in droves now – including some off-duty lads and lasses."

"Keep me informed. This is our first decent murder for quite a while. Let me know if you need anything more – within reason, of course. I'll worry about overtime – eventually." She hung up.

However, also arriving in droves were onlookers. Parents half-expect to receive a 'school closed' text during winter bad weather, but this was mid-summer and lots of blue lights were involved. The people of Somersgill rarely had anything to get excited about.

Seeing him approaching, Ms McAllister climbed out of her car. "What is going on?" she demanded. "Look, it's chaos out there!"

It certainly was. Apart from the almost total gridlock of cars, fifty or sixty pedestrians of all ages were milling about. There were now two constables on the gate but they weren't having much success at establishing a cordon.

"Let's try and help, shall we?" suggested Day and the two approached the main entrance.

Ms McAllister took control. She smiled at the crowd and called out the names of some of the individuals in the gathering. "I'm sorry everyone, but school is closed today. There's been a major break-in and a great deal of damage has been caused. The police are sorting it out.

Please go home, blocking the street is making it very difficult for the police to do their job." As far as she knew, it wasn't a lie – the Deputy Headteacher still had no idea what was going on. Probably.

The crowd began to disperse, those adults with jobs to go to moaning about childcare issues.

"Thank you," said Day, "that was really helpful. Is there anywhere we can go for a chat, not in the office?"

The Deputy Head led the way into a separate building and opened the door to a classroom. In the next room they could hear the muted voices of a DC trying to calm the caretaker.

"Come on, Inspector, what's happened? Why all the secrecy?" she asked.

"Let's have a seat. Tell me, how well do you know Mr Carmichael? Is he married?"

"George, yes - he's married to an ex-colleague. I know him pretty well; I've worked with him for three years. We don't socialise or anything but... What's happened to him?"

Day made a mental note to find out why the wife wasn't curious about her missing husband's whereabouts.

"I'm sorry to have to tell you that we've discovered a body in the school office. We think it might be Mr Carmichael."

Ms McAllister's reaction surprised the detective. "*Might* be him? What do mean 'might'? Do you want me to go over and have a look? Obviously, I'll be able to identify him." Ms McAllister was made of stern stuff.

"No, but thanks for the offer. Does Mr Carmichael have any clear identifying marks?"

"Apart from being jaw-droppingly handsome you mean?" There was no trace of sarcasm in her voice.

Day thought, 'not now' but said, "Anything distinctive on his arms or legs for example."

"I've never seen him naked, if that's what you mean? That's not my sort of thing!"

Day raised one eyebrow. Not a value judgement, just a query.

"He has a rather long jagged scar on his arm… right arm. Motorcycle accident in his youth, I've heard. Has he been disfigured?"

99%! The scar had been clearly visible despite the deep ridges of the cable ties.

"I'd rather not say at the moment. You've been terribly helpful, so far. Tell me, is it possible for you to get me a copy of the full staff address list without going into the office?"

"Of course. I can do it from this PC." She pointed to a workstation behind the teacher's desk.

"Brilliant! Do that would you, then I think it would be best if you went home. It's very important you don't discuss what I've just told you with any of your colleagues."

Day left Ms McAllister to her computer and went next door to listen in on the interview with the caretaker.

DC Dominic O'Neil nodded to his boss and received an instruction to continue in return. "Mr Barker, do you feel able to talk the Chief Inspector through what happened when you arrived at school?"

There was a slight tremble in the caretaker's voice as he began his recount. "Yes. I knew something was wrong as soon as I opened the gate. Mr Carmichael's keys were in the middle of the playground. He's never careless with keys."

"Where are those keys now, Mr Barker?" interrupted Day.

The Caretaker fished in his overall pocket and pulled out a bunch of half-a-dozen keys. "Here."

"Drat!" thought Day - but he was pleased to note that the DC was already offering a plastic evidence bag. As the keys were dropped inside, Day added to himself, "Better late than never."

"I got my car inside and then I noticed the boss' car in the playground. He only ever parks it there when he comes in to work in the holidays."

"Show us where you found the keys; can you remember?"

The caretaker levered himself out of the chair and headed for the door. "Pretty much, yes."

As they walked out of the building, Day asked, "Do you normally go to the Head's office first thing?"

"No, the alarm override switch is in the boiler room so that's always my first job. Wait a minute, though, I've just thought – the alarm wasn't on in the admin block."

"Would that be unusual, given someone was inside?"

"Yes. Well, of course." The caretaker hesitated. "But the doors were locked, even the door to Mr Carmichael's office. I've never known him lock it before. I had to use his own key to get inside." He shuddered.

'Bugger!' thought Day. 'That's the last possible hope for forensics gone.' But that thought also raised a question. "You went inside, saw a terrible sight – and yet you still had the presence of mind to take the key out of the lock and put it in your pocket?"

The trio left the building and walked between two of the three separate blocks on the way to the main gate.

Barker took his time before shaking his head. "No, it's an old habit. I always take a key out before I open any door. Always have done. Sort of automatic; don't know why." He stopped and looked around. Pointing to the tarmac, he said, "Here. The keys were here, more or less."

Day judged the distances. "Tell me, does the main gate padlock require a key to lock?"

"Yes, sir."

"And it was definitely locked when you arrived?"

"Yes, sir."

"Is there a main gate key on Mr Carmichael's bunch?"

"Oh yes. He often comes in at weekends and holidays when I'm not here."

Day did a 360 turn. Dropped or thrown, he wondered.

Day turned to DC O'Neil. "You're a fit young fella, Dom. Could you throw a bunch of keys this far after locking the gate from the outside?"

The DC grinned because he was the same age as his DCI – and nowhere near as fit. He was big and good-looking but was the one member of the team Day had never really warmed to. He was regarded by some female officers as 'full of himself' – a member of the 'I like me, who do you like?' - club.

The Detective Constable took the evidence bag from his pocket and weighed it carefully in his hand. "No problem, sir," he offered. "But why would anyone do that? It's just leaving evidence around for us."

"Ours not to reason why, Dom! Have SOCO grab the lock and check for evidence around the gate."

"Already done, sir."

Day nodded his appreciation, now feeling guilty about his ambivalent attitude towards O'Neil.

He turned to the caretaker. "Thanks for your help, Mr Barker. I'd like you to go and find somewhere quiet away from the admin building and give a full statement to DC O'Neil. If you can find somewhere to make you both a cuppa, he'll be twice as pleasant, I promise."

The DCI had spotted the arrival of just what he needed. Striding through the gate was the tall figure of PC Dipa Sindhu. He waved her over. "In the nick of time, as usual, Ms Sindhu. You're coming for a ride with me; we're going to visit a woman who doesn't know she's a grieving widow – yet."

-

Overlord Derek Day had the kind of early childhood poets write about. From his toddler days, he was allowed to roam his doting grandfather's farm almost at will. He ran, climbed and dug holes. He built dens and played with the livestock. By the time he started school, he was strong and fit – a proper farm boy. Infant School presented no problems. This boy was bright and took learning in his stride. He smiled constantly and was thus usually surrounded by many friends. At the beginning of each school year, the new teacher would raise eyebrows at Derek's name in the register but make no comment.

His problems began in the second half of Junior School. The topic, 'The Second World War' was universally popular with the boys and Derek produced some beautiful work. Then his teacher, Mr Heathcote, asked Derek to take a note to his hero grandfather.

Yes, Arthur Ross VC would be happy to come into school and talk to Derek's class about his experiences in the war. He would even bring in his treasured medal to show the children.

At first, Derek couldn't see a downside – he was already popular, what could possibly go wrong?

The talk was a great success. Captain Ross was unusually modest about his heroism and even allowed some of the children to handle his most valued possession. His description of his part in Operation

Overlord was just graphic enough to stimulate the children's interest. His talk ended with an expression of love for his family.

"You know, children, I have a wonderful family and they all humour me when I want to talk about my medal. Why, I even called my daughter, Victoria. And, of course, you all know my wonderful grandson – Overlord Derek Day! D-Day!"

Most of the children didn't register the name at all, but seven boys turned around and gave Derek some very funny looks.

"Oh, dear!" he thought.

Chapter Three
8.45am

"You shall be my chauffeur, Ms Sindhu," he called as he threw her his car keys. He gave her the Carmichaels' address, settled into the passenger seat and began dialling his mobile. "Oh yes," he added, "I would very much like to arrive in one piece."

The Indian PC acknowledged Day's joke with the tiniest of smiles. She was a decent amateur rally driver as well as an accomplished all-round athlete. She'd just qualified to drive the high-speed pursuit cars. Within a couple of years, she would also qualify to join CID, if she chose. She was a woman of few words. "Sir," she said as the car swept through the gate, barely giving the constable on duty time to make a gap in the tape.

"Mandy, anything useful from Mr Dawson's witness?"

"You bet, sir. She's only the bloody Chair of the School Governors and she lives in a second floor flat overlooking the main gate. She showed us a photo of her and Carmichael together – they made a good-looking couple. I reckon she had the hots for him and I could see why. I told her we'd found a body and she teared up right away. Anyhow, last night she saw some youths on the admin block roof and phoned in. Half a dozen, she reckons. Young teens – fourteen or fifteen she's guessing. About half ten. Obviously, it was pretty dark so she didn't recognise any of them. I don't think it'll be too difficult to find them, though. I thought I might pay a visit to the local secondary?"

"Good idea – but not yet; if they're in they're not going anywhere. I'll want a briefing around noon. We'll organise who's doing what then. In the meantime, get the uniforms to check on the neighbours. Someone else might have seen those kids and might be able to give us a name."

"I've already got a house to house started, sir!"

"Of course you have! Sorry! Any luck with the murder weapon… or the victim's phone yet? What have the two PCs on the call out got to say for themselves? SOCOs found anything helpful? CCTV working?"

"Which would you like me to answer first, sir? Not everyone thinks as fast as you, you know." DS Sharp sounded a little exasperated.

"Sorry, again, Mandy. I know they don't – but I also know that *you* do!" Day lifted one eyebrow in amusement. His DS was already impressive and learning fast – Sharp by name and sharp…

"Fair enough. No to the weapon or the phone – but I've got Phil in the office trying to track down Carmichael's phone details – shouldn't take long. Nothing from the Sci lads - and the two plods from last night simply corroborated the witness statement; but the kids had scarpered before they arrived. The headmaster unlocked the gate for them and the three of them had a good look round and checked all the doors. He told 'em he was going to stick around for a while and he was still in good condition when they drove away. They're good lads though – they both offered to stay and help with the searches. CCTV hasn't worked for ages. Ms Mallender, that's the Chair of Govs. we just interviewed, says they could never find enough spare cash to get it fixed. It wasn't a priority because they didn't have much vandalism. The school's become really popular since Carmichael arrived three years ago. To be 'outstanding' in such a run-down village is quite spectacular – apparently."

"He wasn't very popular with someone, was he? Keep up the good work, Mandy. Call if you get anything useful. We're just arriving at Carmichael's house. See you at twelve if not before."

He then rang County Offices and, despite the early hour, was passed around before someone had the clearance to tell him there were no actual or pending investigations into Carmichael's professional reputation. As far as all the suits were concerned, the man was beyond reproach.

The Headteacher's house was rather more humble than Day had expected; a small semi in the less affluent end of Newbold. Combined with the old sports car Carmichael had been driving, it gave a relatively 'hard up' image. "Perhaps Headteachers aren't paid as much as I understood these days," he thought aloud.

PC Sindhu said nothing; she was steeling herself for the part of the job every police officer hated.

9.00am

They could hear the doorbell ring inside the house for quite a while before the door was opened.

Another surprise. The woman who answered the door was much younger than expected and, despite some evidence of recent tears, was extremely pretty. She was also obviously pregnant. She said nothing but her gaze flicked from Day's sombre face to the PC's uniform and back. Her eyes betrayed many emotions – none of them good.

Day held out his ID. "DCI Derek Day and PC Sindhu... are you Mrs Carmichael?"

She gulped. "Yes."

"Your husband is George Carmichael, headteacher of Somersgill Primary School?"

"What's wrong? What's happened?"

"May we come inside, Mrs Carmichael?"

The look in her eyes appeared to Day to be close to panic. She said nothing but opened the door wider and stood aside. They found themselves in a small, sparsely furnished living room. Mrs Carmichael pointed to a sofa and collapsed into an armchair.

She looked increasingly anxious. "What's he done?" she whispered.

'Strange question,' Day thought. "There's been an incident at school, Mrs Carmichael. We've found a body. Male. We believe it's your husband. I'm so sorry," he said.

What remained of her colour disappeared and she began shaking. "How did he do it?" she asked.

This whole excursion was becoming increasingly puzzling.

"Before we go on, Mrs Carmichael, could you tell me if your husband has a problem with his right arm?"

"Right arm?" she repeated. "No, he's incredibly fit!"

Day saw a flash of optimism cross her face – but then she crumbled. PC Sindhu tensed, ready to leap into comforting action.

"The scar? Oh God, you mean the scar?" The tears began. Through the sobs she stammered, "You didn't answer my question. How did he do it?"

"Do what, Mrs Carmichael?"

"Kill himself."

DCI Day hesitated; he'd been the bearer of bad news many times before but he hadn't experienced a reaction anything like this. "I'm sorry, but what makes you think it was suicide?"

She put her head in her hands and cried for fully five minutes. Sindhu moved over and gently rested her hand on the new widow's shoulder. She offered to make tea but Mrs Carmichael shook her head. The PC looked at Day with wide eyes under raised eyebrows. He could tell what she was thinking. 'Why do women police officers always get the really shit jobs?' Day gave her a slight smile and nodded in the direction of what he assumed was the kitchen.

A few moments later the PC returned with a glass of water.

"Mrs Carmichael?"

Suddenly, she stopped crying and blurted out, "Because it's the last thing he said to me as he went off last night!"

"Go on."

"I took a phone call about nine o'clock. A woman's voice told me George was having an affair with Melanie Price – she's one of his teachers – I'd suspected it myself and when I told him what the woman had said, he denied it and we had a terrible row. The phone rang again about eleven and then he stormed out. As he left, he yelled, "I won't be back. I'm going to put an end to this!". He didn't come back."

"That must have been awful for you. What did you do?"

"I thought it must have been Price on the phone so I did a call back. It wasn't. It was some automated response from the police. It must have been a problem at school; it's never happened before. The caretaker usually deals with that sort of thing."

"Do you mind if PC Sindhu checks your phone to see if it's saved the number of the first call?"

Mrs Carmichael nodded and Sindhu went to the phone. Seconds later, she shook her head.

Day wondered why Mr Barker hadn't mentioned anything about not responding to a police call out.

"That's right. Neighbours phoned in because there were people in the school grounds. Your husband met a couple of our officers and unlocked the gate for them. They all had a good look round and then our chaps left. Your husband told them he was going to stick around for a while. It's possible the intruders came back and he disturbed them."

"You mean he's been killed… murdered?"

"Yes. I'm sorry – but, I think your confirmation of the arm scar means the victim is your husband."

She looked up. "Why do you say that? Everyone at school knows him."

The awkward moment. No point in applying a sugar coating. "I'm afraid he was badly beaten. His face is a bit of a mess."

And then the tears really flowed. "It's my fault! I thought the call came from her so I told him to get out and never come back. I told him I didn't care if he killed himself! I told him I hated him! That's the last thing I said to him – it's all my fault!"

At least that explained him remaining in the office – or did it?

"None of this is your fault, Mrs Carmichael. Is there someone we can call… to be with you?" said Day in his best sympathy voice.

"I'll call my mum when you've gone – she's only a half-hour away."

Day stood up. "Would you like Ms Sindhu to stay with you until your mother arrives?"

"No!" Mrs Carmichael's demeanour had changed. Anger was setting in.

"Okay, if you're sure you'll be alright. One of my officers will be around later to talk a little more about last night. She'll organise any support you feel you might need."

No further words were exchanged. Mrs Carmichael stood, walked to the door and opened it. As he passed, Day handed her his card and smiled sympathetically. PC Sindhu followed her boss to the car.

"Well, what do you think? Woman's first impressions?"

She didn't start the engine but thought for a while. "A bit weird really. Seemed genuine shock at first but then... I don't know. Was she acting?"

"She was rather good if she was!" retaliated Day. "But I share your uncertainty. What did you think of the set up? A bit frugal for a headteacher?"

"Definitely a second marriage. Affair with a colleague – first wife took him to the cleaners. New wife resigns, gets pregnant – both skint!"

"Time you joined us superior beings, Dipa. You've got all the cynicism you need to be a detective." He gave her another address from his list. "Let's go and have a chat with Miss Price, the alleged affair."

Up to that point, PC Sindhu didn't even know DCI Day knew her first name. As she engaged gear, she made another detective-type observation. "It's a bit early in the day to be running a tumble dryer – in July!"

Mrs Carmichael watched them drive away. She picked up the phone but she didn't call her mother. She was shocked that her former colleague, Melanie Price actually answered but she still used the statement she'd prepared for the answering machine. "I told you last night you couldn't have him and now you'll never have him, you fucking bitch!" She slammed the phone down and collapsed in her chair.

-

For some reason he didn't quite understand, young Derek was suddenly on the receiving end of a lot of name calling. At first, it was just his friends having a bit of fun but it soon developed into the kind of hurtful taunting that children excel in. Okay, it wasn't as bad as being a boy named Sue, but the school bullies soon latched on to Derek's granddad's revelations.

Derek was a self-confident, easy-going kid but the taunts began to wear him down. 'Lord Derek' and 'Lord Overday' seemed innocent enough but, when accompanied by exaggerated mocking subservience, soon became tedious. Very sensibly, Derek discussed the problem with his mum and that made it worse. Mrs Day went to see the Headteacher and asked him to intervene. He did. He called in the offenders and very calmly pointed out the error of their ways. All promised to lay off the name-calling and be sweet little boys. That should have been the end of the matter but, at the end of the day, five boys were waiting for Derek outside school.

"Ooh, your mum's all annoyed – I bet you call her cross Victoria!"

Derek could just about swallow insults against himself but his precious mum deserved no criticism. He rounded on the chief bully and put his fists up like the boxers he'd seen on TV.

He got pasted! He managed to make his way home and staggered into the kitchen covered in blood. His mum and granddad were in there – and both exploded!

There followed a massive family row about what to do. Victoria wanted to go back to the school and raise hell but granddad, supported by newly arrived dad, favoured a different approach.

"It's you going to school that got him beaten up anyway!" declared Arthur Ross VC. "I'm going to teach him to look after himself!"

Realising he was too old to do a proper job on Derek's real education, Arthur called in a favour. That's when the boy came under the none-too-gentle influence of Sam Hardisty, former Royal Marines unarmed combat training instructor.

Sam's favourite expression was 'when you're in a difficult situation, there's only one rule...' Trouble was - the 'one rule' was actually several different tactics – but that didn't matter, Derek mastered them all.

"First, think - can I get away from this without fighting? – if you can – do. If you can't escape, work out which of your opponents is leader and study his face. His eyes will tell you if he is going to attack – as soon as you are certain he will - retaliate first! One punch to put him down. Chances are, his mates will think twice about continuing."

Sam then taught his protégé twenty ways of putting an opponent on the floor; none of them bore any resemblance to 'Queensbury Rules'. That didn't matter to Derek, he perfected them all - despite hoping he would never have to use any.

"Now, if you're really outnumbered and in a life-threatening situation - find a weapon – anything that will impose fear or hesitation on an attacker."

Young Derek was fascinated by the ways in which everyday objects could be used to defeat even the most determined enemy. He practised every technique he'd been taught until his prowess actually began to scare his mentor. When self-defence was required, Derek had become a formidable fighter. But those skills, combined with his tendency to go crazy, could be catastrophic for any opponent – and for Derek. He discussed his hidden tendency with Sam. The old ex-marine told him that 'crazy' was not a useful state of mind in a violent confrontation and the boy must do everything possible to perfect a calm control. Derek promised he would learn to recognise the symptoms and always try to maintain his self-control. The boy (and later the man) would keep his promise – most of the time!

By the time Derek left primary school he felt well able to defeat any enemy that came at him. All the training didn't change his personality, though. He was still bright, kind and carefree – when no tormentors were around! This boy now oozed a calm self-confidence – well known to be a great antidote to bullying.

Derek's teenage years would have been less eventful if his granddad hadn't contradicted one vital aspect of Sam's advice. On the day before his grandson started secondary school life, Arthur said to him, "Never start a fight, my boy – but never walk away from one."

Chapter Four

Like almost all her colleagues, Melanie Price had been perplexed when the constable on the school gate told her to go home and wait by the phone. However, she did as she was told. The jungle telegraph began; the staff of Somersgill Primary called each other searching for information.

"It must be serious vandalism or a massive break-in," she repeated to several colleagues. Picking up the fifth call, she recognised Angie Carmichael's voice immediately. The vitriol in the tone shocked her but she had no opportunity to respond before the line was cut.

Melanie folded over onto the settee and cried for a few moments. Suddenly, she sat up and looked around. Like all her colleagues, she was expecting a phone call from the police, but what if someone actually turned up? Time to remove anything that might interest a nosey policeman.

When everything was in its correct place, Melanie spent a good five minutes reapplying make-up. She was just in time; a car with a dark-skinned woman driver pulled up at the end of her drive. From behind the curtain, she could also make out a man in the car. Neither got out. The man had a phone to his ear. Eventually, he put it down and said something to the driver. Both nodded before opening the doors.

-

"Ms McAllister, you got home alright? Do you feel up to giving me some background information?"

"I'm fine, Inspector. How can I help?" The words were right but the voice sounded decidedly shaky.

"Have you had many calls from colleagues?"

"I've been bombarded – but I did exactly as you told me. Everyone got the 'I've no idea what's going on' standard reply."

"Good, much appreciated. You're not going to like this question but has there ever been any suspicion about Mr Carmichael abusing children?"

"Good God, no!" she blurted out. "George loved children – I actually think he'd have killed to protect any one of them. Sorry, that wasn't very appropriate," she almost sobbed. "No, totally unbelievable!"

"Thanks for that. Do you mind talking about Mr Carmichael's private life? Tell me about his wife."

"Angie? She was a teacher with us when George took over. She fell for him hook, line and sinker. She's a good-looking girl and she wasn't subtle about her crush. She pursued him and, eventually she got him. He left his wife and moved into her flat. Angie resigned to avoid any trouble from the local authority. He went through a difficult divorce and they got married. They bought that house last year. He spent a lot of time crying on my shoulder."

Day realised that the Deputy Headteacher was a font of information and gave her the opportunity to talk. "So, not a happy marriage, do you think?"

"Not particularly! George never fully committed; he missed his kids and, I think, his first wife, too – although she was a total bitch during the breakup."

"Mrs Carmichael… Angie, mentioned Melanie Price. She suspected there was an affair?"

"So do we all. It's been staffroom gossip for a couple of months. Strong feeling of déjà vu! But Mel is a totally different kettle of fish to Angie… brilliant teacher. Absolutely driven to do the best for the kids. And she's got plenty of money – independent means - but still comes to school every day and works her socks off!"

"That's really helpful, Ms McAllister, I'd be grateful if you'd stay at home for the rest of the day and keep up the 'don't know anything' act. Someone will be round later today to take a statement. Thanks again." He hung up before she had chance to add more scandal.

Outside Melanie Price's address he told his driver she had been right on almost every count. PC Sindhu smiled briefly; her planned passage into the detectives one step closer.

Day studied the house. A modern detached house in Walton didn't come cheap and a flick of curtain told him they were being observed. The Mini Cooper on the drive confirmed that Ms Price was the woman he'd walked past in the traffic jam outside school.

"Two things to look out for when I tell her the bad news: is it a surprise – and is she the affair?"

PC Sindhu nodded and they climbed out of the car.

-

Derek's first few weeks in Year 7 at Brookside School were uneventful. He was a bright kid and he settled into lessons with enthusiasm. He also made a couple of good friends but the three of them made an unlikely group. Derek was normal height for a twelve-year-old but Aiden Smith was, by far, the tallest kid in the year group. This 'gentle-giant' was also very black with proud family roots back in Jamaica. In complete contrast Kirk McDonald was small and round with a smiley, baby face – he could have passed for seven if he'd needed to. They all worked hard and, during breaks, never stopped laughing at each other's stories. Kirk and Aiden became regular visitors to Derek's granddad's farm.

It was December when the first trouble started. Kirk arrived in school one cold morning in tears, "Some big lads shoved me over and pinched my lunch money," he sobbed to his mates. Derek and Aiden dutifully escorted their friend to the Year Tutor and explained the situation.

"I'm sorry to hear that, McDonald. Did you recognise them? Where they from our school?" Miss Kendal was all sympathy.

"I don't think so; I didn't recognise them and they weren't in our uniform," responded Kirk.

After a few more enquiries, the teacher decided there was little the school could do. She handed him two pounds from her purse, suggested he tried a different route to school and told him to try and forget about the sad incident.

Which would have been just about acceptable if it hadn't happened again the next day.

After they had calmed their distraught friend, Derek and Aiden agreed they would get up early the following day and meet at Kirk's house to walk into school with him. Kirk had been taking a shortcut through the edge of a local park and it was very quiet at this time on a misty cold morning.

Four teenagers were hanging around the swings when they saw the trio emerge into the open. "Oh, look," said the one nicknamed, 'Gobby', "our fag-money kid's got an escort!" The other three laughed and turned towards the group of younger boys.

"Hand it over, shorty!" demanded Gobby, holding out his hand. Aiden was as tall as the aggressors and made the first comment.

"Leave him alone!" he shouted.

In return, he received a sharp poke in the chest from Gobby's finger. "And what are you going to do about it, you black fucker?" Gobby's pals added their own racist abuse before Derek intervened.

"That's not very polite," he said calmly. Derek had already assessed the dynamics of the attackers. Gobby

certainly lived up to his nickname but he wasn't the leader. The lad who was slightly taller, slightly broader and slightly quieter was the dangerous one.

"Ooh, listen to Mr Smoothy!" whined Gobby. "What are you going to do about it, shortarse?"

"I'm going to ask you to give back the money you took from my friend yesterday and the day before." Derek was the soul of pleasantness but inside, a conflict between the promise he'd made to his mentors and the tendency raged.

"Cheeky twat!" yelled Gobby and made to push Derek hard in the chest. The younger boy stepped aside and pulled sharply at Gobby's outstretched arm causing him to accelerate and fall flat on his face.

"Bastard!" snarled Gobby as he rolled and tried to get up. His attempt was stopped by a sharp kick in the ribs - but Derek was only half concentrating on the lad on the ground. The leader was moving in with a roundhouse right cross aimed directly at his face. Unexpectedly, Derek leapt forward inside the incoming blow and jumped up to smash his forehead into the leader's nose. There was an explosion of blood and the lad collapsed in a screaming heap. Gobby was transfixed on the ground and the other two teenagers both took steps back and exchanged puzzled looks.

"I think your friend might need a visit to Calow Hospital. Have you got some bus fare?" The two older boys still standing recognised that the expression on Derek's face suggested there was plenty more trouble if they wanted it. But he was young... and small... this was crazy!

It wasn't – Derek was pleased he'd kept his self-control and executed two of Sam's strategies perfectly.

The two undamaged lads helped their buddies to their feet and limped off.

Derek turned to look at his two friends who were both standing wide-eyed and open-mouthed.
And that was just the beginning.

Chapter Five
10.00am

Day knocked on the door and wasn't surprised when it was opened immediately. The woman he had passed earlier faced him with a puzzled expression. The detective couldn't help himself. 'Wow, she is pretty,' he thought. 'Why didn't I have teachers who looked like that when I was in school?' Then a darker thought entered his head. 'So, our Mr Carmichael liked to surround himself with attractive young women, did he? Maybe McAllister was right - he wasn't an abuser of children – but what about good-looking adult females?'

His hesitation caused Melanie Price's expression to change to one of slight alarm.

"Oh, good morning. Are you Miss Price from Somersgill Primary? This is DCI Day and I'm PC Sindhu." The constable had come to the rescue.

"Yes. Has there been a break-in? Did they smash the place up pretty badly? Oh hell, it must have been if they've sent a detective!"

Day recovered. "May we come in, Miss Price?"

"Of course – and please call me Mel."

"Are you alone, Miss Price?" Day was all formality now.

They were escorted into a large lounge/dining room perfectly kitted out in top quality Swedish style. "Yes, I live here alone." Price noticed that both officers were impressed and felt obliged to tell her much repeated story. "I know what you're thinking. How do I afford this? Simple, my mum and dad won a fortune on the lottery and decided we should go on a world tour. I didn't want to go, I love my job, so they bought me this house and put half a million in my bank account. They buggered off and I haven't seen them for nearly two years! Aren't I the lucky one?"

Day nodded and gave a half smile. If this woman knew about the murder, she was a damn good actor. "Let's all sit down, shall we?" he said. "You're right that there has been some trouble at school, but it's much worse than you've guessed."

Price's expression turned to near panic. "What?" she stammered.

Day wanted a reaction and put the boot in. "The Headteacher's been murdered!" That should give him some impression of the depth of the relationship.

Price laughed. "George? Mr Carmichael? Murdered? You're joking!" but the laughter in her voice had already died. "You're not joking, are you?" Seeing the dour expressions on both officers' faces, she crumbled and began to cry.

PC Sindhu leapt up and found the kitchen. Getting a glass of water was a good excuse for a nose around.

As Price began to recover, she blurted out the inevitable questions. "Murdered? Why? How? Are you sure it was murder?" She realised her mistake and quickly added, "Not an accident?"

"Accident?" he thought. "Was she there?" Could this be another hint at suicide? Why was Carmichael giving off that vibe to people he worked with? "Were you close?" he asked.

"He was my boss and I really liked him. He was good to me. I'm good at my job, Inspector and George gave me a lot of support and help." As she sipped some water, tears began to flow once more.

"He was good to work for, then?"

"Brilliant! He's a great… he was a great man. Really good at his job. He's turned the school around in just a couple of years. It was dire before he arrived!"

"He didn't appoint you?"

"No, I started a year before. It was my first teaching job; I loved the kids but, if George hadn't arrived, I would have quit before now."

Day decided to get the crunch question in before she did too much thinking. "Were you lovers?"

Her eyes met his and grew wide. "What?" she almost shouted. "What would make you ask that?"

"Kind, good-looking boss; young teacher who clearly adored him. It's happened before. You're not denying it?"

"You bet I'm denying it!" she yelled. "I'm his friend! I'm friends with his wife! Angie? Does she know? Have you seen her? Is she alright?" More crying as she put her head down almost to her knees. "Angie's gorgeous... and pregnant. Even if I'd wanted to – I wouldn't have stood a chance!"

"Fair enough," offered Day. "I'm sorry to have to ask but could you tell me where you were between eleven and 3am last night?"

"Inspector, I'm a teacher. I worked all day yesterday marking and planning. By nine, I was exhausted. I went to bed and was flat out until the alarm woke me at six this morning."

"Alone?"

"Alone!"

"When did you last see Mr Carmichael?"

"When I said, 'Have a nice weekend' to him on Friday – about 5.15, I think."

"You've not heard from him over the weekend?"

"Why would I? I've told you – we're colleagues NOT lovers!"

"Thank you, Miss Price. We'll leave you in peace now. Is there anyone we can call to keep you company? We'd prefer it not to be one of your colleagues from school. A boyfriend perhaps?"

"No, I'll manage. I've got plenty to keep me busy. I'll show you out."

As they left the house, a light drizzle began. "Bloody typical July weather!" moaned Day as they walked down the drive. As soon as both were seated in the car, he asked the inevitable question, "What do you think – is she an affair?"

PC Sindhu paused. "I really don't know, sir. Fifty – fifty, no more. You know, I'm sure I've seen her before."

"Pretty memorable face, I'd say," he said. "Think about it. Let's drive. I want to meet the ex-wife before the twelve o'clock briefing."

As the police drove away, Miss Price was congratulating herself. 'Four years doing a drama degree wasn't wasted,' she thought.

Day's mobile rang before they'd got as far as the end of the road.

"Sorry to bother you sir," came the unmistakeable voice of Jimmy Hammond, the veteran PC who sometimes managed Reception at Beetwell Street nick, "but I thought you might like to know about a 'misper' report that's just come in."

"If you think it's relevant, go ahead."

"Scott Grimshaw, aged fifteen, reported missing by his mother. He left for school at the normal time but never arrived. He's at Somersgill Academy; a bit of a likely lad so he's on truant-watch. School rang his mum when he didn't turn up. The School's done a check and all his mates and girlfriend are accounted for. His mother rang us to do the 'good parent' thing – she's frightened to death of Social Services."

Day looked at his watch – still only 10.45. Mrs Grimshaw was certainly protecting her own back.

"Give me the mother's number, please Mr Hammond – I'll give her a call."

As PC Sindhu drove in her unique, assertive style towards their next visit, Day dialled the allegedly distraught parent.

"He's been giving me a right hard time lately, Inspector. Oh, he's not bad when he's here, but he's staying out late – he didn't get in till midnight last night – I need me beauty sleep ya know. He's been horrible at school and even worse in the village – I get phone calls every day – bad influence on younger kids they keep saying! And Social said they'd be after me if I don't sort him out."

It was a tale Day had heard dozens of times before. "You have my sympathy – but don't worry, we'll pull out all the stops to find him. Any idea where he'll be if he's playing truant?"

"They sometimes hang around near the canal – back of Sainsbury's – it's a bike ride away but I think they've got some sort of den there. I was just putting my coat on to go and have a look when you called."

'I bet you were!' thought Day – but he said, "That would be really helpful, Mrs Grimshaw. Ring the station if you find him, will you? I'll send someone down there to have a look as well. Thanks, bye." He hung up before she could get any more moans in, but he had a bad feeling about this.

-

Scott Grimshaw had a good feeling about this. Okay, he'd had to kill time because the old woman said she wanted to see him at twelve noon and, if he'd gone to school, he'd have never escaped. He lay in the clearing, resting his head on his rolled-up blazer and thought about what he'd achieved and how rich he was going to be in an hour or so.

A couple of weeks ago an old woman had stopped him in the street and given him a small box. "It's a present that comes with a job offer – but don't show it to anyone if you want more of the same." She'd disappeared before he'd had chance to think through what had happened but he had the sense to get home and go into his room before opening the mysterious gift. Inside was an old Nokia phone and its charger. More interesting was £50 in new fivers. A note said, 'Keep the phone charged but don't use it – I want this box and everything in it, except the cash, back. £200 more if you do a simple job for me. Tell no one.'

He was in heaven. Someone wanted a reliable helper – was she a spy?

It was two weeks before the phone rang and he received detailed instructions. "This Sunday night at 10.30 get some lads on the roof of Somersgill Primary and make a lot of noise. Don't try to break in – if you set off the alarm, the deal's off. Run for it when the cops come. If you get caught, the deal's off."

Brilliant! £250 for a jaunt that he'd enjoy doing anyway! Being a secret agent was so fucking easy.

Job done – and Scott and his mates hadn't stuck around to see the consequences. He was on his way to school next morning when the phone rang again. "Well done, I'm very pleased with you. Go to the 'Fallen Oak Clearing' at noon. If you come alone and bring the box, you'll get your £200, plus a bonus," said a female voice. "Keep our secret and you'll get more work."

'She must be a spy!' Scott thought, 'She knows where our secret hideout is!'

The 'Fallen Oak Clearing' was in the woods to the north of Somersgill but it wasn't as secret as Scott imagined. It was off the beaten track for ramblers and dog-walkers but it was occasionally visited by furtive young lovers late at night.

A few spots of rain broke Scott's train of thought and he got up cursing to tug his blazer over his head before setting off on the last leg of his journey to wealth. In the films James Bond never gets rained on!

-

Day called DS Sharp. "Mandy, change of plan. Go down to the Academy and see if you can find out about a fifteen-year-old called Scott Grimshaw. He's missing – was out very late last night and appears to have a fan club of younger lads. He might be one of the kids on the roof. Find out where he is; intimidate his mates." Day knew that DS Sharp was good at intimidation.

"Okay, boss. I'm more or less finished here. Pug's got the scene under control. I've spoken to the top woman at Matlock – devastated, although she said she didn't know the victim well. They're going to close the school for at least a week and send out a team of counsellors as soon as the news breaks. One of their senior people is on his way as we speak – he'll coordinate all the education and kids side of things. There's a lot of press gathering outside and I've been doing the 'no comment' thing so they're getting pretty pissed off."

"On your way out, tell them there's been a 'major incident' and we'll release a statement after our briefing – it'll be about one o'clock. While you're at it, we'll move the briefing to the school seeing almost everyone's already there. Get Pug to organise a classroom and some sarnies, will you? Any luck on the phone or murder weapon?"

"No, sir - to the last bit – and 'yes, sir' to all the other bits. I'll set off now so I can be back for twelve." Although DS Sharp worshipped Day, she liked to keep him on his toes with a bit of light sarcasm.

Chapter Six
11.00am

Day didn't laugh until the line was cut. As they pulled up outside a neat little house in Cutthorpe, he said to his driver, "It looks as though somebody's in. Right Ms Sindhu, let's do our third lovely job of the morning and see what the ex-wife's reaction is!"

The woman who opened the door was no 'pretty young thing' – she was a thirty-something classical beauty. Day couldn't help admiring the deceased's taste in women.

"Mrs Carmichael, I'm DC…" he got no further before a brusque interruption.

"No, I'm not Mrs Carmichael anymore. Miss Davison to you!"

Day didn't flinch. "I'm so sorry, Miss Davison. I'm DCI Day and this is PC Sindhu. We've got something we'd like to discuss with you. May we come in?"

She looked at her watch. "Very well, but you'll have to be quick, I've got an appointment at twelve."

"Just a few minutes," offered Day as they were escorted into a pleasant living room. "Tell me, are you the former wife of George Carmichael?"

"Huh!" was all she said but at least she added a nod of confirmation.

"I'm sorry to have to tell you this but George Carmichael was found dead earlier this morning," said Day flatly.

The result was a full minute of silent shock then she looked up and said, "Good!" Another few moments of silence then, "Who's going to pay the fucking maintenance?"

Appearances can be deceptive.

Miss Davison sat down heavily on the edge of a coffee table and rubbed her forehead. "Oh, Inspector, what must you think of me? Poor George – what was it – road accident? He never could part with that damned Honda, could he? Midlife crisis – younger women or a sportscar, that's what they say, isn't it? Pity George wanted both." To everyone's surprise, she began to cry. "Was it a car crash?" she repeated.

"No, we believe your ex-husband was murdered," said Day without emotion.

She looked up with wide eyes. "What? How? When?" she stammered.

Day noted there was no 'who'. "It was late last night – around midnight. I'm sorry but, I have to ask, where were you at around that time last night?"

Miss Davison put her head in her hands. She didn't answer the question but started rocking back and forth and repeating over and over again, "What'll I tell the kids?"

"Last night, around midnight?" Day asked again.

She stopping rocking. "Here," she said.

"Alone?"

"No, I had the children with me, of course!"

"No adults?"

"No." Her demeanour changed abruptly once more and she looked at her watch. "I'm sorry, Inspector, I really must go; I have an appointment I simply can't miss."

"Of course, Miss Davison," said Day, handing her his card. "If you need any support or think of anything that might help us, give me a ring."

"I will. Poor George. Let me show you out. Poor George." All very business-like.

Both officers were happy to take the hint and walked briskly to the shelter of the car.

"What do you make of her, Dipa?" asked Day.

"Still loves him, sir!"

"Really, you sure?"

"Yes – and hates his guts at the same time!"

"So – a suspect?"

"At least a person of interest, I'd say sir. She's on a knife edge; not far from the proverbial 'nutty as a fruit cake'."

"I agree with that last bit, at least. Right, we'll head back to the school. I want another look round before the briefing."

PC Sindhu started the car and was just about to move off when they were narrowly missed by Miss Davison's Fiesta reversing off the drive.

"She really is in a hurry – that appointment must be very important!"

-

The four teenage bullies never did complain to the police about being beaten up by an eleven-year-old but that wasn't the end of the matter. Although Derek had told his two friends not to tell anyone, they were so much in awe they couldn't contain themselves.

By the end of the day, almost everyone in Year 7 knew the story. By the end of the week, everyone in school knew the story – including the teachers.

Derek was sent for and instructed to describe the incident in precise detail. He underplayed his part in the altercation but that didn't stop the headteacher sending a lengthy report to Mr and Mrs Day. That earned him a severe telling off and a grounding from his parents – and a secret gift of a £10 note from his granddad.

Derek was obliged to promise that there would be no more violent behaviour in or out of school.

Easier said than done! A few older boys with reputations for toughness now tried to tempt Derek into fights but he steadfastly refused to be drawn.

By the start of Year 8 everything had pretty much calmed down - with Derek's fighting prowess almost forgotten.

That was before a couple of Year 11s became involved in more racist name calling against Derek's best friend, Aiden. Although it was reported to the teachers, the boys continued their abuse outside school. Eventually, Derek could stand Aiden's distress no longer and he approached the two bullies at lunchtime.

"Hi Jake, hi MJ," he said cheerfully. "I wonder if you wouldn't mind stopping calling Aiden names? It really upsets him and it's not very fair, is it?"

Jake turned to MJ and laughed. "Don't he talk posh!"

MJ poked his finger firmly into Derek's chest. "Push off, prat. Mind your own business!"

"Sorry, can't do that. I must ask you again. Please stop calling Aiden racist names."

Jake said, in a calm, sinister voice, "If you want to discuss it, we'll be by the swings in the park at four o'clock today."

"Will this 'discussion' be one at a time?" asked Derek innocently.

"Definitely!" said both boys in unison.

Derek, Aiden and Kirk were quite surprised when they approached the swings after school; a substantial crowd had gathered. Some expected to see the little boy with the big reputation receive a pasting but the majority had come for general entertainment.

Derek joined the two racist bullies and the circle of onlookers closed around them.

He remembered his granddad's words, 'Don't ever start a fight – but never walk away from one'.

"Look, Jake, I don't want to fight with you – I just want you to stop calling racist names. Please?"

Some of the older girls in the crowd whispered, "Oooh, isn't he cute," but most of the boys laughed.

"We say and do what we want, shortarse! So, put up or shut up!" hissed MJ.

"Last chance?" offered Derek with a smile. "You've nothing to gain, you know. If you beat me, you'll just have a reputation for hitting younger boys – and if I beat you, you'll look like a couple of idiots!"

Raising his voice at the end of the sentence caused just the reaction Derek had expected. Jake let out a howl of fury, leapt forward and took a wild swing at his young protagonist.

Now the words of Sam Hardisty rang in Derek's ears. 'Bullies are cowards, boy. They expect you to be scared and step back – don't'.

Craziness whispered in his ear but Derek resisted. He ducked as he leaned forward, bent both knees, twisted to his right and launched his shoulder into Jake's stomach – crushing every bit of wind out of the bully's body. As he rolled out of the way of Jake's collapse, Derek heard a massive cheer go up from the crowd. He was still on the ground when MJ charged at him. He rolled again towards MJ's feet. He knew he would have to take a kick but timed his move so that it landed on his back. MJ's impetus caused him to trip over Derek and fall flat on his face. In an instant, Derek was up, grabbing the bigger boy's left foot and pressing it back hard into his thigh.

MJ, face down in the grass, screamed as something snapped in his knee. Derek bounced on his leg to ensure it was endgame.

"Get off, you little shit!" roared MJ.

"Say 'uncle'," demanded Derek.

"What?"

"Say 'uncle'." Another bounce – another jolt of pain.

"Uncle – you little fucker!"

"Fair enough," said Derek and he released the leg and began to stand.

Another great cheer went up – but was almost immediately cut short as a burly policeman broke into the circle. He grabbed Derek by the scruff of the neck and hauled him fully to his feet.

Noticing the three stripes on the officer's arm, Derek was quick to say. "Afternoon, sergeant. Good weather for the time of year, isn't it?"

"Oooh!" went the crowd. Even teenagers know that police officers don't take kindly to cheek. A mass evacuation began.

Sergeant Davies looked into the little boy's eyes and saw no trace of devilment. The calm little sod was actually making conversation. After what he'd just witnessed, the sergeant understood that he had an accomplished street fighter in his grip. 'This one's going to be either a master criminal or a tough cop,' he thought. 'I'm going to have to watch him.'

He took Derek home and gave him an almighty bollocking in front of the parents. As he left, Sergeant Davies told Mr and Mrs Day that he would call regularly to make sure the boy was behaving himself. Eventually, the sergeant and the boy would become great friends. Overlord Derek Day's long journey into the police force had begun.

Just before the start of the school summer holidays, Pug's concerns were realised. A teacher accidentally broke the school's promise not to give out the secret of Derek's full name.

As word got around, bullies came from miles around to make fun of him. Everywhere he went, names were shouted and laughter followed. Those brave enough to come close were dealt with very politely. Derek calmly repeated his defence statement, "I think it's funny, too – but I didn't choose it!"

Some were pacified by the honest innocence and walked away. Others avoided conflict when their friends, who were better informed, told them – "Watch out, he's a lot, lot harder than he looks!"

Inevitably though, some had to 'have a go' and it became necessary for Derek to develop a code. He knew craziness had to be contained so this is what he decided:

If he comes for a fair fight – I put him on the ground without too much pain.

If he gets up and tries again – he goes down with a little more pain.

If they come as a group – they all go down in some pain.

If a weapon is involved – he goes to A&E.

This was when Pug Davies found out and suggested politely to Derek's parents that they send him away for the remainder of the holiday. So it was that Derek ended up in Keswick, staying with his granddad's elder sister, Elsie.

Three whole weeks! But Derek loved it. Although Elsie was beginning to get a little frail, she was intellectually as sharp as a razor – and she was a brilliant cook! Best of all she had two border collies and it became Derek's main job to exercise them.

Derek would run miles as the dogs danced around him. He began to love the Lake District and Fell Running. This, combined with Elsie's desire to feed the boy with twice as much good grub as a normal fourteen-year-old actually needed, began to change Derek's shape. He was too heavily built to ever be a top-class marathon runner but he would become a young man with massive stamina.

Despite this, he still cried when he hugged Elsie and her dogs as he said goodbye the day before he was due to return to school.

Chapter Seven
12.00 noon
Just before the deadline Scott moved over to the oak tree and parked himself on a horizontal branch. He took out his own phone and noticed the eighth missed call from his mother. He opened his backpack, pulled out the box and balanced it on the branch beside him. Almost immediately the Nokia inside rang.
"Are you at the oak?" a woman's voice enquired.
"Yep. Have you got my money?"
"Sure have, I'll be there in five."
'Great,' he thought and he rubbed his hands together.
Right on time, a woman emerged from the trees in front of him. This was weird; it was a much younger woman than the one who'd given him the box. Fifteen-year-old boys aren't brilliant judges of the ages of older women but he recognised this one as 'a bit of alright'. At least she was prepared for the rain – her body was completely covered by a lightweight raincoat. But Scott was concentrating on her right hand and the wad of £20 notes it was grasping. As she came nearer, she smiled and held up the cash in front of her face.
'She's 'fit', for an old un!' thought the boy. He was just about to stand and lunge for the cash when he felt a brief movement of air behind him and began to turn. Not quickly enough; the hammer caught him just above the right ear and went straight through this fragile bit of skull. Scott was dead before he'd rolled off the tree.
The woman showed no emotion as she approached the tree, picked up the box and checked its contents. Appearing to be satisfied, she placed the money inside, put the box in her raincoat pocket, turned and walked back the way she had come.
The figure who had wielded the fatal blow weighed the hammer carefully – a brilliant choice of weapon. After

a wait of a few moments for the blood to stop dripping, the killer grabbed the corpse by the shirt collar and dragged it into the trees.

-

12.00 noon
The Briefing
Within seconds of entering the classroom that Pug had converted into a Briefing Room, Day was reminded what a brilliant team he had.

One wall had been stripped and was now covered in crime-scene photographs – an incredibly quick turn-around. A large TV in one corner was playing a loop recording of the gory images inside the headteacher's office,

Just as important, a tea urn was bubbling away and a heap of sandwiches sat on a table in the middle of the room.

This wasn't to be a typical briefing because DCI Day had his own style. He was slightly amused that some of his colleagues called it 'Daysway'.

Everyone who should have been there was present except DS Sharp who had phoned to say she'd made a breakthrough down at the Academy and would be late for the briefing.

"Right – get a mug of tea and a sarnie and settle down – I want us all back out there in half-an-hour!" Day commanded. He paused. "Good – now – time of death – have we narrowed it down?"

Dom O'Neil looked up from his ham and tomato. "Still suggesting midnight to 1am, sir. Doc says he's going to move stuff around so he can do the post mortem this afternoon. He also said formal identification would be a struggle – even the victim's teeth were smashed up."

A nod of thanks. "SOCO – anything useful?" enquired Day.

"No sign of forced entry at all, sir. Whoever it was, the victim let them in. Dozens of fingerprints but, until we've got samples from some of the staff, we've no chance of isolating any from a suspect. Nothing obvious on the gate padlock or keys so far – been wiped clean. Without the murder weapon we've no easy DNA fix but we've collected loads of different hair samples. It's been made more difficult because it's pretty obvious that whoever cleans that office isn't very thorough. Also, the lack of blood splatter meant we didn't get footprints leading from the office towards the gate. Car's no help, either."

"Okay. Pity it's not more helpful but well done on the speed. Good effort with the photos, too." Day turned to his oldest friend on the force. "Any news on the nature of the attack?"

Pug Davies looked at the notes in front of him. "The Doc and Eric the Blood agree he was overpowered with pepper spray and tied up. Marks on his arms and ankles suggest he was tied for only a few minutes before he died. Everyone thinks the chair was pushed violently back and it was the fall into the steel filing cabinet that killed him. Thirty or forty blows to the face were almost certainly post mortem. No defence wounds to speak of."

"So, we're all thinking the PM frenzy equals someone he knew extremely well?" Day's question brought almost unanimous nods. "The sign around his neck leads me to believe this was an organised photoshoot designed to humiliate him – but organisation requires the victim to be in the right place at the right time and, so far, this guy being at school at that time seems totally random. Nothing yet to suggest he was a paedo. If they were taking photos – who for? If they'd not intended to kill him, will they still send photos out – good for us if they do. The kids on the school roof – got to be relevant – were they part of a large-scale conspiracy? We've got to take that seriously. Hopefully, DS Sharp will have something on that when she arrives. Anything else?"

Electronic whizz-kid Phil Johnstone, who had spent the morning talking to very helpful phone companies, joined in.

"The school landline wasn't used during the relevant time but the victim's mobile, which we still haven't found, was. He made two calls almost immediately after our lads left him alone in the school. The first was at 11.34 and the second, to a different number, at 11.41."

"Excellent," said Day, rubbing his hands.

"We have the numbers; the first call, lasting 55 seconds, was to a mobile – owner Mrs C Carmichael from Cutthorpe."

"Oh dear, someone's been telling porkies," laughed Day. "And the second?"

"It lasted 7 minutes 43 seconds and was to an unregistered number – that's very odd."

"Throw-away?" asked Day.

"Yep, looks like a burner."

"Bloody hell, what sort of life was this bloke leading – fancied himself as a spy?" interrupted Pug.

"Or he took his affairs very seriously!" added PC Sindhu.

"Are we certain he was having an affair – or affairs?" Day asked in her direction.

Sindhu gave a 'not sure' shrug but added, "You've seen the ex, the wife and the alleged affair, sir – all very striking-looking women."

"Can you track the burner, Phil?"

"If it was switched on, I might stand a chance but, at the moment, it's off."

"Keep on it. At least now I know where my first call this afternoon is going to be," said Day.

"Do you agree with Dipa that the wife, the ex. and the possible affair are all lookers, sir?" enquired Dom O'Neil.

"I do, Dom, why?"

"Nothing really, although even I can see from his photos what a good-looking bloke he was. He'd give Brad Pitt a run for his money. He wouldn't have any problem pulling."

There were snorts from a couple of the women present. 'It's a good job Mandy's not here yet – she'd have his throat for that!' thought Day. "Well," he said, "let's stick to the sex abuse angle for a couple more minutes. We have to consider that he might have been abusing women, rather than kids."

"The boys on the roof, sir?" offered Pug. "Got to be in on it!"

"Seems so, but DS Sharp has some info on them and she'll be here any minute. Now, the wife, the ex. and Ms Price don't have alibis and at least two out of the three seem to be in a love/hate relationship with our victim."

"What about Ms Mallender, the Governor who lives across the road, sir? She's got a framed picture of herself and the victim on her sideboard – they looked pretty cosy," said Constable Dawson. "She told us she'd gone to bed a few minutes after our lads drove off last night. She assumed the Head had left at the same time – so she said."

"Fair enough, Mr Dawson. I think that's enough to add her to our 'maybe' list," replied Day. "Phil, go and call the PCs who attended last night – yes, I know they've been in already and, if they've any sense they'll be back home in bed, but I want to know if Carmichael drove his motor in when they were still here. That should give us an inkling of just how nosy our Ms Mallender is."

"Will do, sir!" As he opened the classroom door, in sailed DS Amanda Sharp.

"Something useful, Detective Sergeant?" asked Day as soon as Sharp had found a seat and received a mug of tea from an admiring Constable Dawson.

"Yes, sir. The teachers down at the Academy were really helpful. They pointed out the likely lads and phoned the parents to see if I could have a word. Two lots agreed and I chatted to the boys concerned. Both coughed up almost immediately. Scott Grimshaw told 'em it was a test to see if they were cool enough to join his gang. They admitted separately that it had to be exactly 10.30 last night. One of them told me Scott had said no breaking windows – apparently, they didn't want the alarm sounding – just wanted to annoy some neighbours. Seriously weird shit, sir. Still, I'm confident those two won't be doing any more of that for the foreseeable future."

That caused a ripple of laughter.

But Day had already put two and two together. "A break-in would have triggered the alarm and their monitoring service would have called the first name on the contact list – almost certainly the caretaker. Scott Grimshaw wanted a complaint to the police and we all know that Communications keeps the number of every school's headteacher as well."

"So Grimshaw was definitely in on the conspiracy, sir?" asked DC O'Neil.

"I reckon so – but, at what level I've no idea. In any case, we need to find him, pronto. If he's fifteen, he must have left the primary before Carmichael took over – so I can't think what his grievance could be. If someone put him up to it just to get Carmichael here –

this is very much looking like a murder that's been carefully planned – not a spur of the moment thing at all! It's all too vague; how could they guarantee the headteacher would come out – and then stay after our lads had left? Something doesn't fit. Pug, just in case, check with the caretaker if he had a missed call last night."

There was a murmuring across the room. Was this murder of a successful and popular man part of a larger conspiracy? If so – why?

"We need to know a lot more about the victim's life. We've been told he's handsome, bright and charming – but did he really have a sinister side?" Day began writing tasks on the whiteboard. As their names appeared, officers swiftly left the room.

"Mandy, you stay here and help me with the press statement. Then we'll go and visit the Deputy Head – I think she'll be able to give us loads of background."

The 'suspicious death' release was composed and sent off to the Police Press Office and then Day wasted five minutes saying very little to the reporters outside the school gate.

1.00pm

Day looked at his watch. Jess would be home. He had to get to her and deliver the news in person before it hit the TV. "Mandy, follow me home would you? I'm going to break the news to Jess – she used to work with Carmichael. Then you can drive us to Dronfield to see the Deputy."

DS Sharp was happy to sit outside Day's house for fifteen minutes munching a sandwich before he emerged and slid into her passenger seat.

"Jess okay?" she asked.

"Shaken. I didn't realise how close they were when they worked in the same school. She said she knew him well enough to be confident he wouldn't be a child abuser but he was definitely a ladies' man. Would you believe it, she actually admitted she fancied him!" Day laughed. "In a good looks competition, I'm guessing I wouldn't have stood much of a chance."

"No comment, sir," said Mandy. Her thoughts were very different. "He's no fucking idea, has he? So, he's not that spectacular in the good-looks division but he's such a lovely guy. Bloody typical of me – to fall for the only 'one-woman man' in the entire fucking police force."

DS Sharp knew she was attractive but, working in a predominately male team, always did her best to moderate her good looks. She never wore make-up for work and her long blond hair was usually tied back severely. Unfortunately, this made most of the blokes she mixed with fancy her even more. Sod's law!

-

By the time he was sixteen, Derek Day's friend, and now mentor, Pug Davies had become a detective. Derek listened to countless hours of Pug's stories about life as an investigator. To maintain his protégé's interest, Pug played down the hours of remorselessly dreary work and exaggerated the rare bursts of chases and dangerous arrests.

Pug knew he could teach this lad nothing about street fighting so he kept him busy with ever-increasing challenges in long-distance running. To complement his incredible self-defence skill, Derek was now strong and fit – as some of the more disreputable elements of Chesterfield society were about to discover.

Derek and Aiden had been to see a war film at Cineworld and were walking through the town centre towards their bus stop. The trip up Stephenson's Place was interrupted when a large group of fighting drunks spilled out from Church Walk. Both boys sensibly crossed the road to avoid the ruckus, but Derek made the mistake of hesitating and looking.

"What you lookin' at, twat?" shouted the nearest drunk.

Derek never quite knew why he made the reply he did – but it united the drunks and nearly got him into a whole bunch of trouble. "Anything I want – anytime I like!" he laughed.

The eight drunks stopped fighting and focussed their attention on the two boys across the road.

Derek made a quick calculation. These blokes were much older and pretty wobbly on their feet, so he didn't think he'd have too much trouble but he knew that Aiden, despite his size, was no fighter. "Aiden run! See if you can find a cop!" He knew he should have escaped, too – but the little voice in the back of his brain kept saying, "You've had all this training – let's see how good you really are!" Crazy wasn't far away.

Two drunks set off after Aiden without a hope of catching him.

Only six, then. They formed into a shallow crescent and advanced across the road.

Sam Hardisty had taught Derek that drunks should not be taken lightly. "Okay – so they don't move as fast or strike as accurately – but they have no fear and don't understand barriers – they will hurt you, if you let them."

Derek had no intention of letting them.

As soon as the nearest two were in range, Derek did a quick half turn and crashed the heel of his right foot into Drunk #1's right kneecap. Continuing his turn, he thrust his right fist into Drunk #2's stomach. To Derek's dismay, this guy immediately threw up. By this time, Drunk #1, covered in vomit, was writhing on the ground yelling, "Kill the bastard!" Drunk #3 made a lunge at Derek, but the boy sidestepped and kicked him on the back of his knees – causing an immediate, painful fall onto the tarmac. Three down – three to go.

Drunk #4 managed to get behind Derek and grasped him in a bear-hug around the arms. Derek took this opportunity to kick Drunk #5 hard in the balls – before he shot his head backwards – breaking the nose of his captor.

Drunk #6 realised he was the last man standing and hesitated. He looked around at his fallen comrades and decided, with alcohol-fuelled logic, that he must avenge them. He approached Derek warily until they were face-to-face within arms' length. Derek watched the drunk's eyes slip in and out of focus and anticipated when the wild punch would arrive. He easily avoided the fist and grabbed the arm as it flashed over his shoulder and pulled – hard. Drunk #6 fell forward and received a none too gentle tap on the back of his neck from the edge of Derek's right hand. Game over; score 6 – 0.

'Time to leave,' he thought – but he didn't get far. A veteran constable had been watching most of the action. As he had turned the corner with Aiden, the policeman had asked what his friend was called. The response struck a chord – "Ah, Pug's friend."

The constable took hold of Derek's collar and hissed in his ear, "So, you're D-Day! Well this is your lucky day, Mr D-Day. It's such a shame I didn't witness anything apart from a load of drunks fighting. Now – bugger off – before I call for several ambulances!"

As Derek and Aiden set off at a run down Burlington Street, they heard the constable shout, "And pack in fighting – the NHS can't afford you!"

Chapter Eight

It was nearly twenty years since Pug Davies grabbed Derek Day by the scruff of his neck – and now he was calling him 'sir'.

He could have retired years ago, but he was the best Crime Scene Coordinator Derbyshire Police had ever had.

Having tied up all the loose ends at Somersgill Primary, he locked all the doors, checked the integrity of the 'Police, do not enter' tapes and described exactly how they should behave to the two young constables left guarding the scene – he set off to Beetwell Street nick to set up a murder HQ.

2.00pm

Day arrived outside the Cutthorpe house for the second time that day. The Fiesta wasn't on the drive and his knock went unanswered. He phoned Communications at Beetwell Street and told them to track down the number of Mrs Carmichael/Miss Davison's car and put out a call to all response cars. "I don't want it stopped, I just want to know where it is." It was a long shot, but the ex-wife had gone up the 'persons of interest' table.

"Right Mandy, chauffeur me to Dronfield."

-

Ten minutes later they were knocking on the Deputy Headteacher's front door.

"Hello again, Ms McAllister. Thanks for seeing us. This is my colleague, Detective Sergeant Sharp."

The two detectives were ushered into a room that could be best described as a 'riot of pastel patterns'. It wasn't to Day's taste but he had to admit it sort of worked. Photographs were everywhere and confirmed Day's suspicion that Ms McAllister was, indeed, gay.

"Excellent," thought Day. "Everything we hear in the next few minutes should at least be objective."

Tea was served and Day went through the pleasantries as quickly as possible. "I hope you've recovered a little from the terrible shock of this morning, Ms McAllister?"

"It was... still is... a terrible shock – but I'm well enough to help you, if I can. Please call me Valerie, Inspector."

"Thank you. At the moment, we're still struggling to find a clear motive. We simply don't know if Mr Carmichael was killed for personal reasons or if it was some other aspect of his life – possibly even school related?" Day noticed that, despite Ms McAllister's reassurance she was, indeed, trembling. "We were hoping you could give us a brief overview of his position in school."

"Yes, of course. As you know, George started at Somersgill three years ago. The school was in a mess when he arrived. His predecessor was a lovely man but he'd gone way past his sell-by date – he should have retired ten years before. I was doing my best to keep things going and the teachers were doing their best for the children but, without clear leadership, the school went into 'Requires Improvement'. Do you know what that means, Inspector?"

"I do, Ms... Valerie. My wife is a part-time teacher at Highfield Hall."

"Oh, so you'll understand the difficulties that brings?"

"I do indeed. Please continue."

"George was a breath of fresh air. He knew exactly what he wanted from the teachers and most were happy to oblige. He stamped down on indiscipline and, within a couple of months, he had the children and parents on his side. Of course, as far as the mums were concerned, it didn't hurt that he looked like a film star."

"Had you applied for the Head's job when Mr Carmichael was appointed?" asked DS Sharp.

"I did, Sergeant, but in those circumstances, everyone knew an outsider would get the job. I wasn't jealous of George – I really liked him as a colleague – he was very fair. When I 'came out' two years ago he was tremendously supportive. And, as I told the inspector this morning, I supported him when Angie Sanderson got her claws into him and caused a painful divorce. For a while, we became quite close."

"Close for a while – what happened then? And it's Chief Inspector!" said DS Sharp.

"Sorry. Oh, there's nothing sinister, Detective Sergeant. Once George's private life settled down we just returned to a normal professional relationship."

"Angie Sanderson – 'claws' you said?" Day was curious.

"Oh dear, you've caught me out, Chief Inspector. Angie was one of those silly young women who see our profession as just something to do till they catch a man. As a teacher, she was barely adequate."

"Above the office entrance there's a banner that says 'Outstanding School' – how long's that been there?" Day knew that in the current educational climate, this was quite a rarity.

"We were inspected in April and went from RI to 'outstanding' in one go. Quite rare – it made the front page of the Derbyshire Times. Mind you, I'll never know how George pulled it off – our results still aren't that outstanding."

"Oh?" Day was keen to hear this bit and needed to keep up the momentum. Jess had told him that teachers all across the county had been surprised by Somersgill's Ofsted grade.

"Yes, it was strange. Three months after George arrived there was an HMI visit. The Inspector was impressed with what had been achieved in such a short time and told we were well on the way to being a 'Good' school. Then the full inspection happened. We were confident we'd get 'good' but somehow the 'outstanding' grade appeared. We all laughed when she announced it."

"She?" DS Sharp was living up to her name.

"The Registered Inspector was a woman. We all thought George had charmed his way through the inspection."

"This inspector's name?" DS Sharp again.

"Davenport… Mary Davenport I think."

"What did she look like? Describe her please."

MS McAllister's face twisted in concentration. "Mid-forties, I'd guess – short dark hair, slim…"

"Attractive?"

"I'd say so…"

"Gay?"

Day usually loved to watch Mandy Sharp when she was warming up into her brusque 'Gestapo' mode but thought they'd get more information with a gentler approach. "Valerie, you said this morning that staffroom gossip was often about Mr Carmichael and Ms Price. Care to elaborate?"

Ms McAllister looked at DS Sharp and mouthed silently, "Not gay." Then she turned to Day. "Not really. Melanie is very vibrant and she's got everything going for her. Exceptional teacher, private income and, of course, she is rather beautiful."

DS Sharp raised her eyebrows at Day. He nodded. No denying it; Miss Price was very attractive.

Ms McAllister continued. "She was George's favourite – he made a lot of fuss of her and we were never sure if it was because of her skill in the classroom."

"So, Mr Carmichael was a sucker for a looker?" DS Sharp being subtle again.

McAllister raised a half-smile, "Yes, I suppose you could put it that way. And of course, he was such a handsome man, he did attract a lot of interest."

"What about Miss Mallender, the Chair of Governors?"

"Well, she appointed George – I assume because of his talent, not his looks."

"Any relationship beyond the professional?"

"There might have been some hope from her side but George never spoke about her with any enthusiasm. I know they went together to a residential Chairs/Heads training event in a hotel in Bradford, about academy status if I remember correctly, last year. It's anybody's guess what happened there."

"You think she might have a crush on him?" asked DS Sharp.

"Possible."

"Anyone else in his fan club as far as you know?" asked Day.

"There are a couple of young mums who seem to spend a rather inordinate amount of time flittering round him. He once told me that Mrs Tomlinson was like a stalker, sent him notes, made him cakes – that sort of stuff."

"Attractive?"

"Yes, in a tarty sort of way."

"You know the address?" asked DS Sharp, pencil poised.

"Not offhand but it will be easy enough to find in school."

"You said a couple of mums?"

"Oh yes. Janice Rhodes. It's quite a joke amongst the staff – she goes bright red whenever George passes... passed by. I think her husband is still in prison – I've heard he's a nasty piece of work!"

Day's mobile rang; it was Dom O'Neil's number.

"Excuse me, Valerie, I must take this." Day got up and left the room.

"Hi Dom, what's up? Any good news?"

"I reckon so, sir. Did you say that one of the 'Persons of Interest' had a cream mini?"

"Yes, Price, the alleged lover." Day could almost hear the raised level of excitement in Dom's breathing.

"I'm at the White Lion, sir – the pub on the corner just below the school. Landlord's been really helpful and they've got CCTV. It mainly covers their car park but one corner just catches the road."

Day was aware of his own rising excitement.

"Light coloured Mini, sir; passes towards the school at 12.19 and back the other way at 12.34."

"Reg.?"

"Can't see it on either, sir but Phil might be able to do something with it."

"Good work, Dom. Thank the landlord, seize the disc and then drive to Price's house, park out of sight and watch her until we get there."

"Aye, aye, sir!"

Day hung up and went back into the room; he gave DS Sharp the twisted nod that meant, 'time to go'. "I think that's enough for today, Valerie. Now there's been a press release about the 'suspicious death' you might get reporters sniffing around. We haven't given out any information about staff addresses but they have the knack of finding out. If you get bothered, call me." Day handed her his card.

"Thank you, Inspector…" She looked at DS Sharp. "Chief Inspector," she corrected.
"You've been very helpful. If you think of anything else, please call." Smiles and handshakes were exchanged.
As soon as they were in the car, Day ordered, "Walton – the Price address, Mandy – sharpish!"
The DS turned and gave him a very funny look.

-

Derek managed to keep out of any serious trouble through his sixth-form years – he was busy worrying about his granddad's rapidly failing health. Despite his concern, the lad did pretty well in his 'A' levels and, wanting to be close to home, accepted the place he'd been offered in Nottingham to do a Law Degree.

Three weeks before Derek was due to take up his place, Arthur Ross VC died. This was the first great loss in Derek's life and it put a severe dint in his self-confidence.

The funeral was a lavish affair. The 'Crooked Spire' was filled to capacity. A piper played the lament. Four survivors of Arthur's D-Day Company and six other VCs attended. Regimental banners were unfurled. Speaker after speaker declared that a great man had passed, as the congregation nodded and whispered, 'hear, hear!'.

It didn't help the devastated Derek, though. The young man became a boy again and he wept bitterly throughout most of the long service. He would never know if his grandfather had really given him that ridiculous name just to make him tough.

After the funeral, matters were made much worse when it was discovered that, in his later years, Arthur had made some very poor business decisions and his estate was close to bankruptcy.

It was a very sad Derek Day who began his university course not too far from home.

In the first few months he concentrated almost entirely on his studies and began to find the intricacies of the law even more fascinating. His housemates teased him, rather gently, about his lack of social life. His fellow law students found him reserved, particularly with the females. Some thought him gay – but, even though his reputation as a fighter had not followed him to college, it was never said to his face.

Just before Christmas, Derek realised he was putting weight on. He'd abandoned his strict training regime when his granddad died and hours in front of a computer screen or a textbook was no way to keep fit. He began running again and, during a visit to the gym, was spotted as a potential recruit for the Rugby Club. The problem with Derek and most team sports was his lack of ball skills. However, the third team coach recognised his running speed, stamina and talent for fearless tackling so he became a regular member of the team.

This entitled him to membership of the Rugby Social Club; where he was free to mix with the 'giants' of the First Fifteen.

In some cases, 'giants' was a literal term. The captain, Josh 'Cap' Bayswater was, for example, six feet six inches tall and weighed in at a muscular seventeen stone. All the club's social life revolved around him and his girlfriend.

They were a strange pairing; Jessica Raybould was no more than five feet two and thin as a pin. She wasn't beautiful in the conventional sense but her vivacious smile lifted the spirits of everyone around her. She was funny (in a good way) and kind (in every way), taking an interest in all new members of the club.

The second time Derek met Jessica, he decided he would marry her.
The problem:
Derek = lowly first year law student
Jessica = second year teaching student with big boyfriend
'Cap' = third year sports psychology student with huge status.
The solution? Wait until Cap completes his course and leaves. Be patient; no need to go crazy.

Chapter Nine

As DS Sharp drove out of Dronfield, Day was on the phone demanding results and issuing orders. Pug had come through with the caretaker's movements. He hadn't had a callout. "It would have been pointless," Pug reported. "First Sunday in July is the Annual Over-50s Darts Championship at the Working Men's Club – Barker's been the champion for the last five years – everyone in the village knows he'd have been there. And there's usually a lock-in after that!"

"Cheers, Pug. Phone the club, would you, and check what time Barker left. Any news on young Grimshaw?"

"No sign. I've sent Dawson and Sindhu down to the Academy to ask around some more. Which two kids did DS Sharp work her magic on this morning?"

The information was passed on. Day was worried about Scott Grimshaw; it was time to talk to the woman with the money.

Superintendent Halfpenny picked up immediately. "Anything useful, Derek? I'm going to have to release more info. for the six o'clock news."

"Couple of leads, ma'am. What's worrying me is the disappearance of a fifteen-year-old who, I suspect, was involved into the set-up of a very complex conspiracy."

"Conspiracy? I thought you were going down the personal revenge route?"

"Revenge is in there somewhere, ma'am, but it's becoming obvious that this attack was very well planned and I still think it's possible they didn't intend to kill him. Several people were involved and at least one of them is a real nasty piece of work."

"Bugger! What do you need?"

"Boots on the ground. Scott Grimshaw may be the key to this little mystery – I want him found before dark."

"Do it! I'll carry the can for overtime – I'll get the cavalry organised from here. Call me no later than 5.30." She had put the phone down before Day could even say thank you.

The next report told him the ex-wife's car had been spotted in the car park of The Peacock pub – which seemed to suggest she was now doing something as innocent as collecting her children from school.

Day needed to talk to her – and soon - but the priority was Melanie Price. Okay, there were dozens of light-coloured minis around Chesterfield but how many could have been in that area after midnight on Sunday.

He'd only been off the phone for five seconds when it rang. "Sir, it's Dom. I'm watching the Price woman – she's on the drive - cleaning the inside of her car!"

"Stop her!" Day ordered. "Go and talk to her – tell her you've come to take a formal statement – get her to make you a cuppa – anything!" He turned to DS Sharp. "Quick as you can, Mandy – the lovely Melanie is washing her car!"

Even with blue lights flashing, getting through the centre of Chesterfield at school turning-out time is never quick and an earlier shunt on Whittington Moor roundabout didn't help.

DS Sharp killed the blue lights before they arrived at the Price house. Melanie was still on the drive, her hand on a vacuum cleaner. She was looking impatient because a smiling Dom O'Neil was blocking her access to the open nearside door.

"He's chatting her up! The bugger is actually chatting her up!" hissed DS Sharp, as they stopped at the bottom of the drive.

Day smiled inwardly – it was his fault – he had told Dom to do anything to stop her cleaning the Mini. He climbed out of Sharp's car and walked as nonchalantly as he could up the drive.

"Good afternoon, Miss Price. A few more questions if you don't mind? Shall we go inside?" Day was all charm.

"If we must, Inspector but I must put these cleaning materials away and lock the car."

"DC O'Neil will do that for you – won't you, DC O'Neil?" Mandy Sharp could be quite scary at times.

As the DS escorted Miss Price inside, Day gave DC O'Neil instructions. "Put this stuff in the garage, have a quick look inside the car for anything obvious, and then shoot down to HQ and have Phil look at the CCTV you've got. Even a couple of letters from the reg. would be brilliant. Oh, and accidentally take the Mini keys with you. Go!"

By the time Day got inside, Melanie Price was already on the receiving end of DS Sharp's 'third degree'.

After introducing herself, Mandy had gone straight in. "Strange thing – cleaning your car just a couple of hours after hearing of the death of a close friend?"

Miss Price looked close to tears when she replied. "I had to do something mundane to take my mind off it… George. I tried doing school work but all I could see was his face looking back at me from the exercise books. It's just how I cope with any crisis."

"Fair enough," interrupted Day. "Let's all sit down, shall we? Now, Miss Price, I'm going to ask you some questions and DS Sharp will take notes, is that okay?"

"Am I a suspect? Am I under arrest? Do I need a lawyer?" she blurted.

"You're always entitled to have your lawyer present but, to answer your other questions; no, you're not under arrest and you're no more a suspect than all Mr Carmichael's other contacts," Day lied.

"Oh, that's all right then. Shall we have coffee?" A remarkable transformation.

Good. It was rare for Day to try to kill time but he was hoping for a call as soon as Phil had loaded the CCTV onto his trusty computer.

Three decent mugs of coffee arrived courtesy of a very expensive machine.

"Great coffee, thanks. Now, could we just go over what you told me this morning? You last saw Mr Carmichael at about 5.15pm last Friday?"

"Correct."

"And you've not spoken on the phone since then?"

"Also correct."

"And you were alone in bed from about 9pm to 6am last night?"

"This is tedious, Inspector. Yes!"

"Does anyone else have keys to your Mini?"

"No, why?"

"What would you say if I told you a Mini similar to yours was seen in the vicinity of the crime scene around midnight last night?"

Melanie Price shook her head. "I'd say there are lots of cars like mine all over the place; they sell very well."

The slight hint of complacency and sarcasm wasn't doing anything to make Day warm to this young woman. "Midnight on a Sunday? On a street that leads to a couple of dozen houses and flats, a school and pretty much nothing else?"

"Coincidence. Wait, I can prove it. I can prove my car was on the drive all night." Price reached for a sophisticated remote and pressed a number of buttons. The TV screen came to life and, after more input, a beautifully clear picture of the drive, complete with Mini and Sharp's Mondeo came into view. Price handed the remote to Day. "Use that wheel to scroll back in time. I'm sure you'll find what you're looking for."

Day did as he was told – but very slowly. As he went back in time, he saw that the Mini had moved several times during the previous seventy-two hours - but not at the relevant time. Price gave him a staggeringly beautiful 'told-you-so' smile.

"Thank you for that – most helpful. Now, it would be great if you could tell us what you know about Mr Carmichael's life. You know, friends and extra close friends, if you understand what I mean. Any info might be very useful."

"I don't know much about his private life; although Angie and I used to be good friends we haven't really socialised since she married Mr Carmichael. George was a bit of a flirt. He was a very good-looking man and he knew it. I don't know if he ever went further, but he was always talking to the younger, prettier mums; some of the dads didn't like it but he was so charming he always managed to keep everyone sweet. Oh dear, until now."

"He never flirted with you?" asked DS Sharp.

"When he first took over, he flirted with me all the time but then he started a serious affair with Angie and stopped. To tell you the truth, I was very relieved."

"Why was that?"

"At the time I had a much better offer on the table!"

"But not now?" Sharp was beginning to get personal.

Melanie Price laughed. "No, not any more. We almost got engaged but, in the end, I decided Mike was too boring."

"Too safe, you mean?"

"Sort of."

As a welcome break from this line of questioning, Day's mobile rang. It was Phil, the techie from

Beetwell Street. Day excused himself and, leaving Price to the tender mercies of DS Sharp, walked out onto the drive.

"I've had a quick look at Dom's disc, sir, but there's no chance of getting any of the reg – it's just the wrong angle."

Day groaned silently – the easy conviction whisked away.

"Hang on though, sir. Dom said the Mini you were looking at was new. Is that correct?"

"Yep. I'm standing right next to it – 19 plate."

"Well, it definitely isn't this car on the CCTV then, sir. This one's older and in a brief flash of shadow showed a series of dents down the driver's side. Sorry!"

"Okay, thanks for looking so quickly, Phil – cheers."

Day walked back inside and gave DS Sharp his customary 'no go – let's move' twist of the head.

They made their excuses and apologised for the interruption.

As Sharp accelerated away in the direction of the ex-wife's house, Day asked, "Well, what do you make of her?"

"Huh! Does a good impersonation of trying to look humble but, I reckon, she's probably president of the 'I like me – who do you like?' club!"

-

Promising young law student, Derek Day continued to play rugby in the lower echelons of the university teams but he tried to avoid socialising at the club functions. In the three months since he'd made his decision to marry Jessica, he'd bumped into her a couple of times. They'd exchanged a few polite words and moved on.

In the bizarre world of rugby, Derek's talent of tackling hard, earned him the nickname, 'Daisy'. He didn't mind – it was much better than other things he'd been called in the past.

The next time he passed Jessica, she smiled and said, "Hi Daisy, I heard you had a cracking game for the thirds last Saturday!"

He was lost for words! She knew he existed! He gave her a daft grin and muttered 'thanks' before leaving just a little too quickly.

She watched him go – and laughed.

Soon it was the end of term; exams were over and, as for students the world over, the break in tension led to a series of pretty wild parties.

Derek was uncertain. He knew that 'Cap' would be leaving for a job in London in a couple of days and that Jessica would be back for two more years. Should he tell her about his feelings before the summer break or patiently wait for September? In the end the decision was made for him.

His housemates persuaded him to attend the final Rugby Club function of the academic year. As usual, Cap was the centre of attention and downing pints as if expecting a national beer shortage starting the day after. However, there was no sign of Jessica.

Derek wasn't any better at consuming large quantities of booze than he was at chatting-up girls, so he wandered around, talking to team mates while wondering where his 'future bride' might be.

He had made up his mind to leave and strolled into the club foyer. As he opened the door he saw, crossing the car park, three girls with linked arms. He was pretty sure the middle one was Jessica so he retreated inside and waited for them to enter. Jessica caught his glance for a millisecond and then looked back at the way they were headed. It was long enough for him to see that Jessica had a black eye.

As they entered the main room, the three girls were met by a huge cheer. From his position inside the foyer, Derek heard the noise level drop – to be replaced by Cap's booming voice. "At last," he yelled. "Where the fuck have you been?"

It wasn't Jessica's voice that responded but a shrill, "Keeping out of your way, you bastard. Have you seen her eye? You did that!"

"Oh, fuck off, Sylvie! Mind yer own business! Get over here, Jess!"

A drunken roar went up from Cap's first fifteen buddies.

The roar died down, and the room went silent with anticipation. Derek heard Jessica say, very quietly, "No, we're done." It was music to Derek's ears but it caused a different reaction from Cap's team mates.

They all went, "Ooooh!" in the exaggerated way that indicates a challenge.

As Derek entered the club room he found himself behind the three girls but facing a rapidly advancing Cap. The girl on the right went forward to block the bully's way but was pushed sideways and fell into a table full of drinks. The resulting crash made Cap stop. He bent down and put his face a couple of inches away from Jessica's. "I'll tell YOU when we're done!" he hissed.

Much to his surprise, Cap received a face slap that rattled the room.

"Ooooh!" went the crowd.

"Bitch!" yelled Cap but Jessica had already turned away from him – to be surprised that Derek was standing there. She gave him a painful smile and began to walk past him. Cap wasn't done and reached forward to grab Jessica's arm - only to find his wrist in Derek's firm grip.

"Hi, Cap," said a cheery voice. "I think Jessica wants to leave."
"Ooooh!"
Cap's hesitation gave Jessica time to escape his grip but, as she turned again, she saw real fury on her ex boyfriend's face. "Cap – don't!" she pleaded.
Cap stared at Derek's face, then at his wrist, then back at Derek." I think you're out of your depth here, Daisy!" he spat.
Derek smiled innocently. "Come to the bar, Cap. I'll buy you a pint!" He released the wrist.
In return, Derek was given a savage push and he fell and demolished yet another table full of drinks.
"Ooooh!"
'Oh, good,' thought Derek, 'Everyone's seen him start the violence.' As he was clambering back to his feet, Cap made another lunge for Jessica but she side-stepped him.
"Ooooh!"
"I'm sorry, Cap. But I'm afraid I'll have to ask you to meet me in the car park," said Derek as he wiped his beer-soaked sleeve.
"Ooooh!"
Cap turned to him again and laughed. Then, facing his crowd of buddies, he whined in falsetto, "Oh dear, I've been invited outside to pick Daisies!" He waved his arms to orchestrate another roar.
Suddenly, everyone was on their feet heading for the door. Yeah – a bit of fun to end the evening!
Within a couple of minutes, a large circle had formed with the two protagonists facing each other in the centre.
"We don't have to fight, Cap. I'm sure we can agree to differ," said Derek.
"Ooooh!"

In truth, Derek was a little nervous. Okay, he'd fought against worse odds and against drunks before – but Cap was different. He was about seven inches taller and five muscular stone heavier than Derek - and now he was out in the car park surrounded by adoring fans – he didn't seem at all drunk.

Maybe this time Derek Day had pushed his luck too far? If so, he was going to need all his skill and cunning – definitely no time to go crazy!

Chapter Ten
It was a testament to Derbyshire Police's confidence in DCI Day's instincts that a series of searches for an unreliable kid, who had only been missing a few hours, got underway. At the end of the school day, a small detachment of uniforms went down to Somersgill Academy to organise search parties with the help of some of the missing boy's mates. Working on the assumption that now might be the right time to get into police 'good books' even some of their parents had turned up to help.

By 5pm they had exhausted all the suggestions made by the youngsters Grimshaw had taken on the school roof initiation test. Fortunately, the light rain had stopped so areas between the canal and the River Rother were searched without too much discomfort. The dens in the river bank behind the Sewage Works held no surprises. Work on several local building sites was brought to a halt by groups of volunteers.

"I can only think of one other place," uttered young Stevie Bell nervously, "and I don't think he'll be there 'cos there's not much shelter when it's raining."

And so, just before 5.30pm, a group of officers, their guide and his dad set off for the 'Fallen Oak Clearing'.

4.30pm

Pulling up outside Miss Davison's house in Cutthorpe, DS Sharp was relieved to see the Fiesta on the drive.

"You take the lead on this one, Mandy. We want to know why she lied to me this morning – and what that phone call was all about. Be careful, I'm not sure that she's completely grounded!"

Miss Davison looked anything but pleased to see the two police officers at her door. Day introduced DS Sharp and invited himself in.

Two wide-eyed children greeted them as they entered the lounge. One boy, one girl; just a year or two older than Day's two – not frightened, just curious.

"Hi kids," said Day. "We're police officers and we need a quick word with your mum. Is there somewhere else you can play?"

Davison gave Day a furious glance but supported the question. "Go upstairs and get your homework done; I'll be up in a minute."

Both children scouled but left without a word.

"Shall we all sit down?" suggested Sharp.

"If we must!" agreed Miss Davison reluctantly.

DS Sharp allowed a moment of silence before popping the first question. "Miss Davison, last night at 11.34, you received a call on your mobile from your ex-husband, George Carmichael. What did you talk about?"

Davison looked shiftily at Day. "Are you accusing me of lying?" she demanded.

"Yes, I'm afraid we are. The call lasted 55 seconds. What did you talk about?" Sharp repeated.

Realising her bluff had been called, Miss Davison looked down at the carpet for a full minute before responding. "I'm sorry, Inspector, I forgot."

"Forgot!" snorted Sharp. "Huh! Now, for the third time, what did you talk about? And it's Chief Inspector!"

"Oh dear, I feel so terribly guilty. George was pathetic on the phone; almost in tears. He told me he still loved me and begged me to take him back. I suppose if I'd said 'yes' he would have come here and still be alive?"

Sharp ignored the question. "What did you say to him?"

Davison looked over her shoulder to make sure the children hadn't returned. "I told him to 'go fuck himself'!" She started crying – real tears. "I still haven't told the children. I haven't the words. What do I say?"

Day intervened. "I'm going to send round one of our Family Liaison Officers; she'll stay with you for a while and be with you when you give the children the news – if you think it will help?"

"Thank you, Chief Inspector, that's very kind."

But Sharp wasn't done. "Any other lies? You didn't go off and visit your ex after the call?"

"Of course not! I'd never leave the children in the house all alone!" Miss Davison's tears were replaced by almost naked anger.

Day stood and hinted to Mandy that it was time to go. "You'll get a phone call in the next hour. Our FLO will make herself known and ask when it's convenient to call."

As soon as they were outside, Day suggested a visit to Sainsbury's Café; he always thought better on a full stomach.

After sausage and mash, it was time to head to Beetwell Street for the six o'clock briefing but first he had to tell his boss they'd made no progress whatsoever.

6.00pm
The Briefing

As usual, Pug had done a great job transferring all the info from the school to the Briefing Room at Beetwell Street Station. Being an expert on 'Daysway', he'd already written the vic's details and a list of 'persons of interest' down the left-hand side of the screen.

VICTIM: George Carmichael; h/t Somersgill Primary (successful); married + several suspected lovers/admirers (some jilted?) No formal complaints of abuse against children

POI

Miss? Davison – ex-wife (no alibi – call from vic before incident)

Angie Carmichael – wife (no alibi – suspected vic was at school)
Melanie Price – lover? (weak alibi)
Margaret Mallender – Governor (No alibi – knew vic was at school)
? Tomlinson – parent - Stalker?
Janice Rhodes – parent – crush?
Mary Davenport – Ofsted Inspector – affair?
Scott Grimshaw – 15yo – school roof prior to crime
Others so far:
Valerie McAllister – deputy (gay)
Peter Barker – caretaker
+ many(?) jealous former lovers/partners
PRIORITIES
Find/interview Scott Grimshaw
Find murder weapon + vic's phone
Who has burner phone?

-

The troops filed in, most looking tired and dejected. All realised that progress had been minimal; the vital first eleven hours had been a washout.

Morale was slightly restored by the sight of mugs of coffee and a pile of burgers, shipped in from McDonalds. Pug understood Daysway. But Day needed to create some real boosts of confidence, so he opened with his own conclusions to get the ball rolling.

"Thanks for your hard work today. I'd like to say right from the beginning, that I now believe we can rule out a spur-of-the-moment crime of passion. Passion will almost certainly be involved, but what we have here is a cold-blooded revenge conspiracy – more than one person is involved. If Carmichael wasn't a child abuser, he may well have been an abuser of women."

Detective Superintendent Halfpenny entered the room and immediately made a signal that everyone should ignore her presence.

Day pointed to one man who had something new to contribute.

'Eric the Blood' (aka Eric the Red) gave his report. "I've liaised with Doc Smythe, sir. He found evidence of pepper spray on the victim's neck. Blood analysis suggests that the victim was tied up before any other injuries were inflicted. A couple of the cable ties on his wrist were so tight that they did cut into his skin. Splatters on the edge of his desk suggest he might have been slapped or punched in the face a couple of times. There was a large pool of blood underneath his body. The back of his skull was split by a very violent collision with the edge of a metal filing cabinet. Doc says he must have been dead at least five minutes before the face was hit twenty or thirty times."

"Thanks, Eric. Was he naked and expecting the right kind of visitor – before he was disabled?" asked Day.

There was a smatter of laughter but Eric didn't have that kind of sense of humour. "No sir, there was pepper on his t-shirt."

"Could the injuries have been inflicted by a woman?"

"Can't see why not, sir."

Pug added, "Doc's report still says time of death an hour either side of midnight – so, if we take into account Carmichael's phone records, we have a fairly specific slot."

"Thanks, Pug. Let's have a look at your list, shall we? Now, which ones knew each other well enough to organise a murder and had motives? Is it possible that the well-respected Mr Carmichael was a serial 'love-em, and leave-em' type?"

There were a couple of nods from the female officers present.

"We've done preliminary interviews on four of these and nothing obvious has come up. Anyone spotted any links?" Day already had his theory but he liked to give his team the opportunity to shine. There was a pause – who would be first?

As usual, it was DS Sharp who broke the silence. "Mallender's got to be in on it, sir. She's got the perfect position to be a sort of command post – and she was the one who phoned our lads."

"That's right, sarge, but three other locals called in, too," interrupted Dom O'Neil.

Sharp gave him a poisonous glance before continuing. "Mallender knew the caretaker wouldn't be around for a callout."

"So did half the village – everyone knew about the darts match." Dom O'Neil was taking his life in his hands.

PC Sindhu smiled inside. She was well aware that O'Neil was one of the many officers who would have loved to bed the lovely Mandy Sharp. He had just reduced his chances from zero to minus ten.

"Now then children! I have to say I agree with DS Sharp. Mallender is involved – but I don't know how or why. We'll have to be a little bit careful there; the councillor is a friend of the Commissioner and the Chief Constable."

Superintendent Halfpenny nodded.

Day turned to DC Andy Grainger. "Anything from the Ofsted woman, Davenport, yet?"

"Not directly. You told me the deputy head said that Davenport had been over generous to the school, sir but that's in contrast to what I heard today. I phoned Ofsted and, after being passed round half-a-dozen people, I eventually learned that Davenport wasn't working for them anymore."

"Over generous to other schools, too?" interjected Day.

"No, sir. That's the puzzle. Eventually, after I mentioned the 'M' word, one of their top brass admitted she'd been asked to leave because they'd received a load of complaints about her aggressive attitude – bullying and marking schools down!"

"Intriguing!" said Day. "Have you spoken to the lady in question?"

"Not yet, sir. I rang her home phone and spoke to her husband. He told me she was working away – in Chesterfield!" That immediately got everyone's attention.

"Yes. He told me she goes around schools that are expecting an inspection and gives them a practice run – so they can sort out any weaknesses before the real thing. She's working at Mary Swanwick School in Old Whittington today and tomorrow and, her husband said, she was booked in at the Ibis last night and tonight. I tried her mobile and left a message. She texted back and said she was tied up in meetings but would call me at seven tonight."

"Okay, thanks Andy – let me know what you think as soon as you've talked to her."

There was a tap on the door at the back of the room and a PC poked her head inside. "Sorry to interrupt, sir but PC Sindhu is on the phone and she says it's really important. Can I put her through?"

"You can, Ms Archer, thank you."

"It'll be line two." PC Archer left and a moment later the phone rang.

Day picked it up and said, "What can I do for you, Ms Sindhu?"

"I know it's the briefing, sir but I thought you'd need to know this straight away."

"No problem. Go ahead."

"Miss Price – Melanie Price, sir. I thought I knew her from somewhere. I've seen her at a couple of local rally meets – she's usually wearing a helmet so that's why I didn't recognise her earlier. I asked Chris – he drives with me – and he said he knew her – he's got an eye for that sort of thing. 'The good-looking bird with all the money,' he said. Sir, she drives a Mini – a white one!"

Day could feel his excitement growing. "So, if she rallies that Mini, it's got to be road legal, right?"

"That's the club rule, sir."

"Well done, Dipa – we'll go and ask Ms Price where she keeps said Mini as soon as we've finished here." He turned to the expectant faces of his assembled officers. "Ladies and gentlemen, I believe we have a prime suspect – a little liar!"

A buzz ran through the room but, before Day had chance to explain the development, he was interrupted by PC Archer again.

"Sorry sir, line two – it's PC Rouse, coordinating the Grimshaw search."

"Put him through."

The constable was typically blunt when Day picked up the phone. "Rouse, sir. We think we've found Grimshaw!"

Day didn't like the sound of that. "Go on," he said.

"Dead, sir. Close to a place the locals call 'The Fallen-Oak Clearing'. It's off the beaten track, top end of Bluebell Wood, north of Somersgill."

Day groaned. "What state's the body in?" he asked although he suspected he already knew the answer.

"Face bashed in; real mess. Poor lad was just dumped in the middle of some ferns, sir. No real attempt to hide the body." The normally unflappable constable sounded genuinely upset.

"I'll be there in less than an hour but the cavalry will be arriving before then. You got enough help to protect the scene?"

"Yes, sir. No one will find the place without a local, though. Do you know the Somersgill to Eckington road, sir? About half a mile out of Somersgill it passes the edge of the woods – there's a gravel lay-by. My patrol car is there. I'll get someone there to act as guide. It's about a ten-minute walk – and you'll need your wellies."

"Good lad. Control the scene – help will be there soon." Day turned to the meeting. "Grimshaw's dead. This changes everything!" Day looked at Halfpenny. She nodded and mouthed a silent 'carry on' before leaving the room.

Day gave the team the details from Rouse's call and then began handing out tasks.

"I know it's past your bedtime, Pug but we're going to need you in Bluebell Wood. Organise the troops, will you?" A couple of officers laughed but Pug was a popular guy and smiled in return. He was on his way out of the room, phone to ear, within a second of Day's instruction.

"Andy, find out what Davenport thought of Carmichael and if she's met him since the inspection. Also, ask her what she thought of Mallender – they must have met. Remember, she's a person of interest, so listen to the silences. When you've done that, go with Dom and help him charm Price – without chatting her up!"

He turned to Dom O'Neil. "As soon as Andy's ready, get up to Price's and ask if you can look at the security footage again. Just routine, you know the drill. Note the times the cream Mini's been in and out but don't tell her you're looking at today's times as well - we don't know Grimshaw's time of death yet. When you think the time is right – ask her where she keeps her other Mini – and watch the reaction. And Dom, seriously, no chatting up – she's our prime suspect!"

As Day intended, another brief ripple of laughter crossed the room. The briefing ended in a bit of a shambles with officers setting off in all directions. Day had had a bad feeling about Grimshaw since quite early in the morning. Now, he urgently needed to know when the teenager was murdered. That detail might prove to be make or break in this case.

He waved to DS Sharp – neither of them would get much sleep this night.

As they walked out to Sharp's car, Day phoned his wife. "Jess, I won't be home in the foreseeable future, sorry. Kiss the girls goodnight for me."

"Will do, love. And do me a favour, when you catch the bastard who killed George, give him a good kicking for me!"

Day laughed, realising that Jess was doing for him exactly what he had been doing for his team just a few minutes earlier.

-

"You just don't understand the concept of 'captain' do you, Daisy?" said a surprisingly sober-looking Cap as he squared up to the smaller man.

"Oh, I do, Cap. But manhandling women can't be a part of a captain's job description, can it?" Derek hoped his nervousness wasn't betrayed by any tremor in his voice.

"You're a pompous little shit, aren't you?"

"Yes, if you like – and that's the whole point. I'm little at the side of you so where's the kudos in beating me?"

Cap stood still and thought it over. He did a passable performance of looking confused. He stroked his chin. He scratched his head. His audience loved it. Then his expression changed to dark anger. "No kudos – just great fun!"

The onlookers erupted into cheers and jeers. "Ooooh!" Cap looked around and took a theatrical bow. It was a feint; he hurled a massive straight right at Derek's nose.

Derek had been trained to expect tricks like that. He took a short step to his right, ducked and felt Cap's huge fist brush past his ear. Immediately he thrust his own left fist deep into Cap's stomach.

"Ooooh," went the crowd.

Cap staggered back, grasping his middle. His face flashed surprise before he turned away and threw up all over the feet of the nearest members of the audience.

"Eugh!" went the crowd.

All of his street-fighting training told Derek to destroy Cap while his back was turned – but he just couldn't do it. He was, at heart, a gentle man who abhorred violence. He folded his arms and waited to see what would happen.

Cap's back was to him so Derek didn't see the change of expression from shocked pain to outright fury. Losing the contents of his stomach seemed to have invigorated him. Cap wiped his mouth on his sleeve and turned to face his foe once more. He realised he had seriously underestimated Day. He knew his rival's reputation as a fearless tackler for the third fifteen and that should have told him Day was hard and fast. He wouldn't make the same mistake twice; this time his approach would be more considered.

He came forward slowly; his head bent forward and arms stretched wide. He knew that, if he could get Day in a massive bear hug, his strength would be a winner.

Derek knew that too and he had no intention of letting it happen. Cap's posture put his head almost level with Day's and he certainly wasn't expecting an explosive frontal attack. Instead of retreating, Derek went low, bent his knees and propelled himself upwards with tremendous acceleration. His forehead impacted Cap's mouth splitting lips and smashing teeth. Cap roared in anger and pain.

"Ooooh!" went the crowd.

Cap's face was rather harder than expected and there were cuts on Derek's forehead. Within a moment, blood streamed into his eyes.

In a rage to end all rages, Cap came forward again. This time he made contact and scooped Day up in a massive hug. The two of them fell in a heap with the heavier man on top. Derek's arms were pinned to his sides and Cap's massive strength was squeezing the life out of him.

"Now you're going to die, you little shit," Cap hissed in Day's ear.

Realising this was a distinct possibility, Derek took the only action he could think of – he closed his blood-soaked eyes and stopped breathing.

It took Cap a full thirty seconds to realise his victim had gone limp. Through all the booze, pain and rage he began to understand what he had done. 'Fucking hell – I've killed him – I'm a fucking murderer!' he thought.

He pulled his arms out from underneath Day's inert body and levered himself up. He looked down in horror at Day's shut-down face. "Shit, shit, shit!" he uttered.

"Oh, shit!" went the crowd.

But a few of those present knew that Derek Day ran fifteen miles almost every day; his lung capacity was enormous. As Cap looked down in horror, his victim's eyes flashed open and a terrific roundhouse punch arrived on his left temple – completely stunning him.

With considerable effort, Derek pushed the semi-conscious body off and rose to his feet.

Silent – went the crowd.

Derek wiped the blood from his eyes and looked around the circle of onlookers hoping to get a tiny nod of approval from Jessica – but she wasn't there. (He didn't know it then but it would be October before he laid eyes on her again.)

Derek bent down and said in a stage whisper into Cap's right ear, "And let that be a lesson to you – don't hit girls!"

"Yeah!" went a young woman in the crowd. Others joined in and there was even a brief smattering of applause. Two of Cap's team-mates helped him to his feet and led him away.

Cap left Nottingham the following day nursing his injuries and humiliation. Despite his damaged ego, he would have a successful career as a rugby player and coach with a London club. He never forgave Day for the dirty trick and the sucker punch - and resolved to have revenge – however long it took. Five years later he would have his opportunity.

Chapter Eleven

7.30pm

By the time Day and Sharp arrived at the gravel layby there was only space for one more car. A young constable moved a couple of police cones and waved them in.

"Thank you, Mr Collings, are you our guide?" asked Day.

"No, sir, I'm just managing the ins and outs on DS Davies' orders. Will you both log in, please?"

After signatures were in place, PC Collings pointed to a narrow path through the trees. "There's a line of tape all the way to the scene, sir – you can't miss it!"

Pug Davies could only have arrived fifteen minutes earlier but already his extraordinary organisational skills were sorting things out.

The rain had stopped and the evening had turned quite balmy. A light mist was forming above some of the denser parts of the shrubbery.

"Huh!" said DS Sharp. "It's starting to look like a set for a horror movie."

"The whole thing's a horror, Mandy – and I want it sorted by this time tomorrow."

The two detectives followed the line of blue and white tape along a path obviously used by dog walkers then, suddenly, the tape veered off to the right along a barely discernible track through the undergrowth. In the few places they could see the ground, there was evidence of many footprints – the original searchers, then the coppers and the SOCOs had destroyed lots of potential evidence.

Day looked at his watch. "It'll be dark soon, so we'd better get a move on."

It was pretty gloomy and dank under the dense foliage so it was a great relief to have the end of their journey announced by muffled voices up ahead. A couple of bright flashes indicated that the photographer was already at work.

As they entered the clearing they were immediately intercepted by Pug Davies. "Sir, Mandy – another bloody mess – literally! I'm in the process of taping off the centre of the clearing around that fallen tree – I think there might be some useful footprints. I'm guessing that's where the lad was killed. Follow me."

Pug skirted the tree line around half of the roughly circular clearing and pointed to drag marks through the undergrowth. PC Rouse was standing guard. "Sorry sir, sergeant, sarge – you'll have to wait here – DS Davies' orders, sir!" Despite the seriousness of the occasion, Rouse was hiding a smile. Giving orders to senior officers appealed to him.

"Good lad," said Pug with a nod. "Photographer still in there?"

"Yes, sarge. He said he'd need ten minutes, five minutes ago."

"Doc Smythe is on his way; I hope he's up to the route march!"

That earned Pug a friendly punch on the arm from DS Sharp. "He's probably fitter than you, Pug!"

"You might be right, Mandy," Pug replied with an exaggerated rub of the arm. "Full SOCO on the way – they should be here within a half hour."

Day nodded his appreciation and looked around the clearing. The oak in the centre must have died of old age and been brought down by a storm twenty or more years ago. Day mused on the subject of life and death as he waited impatiently to get to the corpse of a tragic fifteen-year-old.

They were standing directly opposite the path they had emerged from. Day guessed that the murderer entered the same way. Whoever it was had a great deal of local knowledge. "Any other obvious routes in been spotted, Pug?"

"Yes, you'll see in a minute, sir. The body's lying close to a vague path – even more obscure than the one you came in by."

Just then, the photographer appeared from behind the group of detectives. "Oh, hello, sir – he's all yours. Bit of a mess - seems similar to that bloke this morning."

"Thanks, Tommy." Day knew that the photographer had seen sights more hideous than most people could even imagine. If he described it as a 'bit of a mess' it must be gruesome in the extreme.

Sharp and Day had already donned the scant protective gear Pug had been able to provide at short notice. They stepped gingerly onto the almost invisible track. Less than ten yards in they found the body. Grimshaw's face was gone; the destruction almost a carbon copy of Carmichael's injuries.

Both detectives stood perfectly still and scanned the scene with experienced eyes. The fragments of facial tissue on the surrounding ferns confirmed that the savage beating, if not the murder, had taken place right here.

"So, killed in the clearing, dragged in here then mutilated post mortem?" suggested DS Sharp.

"Certainly looks that way. I hope the poor bugger was dead before they started on his face. We're going to have to have these ferns removed one by one to look for evidence in this mess. You know, Mandy - the person who did this is a proper nut case. We need to get him pronto."

"Or her?" responded Sharp.

"Still thinking it might be Price?"

"She's still my favourite but she only had a short gap between interviews. I'm still totally convinced there are at least two of them so it could have been the other one!"

Their conversation was interrupted by Pug's gruff shout. "Doc's here, boss!"

Doctor Smythe appeared. He was wearing a dinner jacket that didn't quite match his green wellies.

"What ho, Sharpy? Twice in one day – people will talk! Ah, hello, Chief Inspector – have you done my job for me yet again?" As usual, Doctor Smythe sounded much more cheerful than he looked.

"No chance, Doc!" said Day. "Killed in the clearing and dragged in here for the beating – we hope. We need a time of death asap, please."

"God moves in mysterious ways – his wonders to perform!" replied the doctor as he knelt beside the shattered corpse. "You poor little sod – you've gone through a lot of pain just to get me out of a boring medical dinner," he said quietly – but his audience had already left.

As he re-entered the clearing, Day saw that the evidence gatherers were arriving in numbers. "Come on, Mandy – let's leave the scientists to it. I need to see what Dom and Andy have got out of the adorable Miss Price." Day's brain was buzzing. "How could a young woman who, by all accounts, works so wonderfully well with children, commit such brutal acts? It just doesn't fit."

As they left the clearing Day shouted back towards DS Davies. "Pug, if the doc gives you any indication of time of death, patch it through immediately, please."

"Consider it done, sir!"

They reached the layby with only a few more scratches from protruding branches. As they climbed into Sharp's car, Day told his DS to take her time getting to Walton. He was hoping for some vital information from his two DCs and an approximate time of death before he made a dramatic entrance into Price's posh house. "Let's give 'em all a little more time, shall we? I fancy a coffee."

-

Detective Constables Dominic O'Neil and Andy Grainger arrived at the home of the prime suspect, Melanie Price just after 8pm. They were admitted – but with an 'oh no, not again' set of raised eyebrows.

While Grainger studied the CCTV footage, O'Neil tried his unique brand of charm on Miss Price. At the rear of the through lounge was a pair of French doors, beyond that a deep patio with some high-quality sun loungers and, further on, rows and rows of beautifully tended vegetables.

"Wow! You're some gardener!" exclaimed Dom.

Price laughed. "Not me. I've no idea and no time. My next-door neighbour uses my garden as a sort of allotment. He's retired – and it means I don't have to do any work on it at all. I get all the veg I can use and he takes all the rest – it suits us both fine."

"Great idea!" agreed Dom.

"Excuse me, Miss Price, could you tell me where you went between 4.14 and 5.12 this afternoon, please?" called Andy from in front of the TV.

"This afternoon? Why on earth do you want to know about my movements this afternoon? Bloody cheek!"

"It would be helpful to know," persisted Andy.

After throwing him a glare that would have turned milk sour, she replied, "Morrisons – if you must know! I take Mrs Robertshaw shopping every other Monday teatime. She's a widow – doesn't drive; been a family friend for years. I was with her the whole time if you're checking my alibi for some crime or other – and I used my Visa card at the tills!"

Andy Grainger stood up and turned to face her. "This Mrs Robertshaw, where does she live?"

Dom O'Neil noted that Price's superior, irritated expression was beginning to erode.

"Why do you ask? Do I actually need an alibi – seriously?"

"Possibly," said Grainger with no trace of humour. "Mrs Robertshaw – where does she live?"

Price's manner changed dramatically. "Three doors down on this side, number fourteen."

Dom judged it was time to execute Day's instruction. "Is that where you keep your other car – in her garage?"

Price sat down heavily on her sofa. She was silent for a few seconds – deep in thought. "Yes," she said. "It's my hobby – I've tried my luck in a few local rallies."

"Mini?"

"Yes," she stuttered.

"Light coloured Mini?"

"White."

"Did you go for a drive in your white Mini last night between 11pm and 1am?"

"Yes."

"Did you visit Somersgill?"

"Yes." Melanie Price sat back on her sofa and stared at the wall.

"Okay, we'll leave it there for now." Dom O'Neil smiled broadly as he stepped out of the room to make the phone call. This was going to earn him some serious brownie points.

-

Day declared they should have a ten-minute break in Costa Coffee so they sat in silence for a couple of minutes.

DS Sharp sipped her espresso and looked up at DCI Day seated opposite. His face was a complete blank.

'He's okay looking, I suppose,' she thought. 'Fit though – very lean body. He's such a decent bloke, too; everybody likes him. Wonder if he fancies me? Lots of men I don't fancy seem keen on me – but he shows no interest. So he's got a good-looking wife? So what? I reckon I've got a better figure than her.'

Day glanced at the beautiful face of the deep in thought Mandy Sharp. 'There she is,' he said to himself, 'still analysing the case. Never stops working. Bloody good detective – she'll go far.' He switched off for a moment. 'I wonder how Jess is feeling – I hope she's coping with her loss.'

Then his mobile rang.

-

For Derek Day the Summer would be interminable. He kept his mind occupied with his law studies and keep-fit regime until, with great relief, he returned to college in late September.

He had heard that Jessica was back but he never seemed able to create the opportunity for an accidental meeting. Eventually, one of her friends tipped him off when she would be in the main library building.

With a pile of books under his arm he wandered between the bookshelves until he spotted her alone at a table. He approached and bravely uttered, "Mind if I sit here?"

She looked past him with a neutral expression and nodded.

No words were exchanged for ten agonising minutes. Realising that his hopes were dashed, Derek actually started reading one of the books he had brought. Another thirty minutes passed. Derek was just about to politely excuse himself when, without preamble, Jessica said, "I won't go out with a thug!"

The irony wasn't lost on Derek but he realised that she was considering an offer he hadn't yet made. "I'm not a thug – I only got into that fight to protect you."

"I don't need that kind of protection. I want someone steady, thoughtful and gentle. I want the opposite of Cap; I definitely don't want another bully with a bad temper!"

This confounded Derek. "But I didn't start the fight!"

"You asked him outside – I heard you!"

"True – but only to get him away from you."

Jessica stopped and thought for a moment. "But you are a fighter; I don't want to get stuck with another one!"

That tiny optimistic thought evaporated – for a foolish moment he actually believed he had a chance. Now, the only woman he had ever wanted was in the process of rejecting him. "Look," he said in desperation, "my granddad and his friend taught me street fighting because I'd been bullied when I was a kid. I just got very good at it, that's all! I don't fight for fun – never have, never will!"

Jessica's expression softened a little. "If you want to date me you've got to promise that nothing like that terrible fight will ever happen again!"

Was this an offer? Was she actually suggesting they date?

"I promise! I swear! If you'll go out with me, I'll never get in another fight!"

For the first time she turned and looked at him face to face. He looked so terribly earnest she couldn't help but smile. He returned the smile. The dam broke – Jessica burst into wild laughter.

Poor Derek was mystified; women were so complicated!

Jessica stopped laughing but the broad smile remained. "You're an idiot, you know. I've wanted to be with you since we first met. Why do you think Cap gave me that slap – I told him I was finishing with him – so I could make myself available to you. I didn't tell him that last bit. You really are quite slow sometimes, aren't you?"

Derek's mouth dropped open.

"Oh, very attractive," she said. "Was that a genuine promise because if it was, I will be your girlfriend."

Derek couldn't believe his luck. He took her hand and looked her in the eye. "I promise!" he whispered – and was over the moon when she leaned closer and kissed him on the lips.

In years to come, Derek would break that promise many times. Eventually, he would work up the courage to tell Jessica that he was committed to becoming a police officer – a job which often required the courage to run towards trouble.

But, at that wonderful moment in the library, he was simply ecstatic. They walked out into the fresh air, hand in hand, both grinning like the proverbial Cheshire Cat. At that moment, he wasn't even thinking about the potential of physical intimacy – but he was certainly going to get it – and in the not too distant future!

Chapter Twelve

"Sir, it's Dom."

"Go ahead."

"She's coughed to being in Somersgill at the time of Carmichael's murder, sir! We've got her!"

"What exactly has she admitted, Dom?" Day placed a strong emphasis on 'admitted' to remind Dom he wasn't still working in 'the Smoke'.

"Driving into Somersgill between eleven and one last night!"

"In her other Mini?"

"Yes."

"Good lad, well done. Ask her if she'd like to accompany you to the station. If she refuses, arrest her."

"Charge?"

"Wasting my time! Don't mention the 'M' word – I want to see her face when we drop that on her."

"Will do, sir. See you at Beetwell Street in twenty minutes?"

"Okay. Did Andy have his conversation with the Ofsted woman?"

"He did. He's got quite a lot to tell you. Apparently, she's pretty pissed off with the late Mr Carmichael."

"Sounds interesting but we'll interview Price first. See you in twenty."

"Sir, are you in a café – there's a lot of background noise?"

"Oh, very good, Dom – you'll make a first-class detective one day. We're at Costa near Tesco."

"You wouldn't mind bringing Andy and me a decent Americano apiece would you?"

"Cheeky bugger – but yes, I think you've earned it."

"How about a chicken burger from KFC?"

"Don't push it, Dom," said Day but he laughed all the way to the counter.

9.30pm

The two, now lukewarm, coffees were gratefully received by the DCs as soon as Day and Sharp entered the interview suite at Beetwell Street Police Station.

"She's cried all the way down in the car, sir. We didn't have to arrest her – she says she's going to tell you the whole truth!" O'Neil was so excited he was bouncing from one foot to the other.

"Solicitor on the way?" asked Day.

"No, sir – says she doesn't want one; she's going to tell us everything."

"Excellent!" said Day but he didn't get too enthusiastic about the possible outcome. "Anything from Doc Smythe about the Grimshaw time of death?"

"Usual 'too early to commit', sir but he was prepared to say an hour either side of noon."

That was decidedly helpful. "Where was Price at that time?"

"Well, according to her CCTV, the Mini was on the drive but now, of course, we know that means nothing!"

"Agreed. Take a break, Dom; DS Sharp and I will take it from here. Help Andy compose a report on your chat at Walton – and I want written notes on the Ofsted woman conversation."

Dom was bitterly disappointed but took care not to express it. "Interview Room 2, sir," he said.

"Good work, again. Off you go." He turned to DS Sharp. "Mandy, you take the lead. I'll only join in if I need to."

Sharp nodded and turned the door handle of Room 2.

Price was seated, head in hands, alone at the table. Day nodded to PC Archer and she left without a word. The young teacher looked up at the two newcomers and the tears began again. "I'm so sorry," she whimpered. "So sorry." Down went her head again.

Day thought - was a confession imminent – surely that would be too easy.

"Miss Price," began DS Sharp formally. "You are here voluntarily and have not asked to be represented by a solicitor – is that correct?"

"Yes."

"And you do realise that this interview will be recorded and may, in future be used in evidence?"

"Yes."

"Please confirm your name."

"Melanie Jane Price." She lifted her up head again and looked DS Sharp in the eye. The detective noted that a little of Price's steely schoolteacher gaze had returned. "Look, I know you've got lots of questions but can I just tell you what's happened? I need to get it off my chest."

Sharp looked at Day and he nodded.

"Go on, but expect to be interrupted if we don't like what we're hearing!" Mandy Sharp was disappointed she wouldn't have an opportunity to practise her fearsome interrogation skills.

"I got the job at Somersgill four years ago, the same time as Angie Sanderson, as she was then, and then George… Mr Carmichael arrived a year later. All the women on the staff were gobsmacked; most of us had never seen anyone that good-looking in real life. At first, he was really uptight but, as the school started to improve, he relaxed and his personality came through – not only lovely looking but charming, too. In those early days, Angie and I had a daft bet to see which one of us would be first in his bed. From my point of view, it was a joke but I didn't realise Angie was deadly serious." Price looked up at Sharp, who smiled understandingly.

'What's all that about?' thought Day. "Carry on," he said.

"I've never told this anyone before, but I won the bet – sort of. He propositioned me after the final performance of the Christmas Concert – in the pub. I told him I didn't go for married men and it would never happen. A month later, Angie told me she'd won – they were at it all the time, she said. I guess you already know the next bit – he went off and married Angie even though we all thought it was obvious she wasn't right for him."

"Who's all?" interrupted Sharp.

"The teachers… and most of the other staff. By this time George had become really popular but the mess damaged him. At least that meant he left me alone to do my job. A couple of months after they married, Angie left and George gave me a promotion – said I was a star teacher and needed to show some of the others how to do it. From then on, he started spending more and more time with my class. He would organise after-school meetings, just the two of us. He was really pushy but in ever such a charming way."

Day could see that DS Sharp was getting bored with all this preamble but, before she could intervene, he said, "Please continue."

"I gave in. We did it. I'm not proud of it – he'd only been married a few months. After we'd finished, I had a massive guilt trip and told him that was it – he'd got another notch on his belt – never again. Don't get me wrong, he was brilliant – far and away the best sex I've ever had, but I hated myself. It was even worse when I found out Angie was pregnant. I tried really hard never to be left alone with him after that but he kept after me. Then he started telling me he'd made a mistake with

Angie – he'd wanted me all the time. Said he loved me! But I never let him touch me again. Then he tried a different tack – he kept telling me how unhappy he was and how he'd thought about suicide. I told him there would be no more sex but, if he felt really bad, he could talk to me as a friend, you know. It was stupid looking back on it. And then he told me Angie was already jealous and was checking his phone so he couldn't call me on my mobile because she would recognise the number. One lunchtime he turned up in my classroom and gave me a little box – it was a new mobile. He said he would use it to call me if he ever felt suicidal. At first, I refused it but then, like an idiot, I accepted it. I took it home and put it in a drawer – until last night. I don't know what time it was but Angie rang me and screamed – she called me every name under the sun. She said George had told her everything and gone off to kill himself! At first, I didn't know what to do but then I tried to ring his mobile but it was engaged so I got out the phone he'd given me and put it on charge. Within ten minutes, it rang."

Price's monologue was turning into a torrent and, now she was getting to the nitty-gritty, both detectives were happy to let her carry on.

"He said he was at school – something about an alarm call-out – he sounded sort of angry and distressed. He told me he loved me and begged me to let him come over – but I wasn't having it. I thought if he gets his foot in the door, I'll never get rid. He just grovelled and begged – it was terrible to hear. He had to see me, he kept shouting. Eventually, and I know you'll find the rest hard to believe, but I agreed to drive to school. He told me to park down the road because that nosey bitch, Mallender might be watching – his words not mine. So, I went through next door's garden and got my rally

Mini out – I knew Mallender wouldn't recognise that – and I drove to Somersgill. I parked halfway between the school and the pub and walked to the gate. It was locked. I know I lied earlier but, honestly, it was locked. I stood there, looking and feeling like a complete idiot, ringing his mobile – no reply. There were no lights on in school and I couldn't see his car so I guessed he'd cleared off back to Angie. I walked back to my car and called him a couple more times. Still no answer, so I drove home. I just assumed he'd gone back to Angie. I didn't realise this terrible thing had happened until I got to school this morning and saw the traffic and the policeman on the gate." Price collapsed back in her chair, doing a good impersonation of exhausted honesty.

"Well, thank you for that riveting tale! Can you prove any of this?" asked DS Sharp without a trace of sympathy.

Price stared at her for a full thirty seconds and then admitted, "No."

"Then you're in deep... trouble, aren't you?" suggested Sharp, avoiding swearing on the tape. "Incidentally, would you like to tell us where you were at lunchtime today?"

"At home."

"Can you at least prove that?" DS Sharp thought it was time to exploit Price's vulnerability.

"No, not really... except my security camera will show my car on the drive – and Mrs Robertshaw should be able to tell you I didn't go for the rally car."

"Have you got another one somewhere?" Sharp almost hissed.

Price looked down at the table and whispered, "No."

"Right," said Sharp, "you told us Carmichael called Ms Mallender a 'nosey bitch' – what's that all about?"

"George had told me she was becoming a real pain; visiting the school way more that you would expect a Chair of Governors to do. She spent hours in his office just gossiping; stopping him getting on with important stuff. Time he could have been spending with me – he said."

"Did Mallender flirt with him?" persisted Sharp.

"He said so – said it made him feel sick!"

Mandy Sharp raised her eyes to the ceiling in the classic, 'I'm listening to bullshit' pose.

"Which phone did you use when you were at the school gates, your own mobile or the one Carmichael had given you?" interrupted Day.

"My own, there wasn't enough charge on the other one."

"Where is it now?" demanded Sharp.

"At home, I didn't have time to pick it up when those two detectives brought me down here."

"And the other one?"

"Top drawer next to my bed."

"Right, this is what's going to happen!" Day had now taken over. "You're going to give me your house keys and your permission to go in and retrieve both phones. You're also going to tell me where the keys for the second Mini and the garage doors are kept. If you're telling the truth, I can't see any possible reason for refusal, agreed?"

Price nodded and reached into her coat pocket extracting a single key.

"And now, young lady, you are going to voluntarily offer to spend the night in one of our cells. Yes?"

Price was bright enough to spot a rhetorical question when she heard one. She nodded.

Both detectives stood and headed for the door. PC Archer stepped back inside.

"Ms Archer, Miss Price here is looking for accommodation for the night – please arrange it," snapped Day.

Josie Archer had to turn away so Price wouldn't see her laughing.

Daysway.

-

It was a recipe for disaster. Jessica was a year older and infinitely more experienced than Derek. What could possibly go right?

Everything! Derek was a blank canvas and Jessica taught him everything she knew with great sensitivity. As his experience grew, Derek discovered that he really liked sex and really, really loved Jessica.

It took longer for Jessica to fall in love with Derek. She liked him well enough and his ability to please her in all sorts of ways developed day by day.

At twenty years old, Derek was, despite Jessica's best efforts, still a bit intense. He gave up rugby because the attitude of the other players was, at best, ambivalent.

When he wasn't with Jessica, he worked obsessively on his law studies and his exercise regime. When he was with her, he became a different being. Jessica introduced him to her friends and their boyfriends. Once they all accepted that Jessica intended the relationship to be long term, Derek became a popular member of the group.

As their university year progressed, Jessica knocked the final corners off his intensity and for his third year (and her fourth) they decided to rent accommodation together – as a trial.

By this time, Derek had already proposed four times and been told very firmly to wait. The end of the academic year brought the stress of final exams and, in

that period of enormous relief immediately afterwards, Derek proposed again.
"Okay," said Jessica.
Derek didn't take in that response at first. Her answer was given in the same tone as you might respond to 'fancy a cuppa?'.
"What?" he asked, mouth wide open.
"I said okay – it means yes – I thought someone as bright as you would know that expression," she replied in the same flat voice – but this time with a big smile.
Derek began dancing around the room and squealing like a three-year-old but he stopped when Jessica uttered some fateful words.
"There is one condition!"
Derek suddenly felt the weight of the world on his shoulders. "What?"
"I accept that you want to be a policeman; it's a dangerous job but somebody's got to do it – and I think you'll be good at it. But, promise me, you won't be a daft hero and get yourself killed!"
He was filled with relief and love. "I promise I won't be a daft hero," he said in the least excited voice he could manage.
"Fair enough, we'll get married next August, then," she replied nonchalantly.

With successful teaching practices behind her, Jessica had already been offered a post at New Whittington Primary School – where, in September, she took over a classroom next door to an aspiring young teacher called George Carmichael.
Derek had already received a favourable response from Derbyshire Police. He'd been told he could enter the 'Fast Track' programme after a two-year probationary period if he got a good degree. His 2:1 satisfied that

requirement and he became a police officer on the first of October.
Jessica and Derek rented a flat just off Saltergate and settled into a year of unmarried life.

Chapter Thirteen

Dom O'Neil and Andy Grainger were waiting outside Interview 2 when Sharp and Day emerged. "She confessed?" blurted out Dom.

"Only to being an idiot," replied Sharp. "But at least we've solved the mystery of the burner."

"My impression is that she isn't one of our killers – but she might be mixed up in it. She's not off the hook by a long chalk," said Day.

Both DCs were visibly disappointed but Day wasn't in that frame of mind. He handed Dom Price's front door key. "Dom, go home, get some rest. On the way, go to Price's house and retrieve her phones – both of them. The keys to her other Mini are in her bedside cabinet top drawer. Collect those and hold onto them. Before you go to your bed, call SOCO and tell Eric the Blood to meet you at Price's at eight o'clock sharp. I want him to find me a trace of blood in that other Mini. Bring the two phones in and give them to Phil as soon as you've done that."

Dom turned and left, slightly more positive. Day turned to DS Sharp. "Mandy, you've had the longest day of any of us – go and get some rest. While you're at it, give some thought about the Mallender interview tomorrow. I want you back here at eight – prompt." She didn't look too pleased but did as she was told.

"No bed for you just yet, Andy. Come on, we'll get a coffee and you can tell me about Mrs Ofsted."

The two tired detectives managed to track down some half-decent coffee and sprawled out in Day's office. There was a text alert on Day's mobile. It said, 'Grimshaw - same MO, hit right temple – hammer? – almost certainly fatal – facial damage PM - more to follow – Doc'. Exactly what Day had expected.

He turned back to Grainger. "Dom said you had an interesting conversation with Davenport – enlighten me."

Grainger checked his notes. "Yeah! She rang back exactly on time but was really shocked when I told her about Carmichael – said she'd been working all day and hadn't heard any news – I thought I could hear her choking back tears. Then she said how much she admired him – what a good manager he was, nice man blah, blah.

When I asked about the 'outstanding' result, she was quite open. She admitted the school's results probably weren't as good as they should have been but she gave them the benefit of the doubt because Carmichael was such a good leader – and she was confident the results this year would justify her decision.

Then I asked her if she'd seen Carmichael since the inspection and, straight away, her attitude changed; she became very defensive and said she had not. She let me know, in no uncertain terms, that it wasn't usual for inspectors to return to schools. Any personal relationship? – I asked, as you suggested, sir and she really went for me. The 'what did she think of Mallender?' question got her even more bolshy.

I told her I knew she was working in Old Whittington and asked if she'd thought of dropping in on Carmichael or Mallender – Somersgill's only a couple of miles away. Never entered her head – she said.

Finally, I asked why she was staying over in Chesterfield when she only lived in Leicester. She told me she didn't like the M1 early in the morning."

"Overall impression?" asked Day.

"Her answers suggested she might be worth talking to again if we're looking at a conspiracy with two or more involved."

"Fair enough – is she working at Mary Swanwick School again tomorrow?"
"Yes, sir."
"In the morning, phone the school and ask if she's been there all day today – particularly around lunchtime."
"Will do."
"Good, go home. See you at eight."
Day looked at his watch and decided the investigation would benefit from a few hours sleep; he headed for home. He texted his eta to Jess and wasn't surprised to see a hot snack and a steaming mug of tea when he walked into the kitchen.

His face told Jess the answer before she asked, "Any progress?" It was sort of a tradition when he was involved in a big case.
"Not much, love – few ideas. You feeling alright?"
"Okay, bit sad. I haven't seen him for a couple of years but I did like him – even though he was a bit of a devil!"
"Did he ever make a pass at you?"
"Only once – in my first year at New Whitt. – before we were married."
Day was surprised. "Oh, and just how did you respond, madam?" he demanded in an exaggerated detective-style voice.
"I told him I got all the sex I needed at home – he actually blushed! Never asked again." They both laughed aloud. "Speaking of which – I know what takes your mind off a difficult case." She took his hand and led him upstairs.
"You didn't think to tell me about this... offer at the time?" said Day as he opened the bedroom door.
"Oh yes, that would have been a great idea, wouldn't it? You'd have gone down there and defended my honour

yet again in your own unmistakeable way! And afterwards - you'd have had to arrest yourself!"

They were both still laughing as they jumped onto the bed.

However dark the outside world seemed, Derek always found the perfect escape within Jess' love.

Chapter Fourteen:
Day's DAY 2
DCI Day now had two murders to solve and his team was decidedly overstretched. A request to borrow a couple of uniforms was graciously accepted by his opposite number. Day would have two promising young officers for a week, or until the crimes were solved. Dawson and Sindhu were seconded.
Although he'd been at the station since 6:30am, DCI Day didn't order his team to get together until eight o'clock.
In the company of PC Sindhu, he paid an early visit to Melanie Price's luxurious overnight accommodation to ask her if she'd anything to add to the previous evening's revelations. She hadn't – so he informed her that, should phone records and her neighbour corroborate her story, she would be allowed home by lunchtime. Through bloodshot eyes, she thanked him and promised she would be available for further questioning at any time.
8.00am
DC O'Neil was still in Walton at Price's house but the rest of the team gathered at the required time. Day welcomed DI Trevor Allsop, who'd arrived from Ripley HQ to help out, then he formally introduced both seconded PCs and presented a summary of the previous day's lack of tangible progress. He told them that Price was still a suspect but, in his view, others were definitely involved.
"We've also discovered that Carmichael was no saint. We're getting a picture of a man who flirted and was not averse to a one-night-stand if he got any sort of positive response. If our witnesses are to be believed, just before he was killed, he fell out with his wife and then begged – and I mean begged – both his ex-wife

and his bit on the side to take him in. He was good at his job, but don't be taken in by any 'he was an honourable man' nonsense – especially if you're interviewing a woman.

We're keeping a lid on the Grimshaw murder, hopefully for the rest of today. I'm sure his family will leak it sooner or later but, as far as the press is concerned, it's just a police incident in the woods. So, don't talk about it in your interviews unless anyone mentions the boy – then latch onto it for all you're worth!"

Interviews were allocated and guidance on the nature of the questioning given.

DC Grainger and PC Sindhu were sent off together to interview two of the primary school parents who appeared to have had an unhealthy fascination with Carmichael.

DI Allsop was to be first point of contact in the Grimshaw case but Day made it clear he was convinced the two murders were related. Dawson was told to make arrangements to see Scott Grimshaw's family and friends and begin visits as soon as DC O'Neil returned from Price's house at Walton.

Day saved what he thought was the most important interview for himself and Sharp. Chair of Governors, Ms Mallender would be asked some very searching questions.

Sharp had made an appointment to see Ms Mallender at 9am and, as she drove into Somersgill, Day's mobile rang.

"Sir, it's Dom. I'm just about to leave Walton with the phones. Eric's here and he's going over both Minis with his gadgets. I've spoken to Mrs Robertshaw, the neighbour who lets Price use her garage, and she's pretty certain that the rally Mini wasn't taken out during the day, yesterday. She told me she'd definitely hear it because she'd had her hearing aids in all day. She told me she's hopeless without them – so, I guess, that means she wouldn't have heard Price go out the night before anyway."

"Cheers, Dom, it's what I suspected. Drop the phones off with Phil and report to DI Allsop, would you? We'll all meet up again at 1pm unless any exciting developments occur!" Day ended the call as they pulled up outside the school.

"Now, Mandy, I know it's not your style but I want you to push Mallender; I want to see her when she's rattled."

"It would be my pleasure," she said with a grin.

He raised one eyebrow. "Don't worry about the PCC and the Chief, I'll protect you if there's any comeback." Day checked his watch.

9.00am

"Good morning, Councillor, may we come in?" Day said with his best 'good cop' smile.

"Of course you may, Detective Chief Inspector Day – and I've already met Detective Sergeant Sharp."

Although she had been a town councillor for many years, Ms Mallender had clearly made no attempt to profit from her status. The lounge in her flat was small and entirely functional; one worn two-seater sofa, one newish armchair, a small sideboard and a large desk piled high with formal-looking papers set the scene. The small TV was almost entirely obscured by ring-binders. There was only one picture on the wall – a photo of Mallender shaking hands with Jeremy Corbyn. Sharp went straight into action. "Hello, where's the photo of you and Mr Carmichael, it was on the sideboard yesterday?"

"I've put it away. I couldn't bear to look at it after what's happened."

"This must all be very distressing for you, councillor. You and Mr Carmichael must have been close?" Day was all charm.

"Not really, Chief Inspector – we had a very close working relationship. We both had total commitment to the welfare and success of the children in that wonderful school over there." She waved her arm in the general direction of her large front window. "I think it's going to be hard finding someone of George's calibre to replace him."

Day looked out. There was a perfect view of the front of the school. The office and the 'Outstanding School' sign clearly visible. "Which bit of roof did you see the boys on?"

Mallender joined him and pointed to the larger building next to the office block.

"I'm surprised you put that photo away, it was very good of both of you. You almost looked like a couple," interrupted Sharp – doing as she was told.

Mallender turned sharply but the flash of anger on her face was immediately brought under control. "It might look like that to you, Sergeant but sometimes colleagues have to look good together." She glanced quickly between the two detectives.

'We definitely would,' thought Sharp, without betraying any emotion.

Mallender took the photo out of a desk drawer and handed it to Day. "That was taken at a 'Heads and Chairs' conference at County Offices last year; one of my colleagues took the snap."

"What sort of relationship did you have?" asked Day.

Mallender didn't flinch. "As I said a moment ago, very professional. I admired him for his love of the children and the job. He kept me informed of developments and, if any problems arose, we tackled them together."

"And personally?" DS Sharp again.

MS Mallender hesitated. "I thought that would be coming. Well, to be frank, despite all his excellent professional qualities, I actually found him a bit creepy."

"Define creepy," continued Sharp.

"Hmm, it's hard. I suppose George's great problems were his looks and charm. Ironic, I know, but he gave the impression that women should look into his eyes and just melt, you know?"

"Not really," replied Sharp mischievously.

"Please go on," said Day.

"Oh, come on, Chief Inspector – surely I don't have to spell it out – he thought he was God's gift to women!"

"Was he God's gift to you?" Sharp again.

Mallender suppressed a laugh. "Crikey no, I wasn't in his league – certainly not in his target zone. I'm ten years too old for a start; I wouldn't have had a look in even if I'd thrown myself at him!"

"And did you?" asked Sharp.

"Did I what?"

"Throw yourself at him?" Sharp persisted.

The councillor sighed and shook her head. "No – I wasn't interested. My focus at the moment is preparing the way to become Mayor in two years' time. I'm married to the Labour Party. I've certainly no time or desire to get mixed up with a lothario like George Carmichael."

'Interesting,' thought Day. Everything he was hearing confirmed his suspicion that Mr Carmichael was not the gentleman he appeared to be. "Thank you, councillor," he said. "That's been very informative. Now, I wonder if you'd go over what happened on Sunday night, once more?"

Mallender glared at DS Sharp. "My Sunday evening was exactly as I had already described to the Detective Sergeant. I was working on Council business when I heard a shout from across the road. I looked out of the window and saw half-a-dozen figures on the roof of the Junior Department. I dialled 999 at around 10.45. A police car arrived about 15 minutes later. Two officers got out and stood by the school gate, obviously waiting for a keyholder to arrive. I was surprised when Mr Carmichael turned up – I was expecting the Caretaker – Peter Barker. I watched the three men go into the school – then I lost sight of them. A few minutes later the two constables came out. I talked to them for a few moments and then they drove off. By that time, I was ready for bed – so that's what I did, I went to bed."

"You didn't wait for Mr Carmichael to drive away?" asked Day.

"No, but I heard his car start up and drive away; I assumed that was that."

"You didn't mention that before!" challenged Sharp.

"Didn't I? Oh, how careless of me, Sergeant!"

Day ignored the tension that was building. "You were sure it was his car?"

"Oh yes. That car makes a very distinctive noise," she said as she smirked at Sharp.

"Did you phone anyone else about the intruders on the school roof?" asked Day.

"No, why would I? The police are the people to call if vandalism is taking place – aren't they?"

Day laughed. "Indeed they are, Councillor Mallender. So, you're going to be mayor – are you a local girl, have you always lived in the Chesterfield area?"

"Somersgill born and bred, Chief Inspector – I even attended that school over there, I'm proud to say!"

"Well, now I know where to come if I need some local information. Thank you for your help, councillor, that's all for now. We're going to keep the school under lock and key as a crime scene for the next couple of days. I believe the Education Department want to reopen it next Monday?" Day was at his most polite and business-like, now.

"Yes, that's what I've been told, too. Please go out and catch this killer, Chief Inspector. George Carmichael had his failings but he certainly didn't deserve to end up like that!"

"Agreed, councillor. We'll do our best to catch them!" said Day as he got up to leave.

Both detectives registered the millisecond of shock that appeared on Mallender's face at Day's carefully placed emphasis on the word 'them'.

Sharp tried to take advantage of the distraction. "Did you go out after our chat yesterday, councillor?"

"Err… no. I was supposed to spend the afternoon at the Labour Club but, after the terrible events, I just didn't feel up to it."

"Very sad. So, you just stayed in – on your own?"

"Yes, sergeant – that's exactly what I did!"

No further words were exchanged as Mallender showed them to the door.

As the two detectives walked down the steps. Day said, "Well, Mandy, you gave her every opportunity to ask about the goings on in Bluebell Wood. Not a sausage."

"She must have heard something about it – even if she didn't leave her flat at all! Very suspicious! So, what do you think, boss?"

"Feisty lady – used to being in charge. Probably really good at manipulating people on committees – but out of her depth in murder. She's just gone up from 50% to 90% on my 'probably involved' scale. It's just a matter of figuring out who the others might be. Our Mr Carmichael seemed to have a talent for creating love/hate relationships with all sorts of women."

"She had the hots for him – no question!" stated DS Sharp.

"I agree, but did that fascination ever lead to the dirty deed?" suggested Day. "We'll never know – it could be love 'em then leave 'em – or simply a brutal rejection. Either way, it's beginning to look like the basis of a motive."

"Do you think it's possible she just walked across the road and did for Carmichael within a few minutes of our lads leaving?"

"No, I don't think she's got it in her, Mandy, but I'm pretty sure she's involved in some organisational capacity. It's important we look for any women she knows who've got similar issues with Carmichael. You know, the more I think about our victim, the less I like him."

"Couldn't agree more. Seems like he had everything going for him – looks, brains, job he obviously loved – but he couldn't keep his dick in his pants!" There was no humour in Sharp's tone.

"I wonder just how colossal his ego was? I wonder if he kept a record of his conquests – a sort of score card? While we're here, let's have another look in his office – if there is such a thing it won't be obvious, but we could drop lucky."

"Do men really do that sort of thing?" asked Sharp.

Day laughed. "I've no idea about other men but, if I kept a record, it wouldn't make very interesting reading!"

'I could make it a lot more interesting, given the chance,' thought Sharp – taking great care not alter her expression. "I'll phone the caretaker – see how long it takes him to get here," she said.

The two of them sat on the bonnet of Sharp's Mondeo. The weather was improving steadily but it was still far from being a glorious July day.

"I reckon Carmichael was really weak; his wife more or less kicks him out, he sees a future of being skint so approaches ex-wife and then rich lover to bail him out. 'Man of Straw' I think is the expression!" DS Sharp was not impressed.

Peter Barker took exactly 10 minutes to respond to Sharp's request. "How can I help?" he said as he climbed out of his car.

"Thanks for coming up. I want you to open the gate and the office and deal with the alarm. We'll be no more than half-an-hour," said Day.

"Oh, that chap… Mr Davies said I wasn't to let anyone in without his say-so."

Mandy Sharp looked the caretaker in the eye and laughed. "Mr Davies – sergeant." She pointed at Day. "This guy - chief inspector – open up!"

Day couldn't help but grin. He liked Mandy Sharp and thought her a first-rate detective – but why was she so protective of his status?

The Headteacher's Office was a mess. There had been no attempt to clean up the blood or the finger-printing residue; someone was in for a very unpleasant job in the next few days.

Between them they opened every door and drawer in Carmichael's private domain. No secret score cards were discovered taped to the inside of cupboard doors or underneath drawers. Sharp opened a filing cabinet and said, "Ah, here it is – a file labelled 'Women I Shagged this Month'."

"No?" Day was shocked. A pause and then he laughed. "A joke – oh, very good, Mandy."

Sharp was disappointed by the result but hid her feelings. "Your hunches are usually pretty reliable but this was always going to be the longest of long-shots!" she said. But Day was now deep in thought and staring at the Head's diary.

"Just a minute," he said, "I've been missing the obvious." The A4 Academic Year Diary was full of Carmichael's beautifully precise handwriting. The last entry was less than two days old – 'Alarm call-out 11pm'. 'Strange that he took time to record that,' thought Day.

Before that date, almost every page was full. It appeared that Carmichael liked to write brief aide-memoirs after every meeting or incident. There were also many appointments scheduled for the remaining weeks of term – a lot of people were going to be disappointed.

Flicking through, Day noticed a peculiar pattern. Every so often the circle in the letter 'a' in the name of the day was shaded in. On those pages only, there was a confusingly random row of numbers and letters in the extreme left bottom corner.

"A code?" he whispered as he raised one eyebrow.

"Found something?" said Sharp as she wandered over – half expecting a reciprocal joke.

"Some sort of code. Might be nothing but take a look. Flick through to last September. Check the 'a' in the name of the day; if it's filled in there's a string of letters and numbers at the bottom of the page?"

Sharp took the book and began to turn the pages. "Bloody hell, you're right! There are fourteen entries since the start of the school year – more than one a month. It's definitely some sort of code but could it be about his conquests? It's got to be worth a serious looking at."

"Carmichael's been here three years so see if you can find the previous years' diaries. If he's vain enough to keep those kinds of records, he won't have thrown the old ones away."

Another five minutes searching and Sharp turned up two more diaries.

"Excellent," said Day. "Let's go and interview the ex. Bring all the diaries – this afternoon we're going to play at Bletchley Park."

-

Grainger and Sindhu's first call was to the home of Janice Rhodes, the young parent who was rumoured to become very nervous and/or embarrassed in Mr Carmichael's company. They pulled up outside a beautifully kept council house. The front garden was awash with flowers and the front door was obviously newly painted.

Grainger knocked. It took more than a minute for the door to open and a face to appear in the narrow gap behind the security chain. It was a pretty face, although a little on the thin side and looking decidedly nervous.

'Possibly Carmichael's type?' thought Grainger.

"What do you want? Who…"

"Police, Mrs Rhodes." Grainger help up his ID and Sindhu stepped into Rhodes' narrow line of sight. "I'm DC Grainger and this is PC Sindhu. I assume you've heard about the death of Mr Carmichael from the school your son attends. We're just collecting background information and hoped you might be able to help us?"

At the mention of Carmichael's name, Mrs Rhodes blushed. It was well on the way to being the deepest blush either officer had ever seen. The contrast with her close-cropped blonde hair was startling.

She didn't attempt to open the door any further. "I can't tell you anything, I hardly knew the man."

"Perhaps we could come in, just for five minutes?" Grainger persisted.

"No! I've nothing to say to you about that man!" Mrs Rhodes spat out the response and, amazingly, the blush deepened.

Grainger thought she might blow some vital organ so he backed off. "Perhaps we could call later, when you've recovered a little from the shock?"

"Shock? What shock? I've told you, I hardly knew the man. I really have nothing to say."

Sindhu was concerned by the stress Rhodes seemed to be under. "Is your little boy at home, Mrs Rhodes?"

"No, he's at his grandma's – the school's closed and I have a job to go to." It was hard to tell if the voice demonstrated anxiety or anger.

"Oh, where do you work?" asked Sindhu quietly - while she wrote on her note book, 'Is anyone else in the house with you?'

"The Spar on the High Street." She read the message as soon as it was held in view, "No, I'm alone." Whatever the motion, Rhodes was incredibly edgy.

Sindhu wrote again on her notebook and held it up. 'Are you being threatened by someone inside?'

"No, don't be ridiculous, I'm fine," she whispered.

"Could I ask you about your husband?" asked Grainger. The blush went even deeper. "Ex-husband! Why? What's he got to do with anything?"

Grainger spoke very quietly now. "We understand Mr Rhodes is in prison?"

"He's not Rhodes, he's Petersen. He got life for attempted murder – and he deserved it! He used to beat me up every time he had a drink – and he left me pregnant! Good riddance; I divorced him as soon as he was locked away. I changed my name and the council moved me here. As far as I'm concerned, they can keep him in prison forever – I don't want to see him again!"
Rhodes was so close to hysteria that Grainger decided to call it a day.
"Thanks for your help. Sorry you've found it so distressing. Goodbye."
The door was slammed without another word from Ms Rhodes.

-

"So, it's Petersen, not Rhodes! I know that name from somewhere. Let's get back to Beetwell Street and find out a bit more about him. I reckon she's on the verge of panic about something and it might be an imminent release?"
Less than half-an-hour later they would discover that Gary Petersen had been released from Leeds Prison more than a month previously – and had recently fallen off the Probation Service's radar.

-

The 'powers that be' probably wouldn't admit it, but young constables destined for 'fast track' promotion have to work hard to gain credibility with 'proper coppers'.
PC Derek Day had his opportunity in only his fifth week out on the streets.
It was nine o'clock on an otherwise quiet Tuesday night when Day and his mentor, PC John Treweek, received a call about an affray at the Wheatsheaf pub in Newbold.

Treweek drove fast and expertly but, when they arrived, an ambulance was already parked outside.

"Hmm, it looks as though bloodshed might be involved. Watch your back, son! I'll go in first – stay close," said the veteran officer.

All the lights were on inside but it was deadly quiet. Treweek pushed open the door tentatively. He could see, huddled against the far wall, a group of half-a-dozen customers all staring his way with expressions that ranged from fear to outright terror. On the floor were two bodies. A paramedic, blood oozing from a headwound, was sprawled across another seriously injured man.

As Treweek pushed the door fully open, one of the drinkers yelled, "Look out, mate – he's behind the door!"

The warning came too late. Treweek didn't even have chance to shout 'Police' before a heavy bottle crashed down on his head.

The attacker sprang into view but not towards Day – he ran at the man who had shouted the warning and dragged a broken glass down his face. Amongst the screams, PC Day was able to enter the room unchallenged.

"Police, stop that!" he shouted lamely.

The attacker did. He turned towards Day and it was obvious to the young PC that this bloke was completely wired. His eyes were full of hatred for everything and everyone. He grinned when he saw Day. "Oh look, it's another copper – and this time it's a baby one!" He picked up another pint glass, broke it on the edge of the bar and advanced.

Day watched the two hands and the glasses – one already bloodied – the other soon to be, if he wasn't careful. He'd been trained what to do; his expandable baton was to hand but, for some reason he chose not to reach for it. His streetfighter training seemed to take precedence and PC Day reverted to type.

Simple odds dictated that his enemy was right handed so the glass in that hand was likely to slash forwards first. Fortunately, Day's instinct was correct. As the attacker's hand whipped towards his face, Day stepped to the right. He spun as the glass passed his left shoulder and grabbed the arm wielding it. He accelerated the off-balance thug into the door behind him, giving him a vicious right rabbit punch on the back of his neck. The man wasn't incapacitated, though – some kind of fighting madness kept him motivated. He had dropped one glass as he fell to the floor in front of the door but he was on the point of rising when Day calmly instructed him to drop the other glass. But this guy had gone way beyond making sensible decisions; he rose back onto one knee and stared at Day.

In that instant the voice of Arthur Ross whispered in his grandson's ear. "How many does he have to hurt before you put him down, boy!"

But PC Day knew this was no time to go crazy. Clinical was better.

"You're dead, copper!" the thug shrieked.

He shouldn't have hesitated. The second it took to issue the threat was enough; Day stepped forward and kicked him full in the face, mangling teeth and nose. It was definitely 'game over'. When Day was on top of him applying handcuffs he turned to take in the scene. PC Treweek was staring at him as he spoke groggily into his radio. The five customers still standing were open-mouthed.

But the job was done; the score - Day 1, Thug 0.

Inevitably, Day was suspended pending investigation for allegedly using excessive force. It was only Jess' dogged support that kept him from resigning. However, given the serious injuries the offender had inflicted on members of the public and the emergency services, Day was exonerated and allowed back on duty.

Within hours of starting his first shift, he realised that things had changed. There was no animosity and no hero worship – just a calm acceptance. PC Derek Day was now 'one of the lads'.

He gave evidence at the trial of Gary Petersen and was relentlessly cross-examined about his actions prior to the arrest. Eventually, the judge told defence counsel to stop that line of questioning, telling him it was his client who was on trial not the brave young PC.

Other witnesses described how Petersen had come into the pub looking for the first victim. The attack had been immediate and vicious. There was no argument – the crime had been premeditated.

The jury returned a unanimous verdict on the 'attempted murder' charge.

After the verdict, a list of previous offences was read out. There had been a string of assaults, including several on his wife. The most serious had been an attack on his wife's fourteen-year-old brother, Preston when he had tried to intervene to protect his sister.

The judge called the convicted man a lot of names before sentencing him to 'life' imprisonment. When the sentence was announced, Gary Petersen's lips curled back and he mouthed at PC Day, "One day we'll meet again and then you'll be the one in hospital – or the morgue!

Chapter Fifteen

"Hello, boss – there's been a major fuck-up!" It was Jimmy Hammond calling DCI Day.
Day didn't approve of the word but he worked with police officers, most of whom reserved polite language only for dealing with members of the public, so he was used to it. "Explain!"
"A name from the past, sir. Gary Petersen was released from Leeds a month ago. We did get notice but it got lost somewhere in the system. Andy Grainger's just worked out that he's the ex of one of your P.o.I.s – Janice Rhodes. Apparently, she divorced him when he went inside. She doesn't know he's been released."
"Where's he staying?"
"Dropped off the radar. Missed a meeting at probation a fortnight ago and hasn't been seen since."
"Damn! Where are Grainger and Sindhu now?"
"They'll have arrived at their second interview by now, sir."
Day thought fast. It was ten years since he'd put Petersen in hospital and then in prison. The threats Petersen had made didn't worry him but he doubted that serving the sentence would have turned that thug into a better person. It was the ex-wife he was worried for – and she didn't know he was out. How much would he want to meet the son he'd never seen? "Jimmy, send a car round to Mrs Rhodes' house, sharpish. Tell them to warn her he's out and acting suspiciously. They're to offer to do a security check of the house – that'll give 'em an excuse to look around. Warn the lads Petersen is a violent devil. Then get things moving – friends, family anyone who knew him – chase him down, I want him found, priority one! And make sure the Super knows asap – she'll be livid!"

Jimmy Hammond gulped; someone was going to get a serious bollocking. "Consider it done, sir. We'll find him!"

They would – but, by then, it would be far too late.

-

Having inadvertently started an explosion of activity at Beetwell Street, Grainger and Sindhu were relieved to be able to set off to interview the alleged stalker, Tracey Tomlinson.

Sindhu had already met the wife, ex-wife and alleged lover of the first victim, so was expecting to see another beauty. The woman who opened the door wasn't – she was upset to the point of distraught. To the two police officers it looked as though Tracey Tomlinson had been crying for 24 hours. She had.

"He was so beautiful!" she declared. "I can't believe he's dead!" More tears followed.

Grainger gave her time to compose herself before beginning the questions. "I'm sorry to see you so upset, Mrs Tomlinson, did you have a special relationship with Mr Carmichael?"

"Yes, I did," she replied with unexpected sincerity. "My boy Kirk left last year. He'd always been a bit highly strung and, until Mr Carmichael arrived at the school, no one could cope with him. But Mr Carmichael made the effort to understand him and suddenly Kirk started to behave himself and work hard. I'll always be grateful for that."

"And did you express your gratitude?" asked Grainger, expecting an evasive answer. He didn't get one.

"Oh yes, I let him screw me! Only once mind. He was very good, very attentive – I had a massive orgasm!" The response was so blunt, so understated, so matter-of-fact that, for a few moments, Grainger and Sindhu were shocked into silence.

Tomlinson was surprised by the lull in questioning and gave them both a quizzical expression.

Grainger noticed that Sindhu was desperately trying to suppress a laugh, so he asked a follow-up question. "Only once? It wasn't the beginning of an affair, then?"

"I wish!" replied Tomlinson. "I'd have loved to have had an affair with him. I'd have shagged him every day for a year if he'd let me – but one fuck in his office and that was the end of us! I tried to keep up contact even after Kirk left and went to the Academy but he wasn't interested. Oh, he gave me the occasional smile and even wrote thank-you notes when I sent him gifts – but no more than that – very sad."

Grainger had been a detective for five years and was rarely lost for words but he was so shocked by this open confession that he just mumbled his way through the standard questions. "Where were you at midnight on Sunday? Can you account for your movements yesterday? Do you know of anyone who might have wanted to harm Mr Carmichael?"

Sindhu was quick to interrupt. "Like your husband, for example?"

After accepting seemingly truthful answers, plus an assurance that Mr Tomlinson was so wrapped up in uncontrolled alcoholism, he hadn't even noticed his wife's fixation on Mr Carmichael, the two officers left to write up a colourful report.

11.00am

Day knocked on the front door of Veronica Davison, ex-wife of victim number one. It was opened but the strained face that appeared obviously had no intention of removing the security chain.

"Morning, Ms Davison, we have a few more questions, may we come in?" asked Day in the politest voice he could muster.

"No, but ask away!"

That wasn't an acceptable response and this time Day was anything but polite. "People who have already been caught out lying to police conducting a murder enquiry are walking on very thin ice. Open the door, please!"

The door slammed and remained closed for a full thirty seconds. Day was just about to knock again when he heard the security chain rattle and the door opened wide.

"Come in, if you must!" said a very irritated voice.

They took similar seating positions to the previous visit and Day introduced his colleague. "You remember Detective Sergeant Sharp – one of my top investigators. She's going to ask you some more questions."

"Good morning, Detective Sergeant," replied Davison, in a voice clearly designed to mimic the long, drawn-out replies familiar to school assemblies.

Sharp ignored the sarcasm. "You had an appointment at 12 noon yesterday – where was that?"

This clearly wasn't the question Davison was expecting and, after a short pause, she blurted out, "Mind your own business!"

Sharp didn't flinch. "I'm going to ask that question again and, if I don't get a credible answer, I'm going to take you down to the station – in handcuffs – that should give your neighbours a thrill. Where were you at noon yesterday?" Sharp was well aware that the threat was pretty much empty at this stage but knew a good delivery would usually do the trick.

Now, visibly much paler, Davison replied, "Casa."

"The hotel? What's the big deal about having lunch at the Casa? It's what posh folks do - you must have a dozen witnesses?" Sharp felt her suspicions fall away – but not for long.

"I wasn't having lunch," admitted Davison.

"Oh? I can only think of one other reason for going to a hotel for a couple of hours in the middle of the day! At least you'll have one witness then?" Sharp wasn't letting up.

"Err… yes."

"Name?"

"I'd rather not say!"

"Married?"

Davison placed her head in her hands. "Yes."

It was one attractive woman to another – but Sharp was very much in charge.

"Well, if that's the case, you'd have been better to invite him here. The kids were at school."

Davison almost laughed. "What, with my nosey neighbours?"

Sharp was totally puzzled. "But you're single – what would the neighbours know or care?"

There was a very long pause but Sharp was not in the mood for more delay. "Well?" she demanded.

There was another pause before Davison whispered, "He's famous. TV. He would have been recognised. With the neighbours I've got, there'd be a photo of him leaving my house on Facebook and probably in next week's 'Hello' magazine as well."

"Well, you might as well give me his name – it'll waste five minutes of my time to find out which TV stars were staying at the Casa yesterday."

"I'd still rather not say; as least then I won't feel guilty about dropping him in it – if it gets back to his wife!"

"Ms Davison, yesterday lunchtime there was a second murder which we believe was linked to the death of your ex-husband. I need the name of your alibi!"

The impact on Davison's demeanour was savage; she shrank into a ball. Day thought she was about to slide to the floor and braced himself for a catch.

"Drew Challenger."

Day didn't recognise the name but Sharp did. "Game show host," she said to help her boss out. "Very popular – good looking but a bit smarmy for me."

"Not when you get to know him," retorted Davison, with the hint of real affection in her voice.

"We will get to know him, Ms Davison – and you'd better hope that he tells us you were with him, or we'll be back!" Day stood up and marched out – closely followed by Sharp.

1.00pm

Despite the seriousness of the occasion, there was laughter in the Briefing Room as Day entered with Detective Superintendent Halfpenny.

"Okay, what's the joke?" demanded the senior officer.

Most of the detectives present made very good attempts at innocent expressions and waited for someone else to respond.

Eventually, it was Pug Davies who answered the question. "Detective Constable Grainger was regaling us with a graphic account of his interview with Mrs Tomlinson, the alleged stalker, ma'am. Apparently, she was very frank! The lad gave us a good laugh – broke the tension." Pug had known the Superintendent for many years and knew his stock was high with her – he hoped he'd done enough to protect Grainger.

In the corner, Grainger was looking like a rabbit caught in headlights.

DSupt. Halfpenny glared in Grainger's direction and then said, in a falsetto, 'schoolma'am' voice, "See me after class, young Grainger." Then she smiled. "I could do with a laugh, too!"

Everyone relaxed. The business could begin.

Halfpenny opened the meeting. "DCI Day and I agree that the murders are linked and we have a conspiracy involving two or more people on our hands. I'm not as convinced as he is that Councillor Mallender is the ringleader but, history convinces me that I should stand by his theory until proven otherwise. I know you'll work hard to resolve these crimes. Total effort everyone, please – I'll worry about the overtime when you've caught the bastards!" She walked out without another word.

Day, pleased at the unspoken vote of confidence, said one word. "Petersen?"

"Word's gone out, sir. Everyone in the county's looking for him. Other forces are aware of the situation," replied Pug Davies.

Those officers who, earlier in the morning, had known nothing about the Day/Petersen clash certainly did now. Day's status within the team went up another notch.

"What are the chances of him being involved in our murders?" asked DI Allsop.

"Just a hunch, Trev. No logic yet. Both murders were committed by a vicious devil – and he fits that description."

"Is it possible he found Rhodes and the kid and she told him she had the hots for Carmichael – so he was removing a rival?" suggested DS Sharp.

"Same thought's crossed my mind, Mandy – but we've got to stay open minded. Petersen could be living it up in London for all we know," Day added.

"Rhodes was very edgy when we interviewed her, sir," said Grainger.

"Pug, who went round to tell her Petersen was out? What did they make of her?"

"Rouse and Adams, sir. She wouldn't let 'em in. Rouse said she seemed more shocked than surprised."

"Do you think it's possible Petersen's in the house holding a knife to the kid's throat?" asked DS Sharp.

"It's a grim, unlikely possibility but we'll have to take it seriously. Surveillance – Pug, set up a rota, please. Does Rhodes have access to a car? Find out, please Mr Dawson. Does she have any links to Mallender? Some years ago, she was in difficulties and the council agreed to move her – did Mallender help her out – is she owed a favour? Do your best with that one, Dom."

That's enough on that particular theory; let's look at other angles. Price first."

"No blood in either car, boss," contributed Eric the Blood immediately.

"Phone records support her story, too," said Phil Johnstone.

"Neighbours' stories agree with what she told you, sir," said Dom.

"Fair enough. Apart from one more little question, we'll put her on the back burner for now. Her stupidity has, at least, allowed us to pinpoint Carmichael's time of death very accurately. We know he put his phone down at 11.49 and Price arrived at the school gates only a few minutes after she passed the pub camera at 12.19. A little over half-an-hour. That's quick work – very well organised. Phil, check every camera within a five-mile radius around those times.

Now, we might have struck gold regarding Carmichael's love life. DS Sharp and I noticed what appears to be a system of codes in his diaries going back three years. We think they might record his conquests! We're going to have a good look at it after the briefing – what we need is a 'key' to get started. Ms Sindhu, that's where you come in. Go and see Price and, whatever it takes, persuade her to admit the date, place and time when she had sex with her boss; that could set us going. Andy, you do the same with the woman from 'True Confessions' magazine – you seem to be the one to get her to open up."

"No pun intended," added DS Sharp.

Laughter broke the tension.

There followed detailed reports from SOCO and the doctors about Carmichael's post mortem and Grimshaw's attack. Doc Smythe reported that cause of death for Carmichael was the blow on the back of the head from the collision with the open filing cabinet drawer and was therefore possibly unintended – but the boy had been hit from behind in an unmistakably deliberate murder.

Little had been gained by interviewing Grimshaw's family and friends. One sliver of hope, though was a throwaway comment the boy had made to a friend a couple of weeks previously. Grimshaw boasted that 'an old woman had recruited him to work for MI5'.

The call to Mary Swanwick Primary School had also thrown up an interesting fact. Mary Davenport, the former Ofsted inspector who had claimed she had been at the school all day Monday, hadn't arrived until 2pm – to conduct an after-school staff meeting. It would be interesting to see if she was on Carmichael's conquest list.

Drew Challenger was furious when he was tracked down and asked about his liaison with Miss Davison. At first, he strenuously denied even knowing her but, following assurances he would not be named, he admitted he had been having an occasional fling with her for nearly a year. Yes, they did meet at Casa yesterday, but she was 90 minutes late – so it was only a 'quickie' because she had to pick up her kids from school – he told the officer.

There were a lot of women suspects in this case – and all of them were bloody liars!

As the reports continued to come in, Day wrote follow-up tasks on his whiteboard. "Unless we have a breakthrough, I'll see you all back here at 6pm. Phone me immediately if you think you've found something useful. Now, get to it!"

-

Jess had organised a simple wedding; twenty minutes at Chesterfield Registry Office followed by a reception for just forty guests at the Sandpiper Hotel.

Living frugally in their first year of employment had allowed the happy couple to accumulate some savings. Colleagues at school and police station, realising the couple's ambition to get on the housing ladder, had been generous. But it was the parents who made all the difference. Both pairs gave more than they could really afford to turn the savings into a deposit. Just before the wedding date, Jess and Derek moved into a small semi in Brimington. In those difficult days of financial crashes and bankruptcies – a rare feat indeed.

The honeymoon was spent stripping woodchip, painting – and every other form of DIY imaginable. Derek's skills were limited but Jess seemed to be able to turn her hand to everything.

Three weeks after the marriage, Jessica's cousin Grace sent them an email. She was going away for a while and would the newlyweds like to spend a few days in her flat in London?

Derek had a couple of days leave available and Jess wasn't due to return to school until the following week, so they agreed they deserved a break and a brief trip to the capital would be fun.

It was a decision that would almost put an end to Derek's career – again!

As a belated wedding present, Grace had left them a couple of tickets to a West End show. After an evening of great entertainment, they decided to take a walk back to Grace's flat. Their A to Z told them it would be a long walk but failed to indicate that the route would take them through some pretty dodgy neighbourhoods.

They heard the trouble before they saw it. Two men were curled up on the ground receiving vicious kicks from a gang of more than a dozen.

"999!" Derek whispered to Jessica as he set off towards the fracas.

"Stop! Police!" he yelled, in the firm hope the attackers would run away.

They didn't. Almost as one, they stopped their attack and turned to face the new threat. Derek could almost analyse their thoughts. One ordinary bloke in civvies didn't seem much of a challenge – even if he did claim to be a copper.

Derek listened to Jess calmly giving their location down the phone as he studied the opposition.

Skinheads – more tattoos than teeth. Although some were obviously injured, it was still too many; Derek realised he was going to get trashed.

Behind the semi-circle of thugs, Derek was relieved to see both the victims were attempting to get to their feet. They were big men and, despite the blood and the darkness, it was possible to see that one was black and one white.

'Racist attack,' thought Derek, 'Bastards!'

Suddenly there was an exaggerated shout. "Bloody hell, is that you Daisy? Are you really a copper?"

Derek recognised the voice. Of all people – Cap! A bad situation had become a whole lot worse. Derek was facing thirteen skinheads and the odds had just increased.

He was wrong. The skinhead nearest to Cap had turned towards the shout and received a brutal punch in the face from his former victim. He dissolved onto the tarmac. Derek had a split second to think it was a good job Cap had been injured - otherwise that stupid man would have been dead.

There was now some confusion in the ranks of the twelve remaining thugs. The black guy was also rising unsteadily to his feet – and he was huge! Derek could see the thugs reassessing their situation. Okay, so twelve onto three wasn't as favourable as thirteen onto two – but the new arrival claiming to be a copper didn't look much. However, he was as yet uninjured, so he had to be the first target.

Derek heard his grandfather's voice: 'Keep calm, identify the most enthusiastic attacker and put him down first – the others will hesitate – and that fraction will give you an opening'.

Derek identified the leader. He was the guy who yelled, "Jacko, get the bitch with the phone!"

Derek's calculating calm wavered. Jess was under threat! The man he assumed was Jacko was well to his right – out of immediate reach.

The gang leader regretted his instruction less than two seconds later. Derek jumped at him and twisted the full weight of his body through his left elbow into the thug's vulnerable right temple. The momentum pushed Derek in the direction of Jacko - who was now within arm's length of Jess. He was too late! He saw had Jess put away her phone to face her attacker. As he came into range, she took a mighty swing that just clipped the end

152

of his nose. The blow startled Jacko but didn't stop his charge and he knocked Jess to the floor. His attempt to jump on top of her was interrupted by a devastating kick into his ribcage from Derek's right foot. Two down.

Derek saw that Jess was stunned but trying to get to her feet when a new threat emerged. A fist swung violently towards his head but the automatic duck was perfectly timed. He twisted sharply and slammed his right fist into the guy's stomach. Three down.

Derek had a moment to look up and see that his intervention had given the two earlier victims the opportunity to recover and begin to do some damage to the gang.

Although the odds were still very much in their favour, it was clear that some of the gang were hesitating. However, three of the more determined were giving Cap a hard time. Derek grabbed the nearest by the back of his T-shirt, spun him round and speedily applied three sharp left jabs to his face. On the third blow, strong arms seized him from behind. He reacted instinctively and shot his right elbow backwards into his new attacker's face.

Oh shit – it was a copper! Derek hadn't registered the sound of approaching sirens – and now he'd assaulted a police officer!

Derek's lame 'sorry' didn't gain him any sympathy. He didn't resist and, within seconds, he was manacled on the ground.

Five minutes later he was pushed into the back of a van. Four others were already inside. Cap and his giant friend were accompanied by two scowling skinheads. As the van drove off, Cap broke the silence.

"So, Daisy, are you really a cop – be honest, now?" He was actually grinning through the blood.

"Yes, I'm afraid so – but, I suspect, not for very much longer!"

"Well, I'd like to express my gratitude," said Cap's friend. "My name is Marcus Reivers and I'm very pleased to meet you. In other circumstances, I'd shake hands." Although he too was covered in blood, he began to laugh.

Derek, though was in despair. He'd lost sight of the love of his life and now he'd almost certainly lost his job.

Chapter Sixteen

1.00pm

Margaret Mallender was scared. Her successful career as a Town Councillor was over – her dream of becoming Mayor of Chesterfield shattered. Prison was perhaps the best she could hope for?

She was bright enough to know that the senior detective was convinced she was involved in this stupid conspiracy. It wasn't fair; she'd just wanted Carmichael to be terribly humiliated. They'd discussed stripping him and tying him to a chair with a sign around his neck so they could put pictures on the internet. That would be sufficient revenge – he'd be investigated, his career would be over and he'd never even be able to go out in public again. It had been incredibly difficult to organise and this had been the third attempt. They'd needed to get him alone and vulnerable and Mallender had used her local knowledge to hatch a series of complex plots. At no time had she agreed to a murder but now she suspected she'd been used – had the others intended to kill Carmichael all along? She'd totally blundered. Out of the dozen or so women who'd complained to her about Carmichael she'd chosen just three she thought would have the bottle to seek revenge without going too far. How was she to know one of them would involve a bloody psychopath in the plan?

All the women involved had the same motive for wishing to see Carmichael humiliated. All had been seduced in 'one-night stands' by that smooth-talking ruthless bastard. It was that bitch of an Ofsted Inspector who'd provided the spark. As Chair of Governors, Mallender had met Davenport during the very positive inspection feedback. A couple of weeks later the inspector had arrived unannounced at Mallender's door.

She admitted that Carmichael had dumped her the second the 'Outstanding' verdict was in the bag. She had been humiliated and wanted some 'off the record' revenge. Mallender couldn't believe she'd been stupid enough to admit to Davenport she'd made the same mistake and discuss various vengeance strategies.

Carmichael had made Mallender feel so young and desirable. She had become a giddy sixteen-year-old who gave herself willingly even in the unromantic surroundings of his office. Although she'd had a few sexual partners before, they'd been meandering amateurs compared with the progressive artistry of George Carmichael and she'd discovered ecstasy. When they met the following day, she expected a positive reception and to be appointed his long-term lover – but he never treated her with affection again; he never even mentioned that hour of so-called passion. After many weeks of distress and humiliation she had resolved to punish him – but never to kill him.

The co-conspirators had suffered similar fates but, unknown to her, at least one wanted much more in revenge. They needed Carmichael in school alone – preferably after dark.

Then a breakthrough; he had confided in her that his marriage was on the rocks. She did her best to appear sympathetic while, all the time, planning a third attempt - a complex plan that had at best a 50-50 chance of succeeding – how was she to know that it would be so totally successful - until one of the recruits went too far?

She knew the phone call to the police would have to be genuine, and not just from her, so she had dressed as a much older woman and recruited that stupid boy to organise a disturbance that would generate lots of phone calls on a night when she knew the caretaker would be busy.

She'd told the others that Carmichael's marriage was in difficulty and how she would try to tip him over the edge that night. From her commanding view of the school entrance, she had called the others up when it became clear the plan was working.

She was just as guilty as the rest of them, wasn't she? No, of course not – she'd never even thought of murder, just humiliation. Okay, she'd supplied the phones, the pepper spray and the masks they'd been instructed to use but that didn't make her a murderer.

After Rhodes had told her of the 'accident', Mallender had cried and moaned throughout a sleepless night. She was having difficulty assimilating the facts until the two police officers knocked on her door on Monday morning, confirming the death. How she held it together then, she'd never know. And now they'd killed Grimshaw, too; his only crime was stupidity.

She was done for… but that wasn't the worst of it. She was no longer in charge. The call she'd had earlier had been very reassuring – at first. "Stick to the agreed story and everything will be fine, go to your regular meeting." the caller had said. The tone made it abundantly clear that if she didn't 'stick to the agreed story' there would be serious consequences.

She was facing prison or death threats – what a choice!

2.00pm

Davenport was also panicking. The text message had been very clear. 'MM is cracking. Silence her or we're all done. She'll leave her flat at 3.30'.

At first, she tried to convince herself that 'silence her' meant persuade Mallender to be strong and quiet but, it soon became clear, she had to admit to herself that a more drastic solution was required. The councillor, although a great organiser, had always been the weakest link in their conspiracy. Davenport had been shocked by Carmichael's death – but now had to admit he deserved it. Even that pathetic teenager's murder would benefit society in the long run - but this series of events was now getting out of hand.

What could she do? She had no gun or knife – or the skills to use them. She couldn't even look at a hammer without throwing up after what had happened in the last couple of days. She had a fast car and was a pretty decent driver – learned during a dangerous upbringing sharing her big brothers' desire to drive very quickly in cars they didn't always own. Her contact had said Mallender always left for a regular meeting at around 3.30pm. Davenport concocted a simple scheme and then began to plan her escape.

-

Being locked up in a police cell in the capital overnight was a novel experience for young PC Derek Day. The two detective constables who interviewed him the following morning made a point of demonstrating no favouritism.

"If you're a policeman - if - you should have known better," said one.

"It's people like you give us all a bad name," said two. "You come down to the capital for a scrap – that's a definite no-no. Tell us what happened, make it good!"

"Of course," said Derek with all the restraint he could muster. "But, first could you tell me what happened to my wife, please?"

The younger DC looked at his notes. "Yes. Mrs Jessica Day was released from hospital a couple of hours ago.

They'd kept her in for observation but luckily the concussion was minimal."

"Phew, could you tell me where she is?"

"Here, in the waiting room next to reception."

"Thanks for that, gentlemen." Derek then made a long and completely accurate statement.

Both DCs scowled throughout. "You do realise one of the blokes you hit might have permanent brain damage?" asked one.

Unfortunately, this was not a surprise to Derek – but the man had ordered an assault on Jess – and he was in the way. "I'm genuinely sorry to hear that," he lied.

At that moment the door of the bleak interview room opened and a uniformed sergeant strolled in. He looked at Day then bent to whisper in the closest detective's ear. Both DCs sat back in their chairs in apparent disgust.

"Okay, Police Constable Day, you're free to go. Your wife's waiting for you in reception," announced the sergeant. "You seem to have powerful friends. Piss off back to Derbyshire asap, will you?"

Derek didn't know he had 'powerful friends', he just wanted to see Jess. And there she was, sitting in a small waiting room chatting to her former boyfriend and his truly massive friend. All three were the worse for wear. Jess was pale grey and the two blokes were decorated with bruises and steri-strips.

Derek felt almost guilty; there wasn't a mark on him. Jess looked up and immediately ran to him. "Ouch!" she exclaimed as he hugged her, so he hurriedly let go.

"Where does it hurt?"

"Just general soreness," she said. "I had quite a tumble!"

"So, Police Constable Daisy, we are assured beyond reasonable doubt that you are a real, genuine copper!

And you married Jessica!" interrupted Cap. His voice gave no clue to his mood – until he broke into a wide grin. "I owe you one."

"Me too," said Cap's friend.

"Are you two my powerful friends," laughed Derek.

"Not me, Daisy," Cap nudged his friend, "Him."

"Yes, it's me I'm pleased to say. I'm a barrister and I sometimes work for the CPS. I've worked with several of the senior officers here."

"And played rugby with them," added Cap.

"So, what did happen last night?" Derek wanted to know why he had put his career at risk.

"My fault, I suppose," admitted Cap. "We were walking along minding our own business when that gang of idiots started shouting abuse at Marcus. He told me to ignore them but I'd had just the wrong amount of beer and I shouted, 'Piss off, racist twats!'. They seemed to take exception to that. In fairness we did put a couple of them down before we both ended up on the tarmac!"

"There won't be any charges against you," said Marcus to Derek. "When they heard the full story from me, they believed it. You did warn them you were a police officer and it was your lady who phoned the police. Five of the gang were arrested last night and they've all got form. However, I'm sorry I won't be able to protect you from possible disciplinary action when you get back to work."

But Marcus did have a couple of tricks up his sleeve. That night, the Evening Standard ran a story on page five under the headline 'OFF DUTY POLICEMAN SAVES BARRISTER FROM BRUTAL ATTACK'.

A few days later the same story would appear, with a rather more sensational headline, on the front page of the Derbyshire Times. '*CHESTERFIELD PC STOPS RACE RIOT IN CAPITAL*'.

Derek never found out how the event became exaggerated, but it did save his career.

All his superiors, from his sergeant upwards, gave him a series of severe bollockings – and some even managed to keep straight faces.

Chapter Seventeen

With information from two of Carmichael's conquests, Day and his team began to make sense of the codes in the school diaries.

After checking her own diary, Melanie Price reluctantly confirmed the date, time and venue of her one sexual encounter with her boss.

There was a row of letters and numbers on the date page she indicated:

er19.5od10md

Tracey Tomlinson was more enthusiastic about passing on her details:

ro19od4m - was the shorter code on her page.

Phil Johnstone quickly worked out that the first two letters represented the second letters of the conquest's name – nothing so obvious as the actual initials. Information received suggested that the first set of numbers was the time of day. It didn't matter that no one was sure if 19.5 was 7.30pm or 7.05pm – or the start or finish of the seduction.

Both women told their interviewers that most of the action took place in Carmichael's office – principally across his desk! So 'od' was assumed to be 'office desk'. The remaining information was more problematic until Day realised the next number was Carmichael's score for the encounter. Melanie Price, the woman he really wanted, scored 'the perfect 10'. Day wasn't worldly wise enough to interpret the letters at the end – but DS Sharp was – she didn't think it necessary to tell him but, given the chance, she would have been happy to demonstrate.

"Right, Mandy, Phil – we'll take a diary each. Look for 'aa' – if our theory is correct, we need to find the date he seduced Mallender asap."

It took less than five minutes for two lots of 'aa' to be found. The first was at 21.00 the previous December – the entry was immediately after the evening Carol Concert. "That's got to be Mallender!" exclaimed Day. "That's enough to bring her in!"

The other 'aa' entry was a unique double – two sessions in the middle of the Ofsted inspection! "Mary Davenport – it seems she got a double helping in return for her generous grading. Now she's going to have to answer some tough questions, too! Phil, call Andy and Ms Sindhu – tell them to find Davenport and bring her in. If she won't come voluntarily, they're to arrest her for wasting police time. When you've done that, go through all the diaries and list the initials to check if any more tally with our P.o.I. list. Come on, Mandy, let's go and get Mallender."

3.00pm

The earlier call had been the last straw for Margaret Mallender. She admitted to herself that her life was in ruins – but that was preferable to becoming the next murder victim.

Delusion was setting in. She reckoned if she gave herself up and told the complete story, she'd get away with a relatively light sentence – perhaps even non-custodial. Yes, she thought, I've always been an upstanding citizen and supported the police. If I tell them it was only supposed to be a humiliation, of course they'll believe me.

But first, she had things to do. She made a pot of tea and sat at her desk. Tears rolled down her cheek as she wrote a letter of resignation to the Town Council. She then phoned the Town Hall and presented her apologies for the Housing Committee meeting scheduled to start at 4pm. It was the first Tuesday of every month and she had been so proud never to have missed one in her nine-year tenure. More tears.

Having put all her affairs in order for a brief absence, she steeled herself and locked up her flat. She would go straight to Beetwell Street Police Station and ask to meet with DCI Day. He was a reasonable man; he would understand her position. Far better to walk boldly into the station than be arrested in her flat and led out in handcuffs. She'd get it all off her chest and would provide the key to solving two murders – why, she'd be the hero of the hour! Now feeling positively light-headed, she marched confidently down the steps and into the courtyard behind.

At this time of day, the area between the rows of garages was normally deserted, but not today. A BMW she half recognised was parked right in the middle. She ducked down to get a view of the driver and flinched when she realised it was the Ofsted woman. Mary Davenport turned her way, smiled, waved and reached over to open the passenger door.

Mallender approached warily. She bent her knees and, to steady herself, held on to the low-slung car's inner door handle with her left hand. "Hello, Mary…" was all she managed to say before the car hurtled backwards and knocked her sprawling on the tarmac.

She was vaguely aware that the BMW had shot forwards and she tried to pull herself onto her feet. She was five seconds too slow; the car reversed at speed and hit her on the left shoulder, spinning her round and knocking her unconscious. That was a strange kind of blessing; she was totally unaware of the pain when the car's front tyre drove over her head.

Margaret Mallender had resigned from more than just the Town Council.

-

There was spring in the DCI's step as he held open the door to the car park for his DS. "I've got a good feeling about this, Mandy. Mallender will give it all up – we might both get to bed at a reasonable time tonight!"

'What, together?' thought DS Sharp.

"Sir!" A shrill shout from behind stopped Day in his tracks.

He turned to face PC Archer who had obviously been pursuing him down the stairs.

"Hit and run in Somersgill, sir. Sounds like it's near the primary school! Paramedics on the way."

"Anything else?" Day had a deep sickening feeling in his stomach. Grimshaw's murder had obviously been part of a clean-up operation – were they about to witness phase two? "Please don't let it be Mallender!"

As DS Sharp tore up the A61 in the direction of Somersgill, Day's worst fears were realised; it was the councillor – and it was a fatality.

After arriving at the scene, it took Day less than five seconds to decide this was no cruel accident – it was a cold-blooded murder.

"What do you think, Mandy?" asked Day as a paramedic lifted the blanket.

"Hard to tell. Car definitely went over her head."

"Look at the skid marks. Reversed to knock her over, then forwards – reversed again and then and forward for the fatal blow – that would have left the assailant pointing towards the escape route," said Day.

"Deliberate, merciless!" added DS Sharp.

"Agreed," replied Day and he turned to the PC who was first on the scene. "Mr Smith, any witnesses?"

"Not the actual incident, sir, but a lady saw a car going down the street 'rather too fast', as she put it. She said the back light was damaged. Sporty black thing, she said - didn't get the reg. I've got her name and address, here, sir. I've put the word out; everybody's looking for a black car with a damaged rear end."

"Thanks." He handed the constable an evidence bag and a pair of gloves. "Put those rear-light fragments in there would you, please? Any reports of stolen motors in the past few hours?"

"Nothing from Coms., sir."

"Okay, thanks. Mandy, get down to the White Lion, will you? Ask them to show you the CCTV. They might have caught some info on the car," ordered Day.

"Aye, aye, sir," she said and set off at a run – the pub was so close, it wasn't worth moving her Mondeo.

"Who's watching the Rhodes house, now Phil?" Day said into his mobile.

"DC Malysz, sir."

"Okay, I've got his number, thanks." Day dialled the number of one of his latest recruits, a tough little Polish guy called Kamil.

"Hi Kam, it's Day. What's happening at the Rhodes house?"

"Absolutely nothing, sir. Curtain moved about five minutes ago so I'm pretty sure somebody's in and her car still parked on street." The young detective was obviously pleased have a distraction from the monotony.

"What's her car – colour and type?"

"Blue Corsa, you want reg.?"

"Not necessary. What can you see from your current position?"

"All the front, the side door and about half back garden, sir. Any problem? You want I should knock on the door?"

"No Kam, I'll let you know if want you to invade the property." Day put the phone down to the sound of his colleague's chuckling.

The unit of eight garages was a little distance from the flats it served but the whole turning area must have been visible from the third floor. "Mr Smith, up to the top floor of the flats, if you please. Knock on all the doors – someone must have seen or heard something."

Doctor Smythe appeared at the end of the drive through to the road. "Ah, Chief Inspector, I've just seen young Sharpy entering the pub. I hope you ordered one for me?"

Day wasn't in the mood for the doctor's dry humour so he lifted the blanket covering the victim.

"Bloody hell, Mr Day, you're accumulating some very messy bodies this week!" Even with long experience of police work, the sight of Margaret Mallender's crushed head made the doctor wince.

With his best lead deceased, Day decided it was time to go back to the team analysing the diaries to see if any of the other one-night-stand conspirators had been identified. Some of them might have partners or husbands who wouldn't be too impressed with Carmichael; all this bloody shambles revolved around that bastard's callousness.

-

It was pretty clear to Grainger and Sindhu that the Headteacher of Mary Swanwick Primary School was annoyed. Davenport had gone. "Yes, she's been in school most of the day doing lesson observations but she just buggered off without a word – and she's supposed to be leading a second staff meeting. If she thinks she's getting paid…"

Andy Grainger cut her short, "How long ago?"

"I didn't see her go but I've been told she read a text message and left without a word." The headteacher glanced at her watch. "Must have been about 2.30."

"Distressing for you. Did you see the car she came in?"

"Yes, a black BMW – very flash."

"Okay, thanks, Mrs Wheatcroft, we'll be leaving now."

Their speedy departure did nothing to improve the headteacher's temper.

As the two officers ran back to their car, Grainger phoned Day. "Davenport's done a runner, sir. What shall we do?"

"Any info on what car she's driving?" asked Day.

"Black beamer, sir."

"How long ago?"

"Two-thirty-ish, the head here thinks."

"Plenty of time to get to Somersgill and then away. My money says she'll head for home – she won't know we're onto her yet. Set off towards Leicester. I'll see you get the info you need," said Day. "The BMW might have rear damage. If you catch up with her, be careful – she's a real piece of work. Let Ms Sindhu drive!"

Grainger threw the car keys across. "You drive, Dipa. Head for the M1 South. Blues and twos, go for it!" They were flying out of Old Whittington towards the A61 before Andy Grainger had fastened his seatbelt.

"Hold tight! And Andy, soon as you get the info, get onto Traffic and tell them to look out for her car. Any of the traffic lads see her, they're to stop her on my authority; she's now a triple murder suspect!" Day was trying hard to cover the heady mix of anger and excitement in his voice.

"Another one? Bloody hell!"

"Yes, the Councillor – deliberate hit and run; almost certainly Davenport's BMW. Tell all our people she's dangerous and I'm guessing she'll be pretty desperate when cornered."

"Will do, sir."

"Good lad."

The chase was on.

Derek Day decided to phone his wife.

"How's things, love?" she said. "Any nearer to catching your killer?"

"Killers, I'm afraid. Someone's bumping them off faster than I can keep up with."

There was a sharp intake of breath. "Not more?"

"Yes, I can't give you any details but I did want to ask you about your friend, George. You said he made a pass at you just once?"

"It's not like you to be jealous – especially of the deceased!"

"I'm not being funny, Jess – I'm trying to get a more accurate picture of the man. Why only once? You're still gorgeous now but back then you were something else!" Derek Day was trying to choose his words carefully.

"Listen, love. Since the murder hit the news I've had a chat with some ex-colleagues. Dot Mellors, do you remember we started at New Whitt at the same time? She says George was an absolute pest for weeks until she complained to the head. She said she never gave in and hadn't got a good word to say for him."

"You think he left you alone because he was scared of me?"

"I know he did. The first pass he made was when you were suspended for that incident in the pub. I put him back in his box and then, when you were reinstated, news of what had happened that night began to drip through. I imagine, as far as George was concerned, you were just too dangerous," she laughed.

Derek laughed too, but without much humour. "I'm afraid to say, Jess, that the more we find out about your former colleague, the more I dislike him."

"I guess I was just lucky to be married to the right man? What do you think?"
"You still are. Bye love."

-

A shortage of manpower might have been one of the factors in Mary Davenport's good luck. She made it home to Leicester without interception. Her husband was surprised to see her but he was used to her comings and goings so thought it best not to comment.

When she picked up her pre-packed international travelling case, he didn't doubt her story about a lucrative job in the English School in Dubai being brought forward. She kissed him on the cheek and told him she'd phone from Heathrow.

Less than twenty minutes after she left, Grainger and Sindhu arrived at her house.

As soon as Mr Davenport had explained about an important job that had been in her diary for months had suddenly been brought forward, Grainger called Day.

"Husband says she's heading for Heathrow for a flight to Dubai. Jobs been on for months but she's been asked to go earlier."

"And if you believe that…," Day replied. "All right, you two, there's no point chasing her down the M1 – even if we believe she told her husband the truth. All the forces have been notified and airports and ferries, too. She won't get far in a damaged car. Get as much info as you can about her movements in the last three months and then head back up here."

-

Mary Davenport's luck ran out when a traffic cop spotted her damaged tail light as she drove at exactly 70mph on the M62 heading towards Hull. It would have been a routine stop but, when she accelerated away, the two officers checked the registration and spotted the alert from Derbyshire police. They set off in pursuit.

Davenport was a decent driver and was at the wheel of a powerful car but her skills were not at the same level as the PC driving the police Skoda. Even exceeding 120mph failed to shake off the pursuit. More police cars joined the chase and eventually Davenport found herself boxed in by four cars. As the police drivers skilfully manoeuvred to force her onto the exit sliproad, she took a terrible gamble; she accelerated hard, hitting the left rear of the car in front. It spun sideways and the police car following missed it by only inches. But Davenport's BMW was in trouble, too; the car began to fishtail and even as she fought the steering wheel, she knew the battle was lost. Her car's back wheel clipped the apex of the sliproad and the vehicle flipped over – three times!

It had been an eventful day for Mary Davenport – and it ended in total blackness.

Chapter Eighteen

6.00pm: Briefing Room

"What we have here folks is a complete Jekyll and Hyde character. By all accounts a headteacher of astonishing talent – admired by almost everyone who came into contact with him professionally. On the other side we have apparently, a serial womaniser without conscience. As far as we know, he did nothing illegal but, as far as I'm concerned, he was totally immoral."

'You would,' thought DS Sharp.

"His selfish action has brought about three brutal murders – including possibly his own. Now, what do we have on the hunt for Davenport?"

"Just in, sir. Spotted on M62 heading towards Hull with local bobbies in hot pursuit. Should be sorted soon," offered Phil.

"Excellent! Given her recent actions, I think we can conclude that Davenport is at the centre of this shambles. Seems clear she killed Mallender and then made a run for it. There's not much doubt in my mind she was at least present when Carmichael was killed. She's going to tell us everything! Pug, organise a car to go up to Hull to collect her as soon as we get word she's in custody."

"I'll go myself, sir – if I can borrow Ms Sindhu to drive?"

Day laughed. "Your nerves are stronger than mine, Pug. But the answer is yes."

Everyone joined in the laughter, especially Dipa Sindhu, who realised her extraordinary skill meant she had been accepted as one of the team - in record time.

"Anything on Petersen? Has he turned up, been spotted anywhere?"

A chorus of, "No, sir!" met Day's enquiry.

"Damn! Now, what about Rhodes. Is she as shy and nervous as she makes out?" asked Day to the whole group.

"I thought she was going to have some kind of fit on the door step when we first went to interview her," replied DC Grainger.

"Any idea why?" enquired Day.

"She was married to Petersen; nobody knows better than you what a complete arse he is. I can't imagine how awful that must have been, sir – she's got to be traumatised!" said DC Grainger.

"Agreed. But does that make her less or more likely to resort to violence against another abuser?" offered DS Sharp.

"According to the school diary, someone with the second letters 'ah' was seduced last year. Given her attitude, it must be favourite it's her?" Day's question caused a series of nods around the room.

"Could she be hiding Petersen, sir? She insists he's not there but apparently gets very upset when asked?" called out Dom O'Neil.

"We're watching the house and we know the little boy isn't there, so there's not much more we can do without some evidence. Davenport's the key now. If Rhodes is involved, we'll know before the night is out. If not, we'll need some more help with the codes in the diary; Trev, Dom, will you go to see Mrs McAllister tomorrow and show her the sets of initials we've got – it might just jog her memory and give us a couple of new lines of enquiry. But, be careful, I don't regard her as a suspect but it's not impossible." Day always liked to have a 'Plan B'.

"What's McAllister's first name, sir?" asked Dom.

Day looked at his notes. "Valerie. Why, is there an 'ac' in the diary?"

"Yes, sir. Almost exactly two years ago."

"Intriguing. McAllister made it clear she's gay. As far as we know, she has a permanent female partner. What do you think, Mandy – could she be ac/dc?"

DS Sharp looked around the room, carefully studying the faces. "I don't know, sir. Given I'm a committed heterosexual, I guess if there were no attractive men available, I might consider trying out a good-looking woman!"

As intended, this caused a few seconds hilarity but Day wanted a considered judgement and gave Sharp a quizzical look.

"To be serious, my impression of McAllister was that she's comfortable with being gay, sir. I know Carmichael was spectacularly pretty for a bloke and very persuasive but I'd be very surprised, shocked even, if a gay woman in a stable relationship would fall for his charms."

"Thanks, Mandy, that was my impression, too," said Day. "Dom, ask her anyway and report the reaction. And Dom, be subtle!"

More laughter indicated that the team was beginning to feel a little more positive now Davenport was in their grasp.

"Most of you can go home and get some sleep – I have a feeling we'll be kicking doors down very early in the morning!" Day's statement was deliberately intended to raise morale and it ended the meeting on a high note. Day, Sharp, Pug Davies and Dipa Sindhu remained. Pug was on the phone and suddenly his expression turned very grey. He looked up at Day and rolled his eyes – a classic sign something was wrong.

Day waited for the call to end. "Dead or escaped?" he asked wearily.

"Neither," replied Pug. "She crashed into a police car and rolled over. She's unconscious and badly injured; major surgery imminent - would you believe the medics are talking about inducing a coma!"

DCI Day rarely became agitated and never panicked but he now had a strong feeling that 'somebody up there really didn't like him'.

This chain of events was spiralling out of control. Every time they made a breakthrough, it was snatched away. "Pug, phone back and find out which hospital Davenport's in and who's in charge of her treatment – I need to speak to that doctor before they do anything I'll regret."

Then Day did what he always did when he was perplexed – went to his whiteboard. Daysway.

"What do we actually know?" he asked Mandy Sharp.

As the two of them discussed the case, with occasional interjections from PC Sindhu, Day wrote:

Carmichael killed by two or more – poss. unintentional? Complicated plan. Robbery was cover?

Grimshaw involved in conspiracy – was he in the room when Carmichael was murdered? Doubt it.

Mallender definitely involved - was she in the room when Carmichael was murdered? Doubt it.

Grimshaw murder – at least two involved – he knew too much?

Both disfigured after death – psycho!

Mallender murder – definitely Davenport's car – so Davenport 90% guilty – was she alone, was she driving?

Mallender wrote a resignation letter earlier today – was she on way to us to confess? Search her flat more thoroughly – there might be a confession

In Carmichael's office at time of death: Davenport? Price? Rhodes? Any number of others!!

Where's Petersen?

Pug Davies approached the whiteboard and looked it up and down. "More bad news, I'm afraid, sir. I've spoken to the hospital and Davenport's due on the operating table any time now; surgery will take hours and there's no guarantee she'll recover."

"Okay, then there's not much more we can do tonight. Go home and rest. Give me the hospital details, Pug, I'll ring 'em first thing. If it's not worth driving to Hull, we'll pay a visit to Miss Rhodes – and she *will* let me in. Back here at 8am, please."

Four rather dejected police officers drove out onto Markham Road that evening.

-

There'd been a major crackdown by Chesterfield Police on the late-night town-centre drug dealing that had been something of a local scandal. It was working - and the dealers were finding it ever more difficult to find bases away from prying eyes. Moving further out of town, one particularly successful group of dealers set up in and around parks. The police watched them – and they watched the police.

The target for that Tuesday night's raid was Holme Brook Valley Country Park to the west of Chesterfield, and newly-promoted Detective Constable Derek Day was excited to be involved.

Holme Park is large and, although its two main car parks were locked before nightfall, there are dozens of pedestrian accesses – some in places only known to locals.

The groups of teenagers that often roamed the park after dark had previously been drinking copious quantities of cheap alcohol but now they had become lucrative targets for unscrupulous drug dealers. Thefts in the surrounding estates had increased dramatically as the kids looked for cash to sustain their new habits.

It was to be a large operation. A dozen officers were to enter the park on foot with their back-up cars only minutes away. Park Rangers were on hand to unlock gates for emergency vehicles if required.

DC Derek Day and his colleague, DC Alan Radford entered the park from the north via a pedestrian pathway from Little Brind Road.

It was clear from the outset that things weren't going to plan. Shouts and screams were heard within seconds of the coordinated assault; any competent dealers would have been alerted immediately and be off along their carefully prepared escape routes.

Day and Radford had studied grainy photos of the main target of the police operation, a mysterious individual known only as Frisco, so it came as quite a surprise when he ran right across the path in front of them. It took a full five seconds for Day to recover and set off in pursuit and another five for Alan Radford to follow on.

Frisco was fit. He cut right off the gravel path and hurtled down the steep grassy bank, through the old children's playground and towards the trees and stream that lined the valley bottom. Derek Day ran half-marathons for a bit of light relief and had no doubt he would catch the villain. Alan Radford ate Snickers for fun and quickly fell way behind. Eventually he stopped and radioed the team leader to describe what was happening.

Frisco made the tree line ten strides ahead of DC Day but the young copper didn't hesitate and charged into the undergrowth. Crash! He was immediately struck down by a blow to the chest. As he reeled, semi-conscious in the mud, Day realised he'd been ambushed; one of Frisco's minders had been waiting for his boss and any pursuer. The baseball bat had hit low because Day was in the process of jumping a small shrub when the blow connected. That shrub had saved Day's life. But it wasn't over yet.

Frisco had stopped and turned. Three other figures appeared from amongst the trees.

"Finish him," hissed the leader. "It's time to set an example!"

Day realised he was in deep trouble as the guy with the baseball bat came towards him. He had to get to his feet and get in close. His attacker grinned as he pulled the bat back to make a crushing swing. "So long, copper," he said.

Hundreds of hours of training at the hands of an unarmed combat expert saved Day. His reaction was automatic, instinctive. He managed to get halfway up and propelled himself forward under the blow. Three stiff fingers of his right hand shot into the exposed left eye of the thug, ruining it forever. He dropped the bat and screamed like a stuck pig. That horrendous noise so close to his face shocked Day back into some kind of alertness. He picked up the bat and studied the dealer and his three buddies. All four were paralysed with shock, looking at the man on the ground rolling in agony, blood oozing through his fingers, still screaming.

"Get on your knees, you're under arrest," yelled Day but his command had the opposite effect.

Frisco turned and ran but his three mates faced Day and made an effective barrier. For a few moments he was stunned by their loyalty – and stupidity.

"You're still under arrest," he said as he waved the bat in their faces.

All three took a step backwards but they were still blocking the path to Day's main target. They'd seen their mate destroyed but calculated it was the copper's luck rather than skill and three to one was pretty good odds. The man on the left looked to be the most determined so, after a feint in the other direction, Day broke his right collar-bone with a swift downward jab. As the man collapsed, Day redirected the bat into the right ear of the middle man – with just enough force to stun. The third man cut and ran but he wasn't of interest to Day, he wanted Frisco! Day dropped the bat and set off in the direction the dealer had disappeared.

As he broke into open ground, Day caught a glimpse of movement in the deserted car park. A dark figure ran around the barrier and into Linacre Road. Day's chest was hurting and breath came hard. He knew it was time to call it a day and stop to summon assistance but, as he grabbed at his radio, he realised it had taken the full force of the blow to his chest. No help there. He set off again.

As he passed the barrier, Day saw Frisco running to the left and turning into Milldale Close – he was heading back into the park – or did he have a car stashed down there?

Day struggled up into a fast jog.

Frisco did have a car parked on the Close but he was tiring fast. When he turned as he opened the driver's door, Frisco was horrified to see the copper only a few steps behind. The dealer pulled a knife.

Day saw the blade and didn't hesitate. He ran full tilt into the car door, slamming it into Frisco's arm. It was just as well that the manoeuvre broke the dealer's wrist because Day was now out of the game. He just had the energy to kick the knife away before he fell to the pavement and gasped for breath. Frisco looked him in the eye and said, "Bastard!" before fainting.

It seemed like hours before a back-up car swept into the road and pulled up next to Frisco's car. As two officers dragged Frisco to his feet and, without any consideration for his injury, thrust him into the back of their car, a second vehicle pulled up. Out stepped Detective Inspector Halfpenny. She took in the scene and said, "Well done, young Derek. Want a lift?"

Although Derek was far from a show off, his colleagues insisted on seeing the massive straight-line bruise across his chest. The imprint of the destroyed radio caused much amusement. Photos were circulated. One young officer was particularly impressed; PC Amanda Sharp was to become a fan for life.

Chapter Nineteen
Day's DAY 3
7.00am
"The outcome is going to be very uncertain, Chief Inspector, and there's no guarantee she'll ever be lucid. We've released the pressure on her brain but, even if she makes a full physical recovery, I can't promise she'll be able to help you," replied the very tired consultant surgeon who'd been working on Davenport though the night.

Day tried not to sound too disappointed. "Okay, doctor, thanks for taking the time to talk and for keeping her alive – you sound exhausted."

"Bed for me now but, I guess not for you?"

"No, sir, just another day at the office. Thanks again; I'll be in touch." Day put the phone down and groaned inwardly. DS Sharp had just entered his office. "Mandy, check who's watching the Rhodes' house, see if there's any action or if the lady of the house is at home, please?"

"Good morning to you, too, sir," she replied with none-too-subtle sarcasm.

"Oh, sorry Mandy, good morning."

She gave him a sympathetic smile that would have melted the hardest heart. Day didn't even notice; he was still searching for links in this bizarre crime wave. Who were the others?

Five minutes later DS Sharp returned. "Bedroom curtains opened ten minutes ago, sir. Charlie Haslam couldn't see who it was but obviously someone is in."

"Right, no time like the present – let's go and spoil her breakfast."

"Just a minute, we still don't know where Petersen is. If he's in there, he's not likely to be happy about the two of us barging in!"

For one terrible moment, Day actually wished for a confrontation with Petersen. Beating the crap out of that unpleasant waste of space would have been a wonderful antidote to his frustration, but the professionalism burst through. "Okay, get an area car to meet us there in twenty minutes. With Charlie, that'll make five of us. Have you got a Taser in your car?"

"Not at the moment, but I'll take one with me," suggested a very relieved DS Sharp. She reckoned she could give Petersen a run for his money on her own, but she didn't want her boss damaged in any way.

9.00am

The five officers gathered for a planning meeting just up the road from Janice Rhodes' council house. There had been no further sign of movement from within but Charlie was confident no one had left, so Day decided that they would take one of the uniforms to the door while the other stood by the observation vehicle – just in case.

Day tapped lightly on the door, hoping not to create any tension. To his surprise, it was opened almost immediately by a smiling, rather attractive woman. Janice Rhodes had undertaken some kind of transformation.

She looked at the uniform and correctly concluded that all three were police officers. "Good morning gentlemen – and lady," she said cheerily, "what can I do for you?"

Day was slightly taken aback by this surprisingly positive beginning. "Good morning, Ms Rhodes," he stammered, "I'm DCI Day, this is DS Sharp and PC Travis. May we come in for a few minutes, we need a little help trying to get our heads around some of the tragic events that have been blighting the village in the last few days?"

This was crunch time number one, how would she react?

"Oh yes, do come in, I'll put the kettle on!"

Day was flabbergasted then he thought, tongue in cheek, 'It must be my natural charm.'

DS Sharp was also surprised, she had been bracing herself to give the other woman a good shove so she could get through the door.

The three officers were led into a small lounge/diner. The furniture inside was old or cheap but the overall effect was in surprisingly good taste and it was immaculately clean.

"How would you like your tea, or would you prefer coffee?" Ms Rhodes was playing the perfect host.

Orders were placed and, five minutes later, a tray of steaming drinks appeared.

As she poured milk into cups, Rhodes asked, "Now, how can I help?"

Day began "As you know, your ex-husband, Gary Petersen, was released from prison a few weeks ago. Given you divorced him and gave birth to a son he hasn't seen, we thought you might be in some danger. Has he contacted you in any way?"

She didn't flinch. "No, not a sausage. DCI Day? Hang on, you're not the young PC who gave Gary what for in that pub fight are you?"

"Yes," he replied bluntly.

"Chief Inspector, now - you've come up in the world, haven't you?" Rhodes smiled and flashed her eyelashes at Day.

DS Sharp fondled her Taser.

Day, of course, didn't even notice the flattery. "I don't want to cause you any distress, but would you mind looking at this photo of your ex – it was taken just a few weeks ago. I'm guessing he looks very different from your memory of him; would you recognise him if he passed you in the street?"

Rhodes studied the photo very carefully. Day noticed that the shape of her mouth changed almost imperceptibly – was it a smile or a sneer? "I agree, he does look very different but, don't worry Mr Day, I'd know that man even if he was wearing a full body monkey costume!" Whatever emotion she was trying to disguise, it was enough to increase his interest in this woman.

Day continued, "Given his past record, I was hoping we could have a look around your house and make sure it's secure, should he come knocking. How would you feel about that?"

Crunch time two.

"Of course, that would be reassuring. Feel free, or would you like me to give you a guided tour?"

"A bit of both, I think. Where shall we start?" said Day.

"Why don't you nip upstairs first? Two bedrooms and a bath. I hope you like it. The window catches are pretty old, will you test them for me?" Rhodes couldn't have been more obliging.

"Mr Travis, you stay here and finish your tea. DS Sharp and I will do the check upstairs," Day's order left the young PC in no doubt that he was there to stifle the possibility of their genial host doing a runner.

Sharp followed Day up the stairs, her imagination at full stretch.

The three rooms were beautifully decorated and perfectly clean and tidy. The two detectives could find no evidence of any man being there in the recent past. Sharp pointed to the hatch on the landing ceiling and raised one eyebrow – just as their host appeared on the stairs.

"All right, Chief Inspector, this charade's gone on long enough. It's pretty obvious you think I'm hiding Gary for some reason I really can't fathom. Look in the loft – in fact, you have my permission to search the whole property." Not quite as friendly now, but still far from hostile.

So they did. And found nothing, just an immaculate house with two perfectly manicured gardens. Even the inside of the shed, although cluttered with gardening paraphernalia, was clean and tidy.

"You have a beautiful house, Ms Rhodes," said Day when the search was completed to his satisfaction.

"Thank you, you're very kind. Is there anything else?"

Day picked up a framed photo he had noticed earlier. It showed Janice sharing an adoring glance with a giant of a man. "May I ask who this is?"

Rhodes laughed. "You mean you don't recognise Preston – you must have seen him at the trial?"

The brother? Day was shocked; this wasn't a typical brother/sister picture. "Good heavens, Preston! I can't believe it. He was just a little lad last time I saw him; what's he up to, now?"

"He works security in town, mainly night clubs."

"Well he's certainly built for it, give him my regards if you see him. Do you see him often?"

"Yes, he calls three or four times a week – the beatings we shared made us very close. Anything more?"

"Yes, there is, Detective Sergeant Sharp would like to ask you a few questions, I assume that is okay?"

"Of course, go ahead sergeant."

"Seventeenth of September last year, about 7.30 in the evening, did you have sexual intercourse with Mr

George Carmichael, headteacher of Somersgill Primary…"

"Certainly not," interrupted Ms Rhodes.

"…in his office?" continued DS Sharp.

"No," she stated firmly, but her cheeks had begun to turn red.

"I'm afraid your face tells me otherwise, Ms Rhodes," said DS Sharp.

Rhodes shook her head but her colour deepened. Her shoulders drooped in the classic admission of defeat but there was still some fight in her. "I'm going to ask you a question, sergeant. If you'd been raped, would you like to hear it described as something as ordinary as 'intercourse'?"

That question put Sharp off her assault for a few seconds but then she latched on to the admission. "Are you saying that George Carmichael raped you in his office on September 17th last?"

"Yes, that's exactly what I'm saying!" And Janice Rhodes began to cry.

The two detectives let her get on with it and, for a couple of minutes, they communicated with each other in a well-practised sign language. PC Travis left and returned with a glass of water. Day nodded and the constable was relieved to note that his presence was no longer required.

"But you didn't report it to the police?" asked Sharp as soon as the tears had subsided.

"No."

"May I ask why?"

"Who would have believed me? He's a lot more important than me – what am I – just a shop assistant!" The classic, tragic response that had deterred women from reporting sexual assaults for centuries.

"You have my sympathy, but you realise, you've just admitted a motive for murder?" Sharp asked at a whisper.

Rhodes' blush disappeared and she turned pale grey. "I swear on the life of my child, I didn't kill him! Oh yes, I hated him and, I admit, I wasn't unhappy when I heard he'd been killed, but I had nothing to do with his death!"

Time for a change of tack. "Do you know Margaret Mallender?" asked Day.

Rhodes was obviously relieved by the variation. "The councillor? Yes, she helped me get this house when you sent Gary to prison."

"Met her recently?"

"I've seen her in the school yard a couple of times this summer. Why?"

"Where were you around three o'clock yesterday afternoon?"

"I was working at the SPAR up the road."

"So you'll have plenty of witness to corroborate that?" asked DS Sharp

"Dozens," she said.

"I doubt it. One of our officers was outside the house looking out for Petersen; he said you didn't go out."

Rhodes was looking increasingly confused. "What day is it, today?" she asked, seeming genuinely puzzled.

"Wednesday," said Sharp impatiently.

"Oh heck, I'm really sorry. I missed a day; it was Monday I was working. You're right, I didn't go out at all yesterday. Sorry." Rhodes smiled innocently.

"Anyone can make a mistake," suggested Day, "What shift did you work on Monday?"

Rhodes appeared deep in thought for a few seconds. "Two till eight. Yes, that's right, two till eight."

"Thank you. Have you ever met a lady called Mary Davenport?" asked Day.

"No, I don't think so." But the tiny hesitation and flicker of the eyes gave both detectives a hint she was lying again.

"Ms Rhodes, I know it's painful for you, but I want to talk about Mr Carmichael's sexual assault," said Day.

"Rape, Inspector – let's give it it's proper name!"

"Fair enough. Do you know any other women who've been raped or assaulted by Mr Carmichael?"

"No. It's not the sort of thing that women go around bragging about – is it Sergeant Sharp?" Sharp didn't respond, she was too busy analysing the second lie.

Day did respond. "Okay, Ms Rhodes. Even though you didn't report the crime at the time, we could still provide some help. We have female officers specially trained to support women in your situation. Would you like me to put you in touch with one?"

"No, thanks, I've put it all behind me now; it's dealt with."

"Okay, that's fair enough; if you change your mind, let me know. Now, I need you to be aware that we are watching your house. This is for your protection in case Petersen pays you a visit with any revenge in mind. I intend to keep this up until he's been traced and sent back to prison for breaking the terms of his parole, is that all right with you?"

"All right? It's far more than all right, Chief Inspector, I'm very grateful!"

This woman was displaying almost perfect innocence but, thought Day, the important word was almost.

As they got up to leave, the detectives were both dwelling on these words: "No, thanks, I've put it all behind me now; it's dealt with."

Rhodes must have been involved, but how?

10.00am

"Thanks for offering to talk to us, Mrs McAllister," said DI Trevor Allsop, as the two detectives were ushered into the Deputy Head's living room.

"Not a problem, gentlemen. I do hope you've come to tell me you've made some progress?"

"Some, but nothing conclusive yet. In fact, the situation's getting more complicated; there have been other deaths." Day had instructed DI Allsop to be very matter-of-fact while Dom O'Neil was to observe reactions.

"Yes, I heard about Scott Grimshaw. I used to teach him. He was one of those kids who wasn't over-bright and was mildly disruptive in class but I liked him. He was a bit of a lost soul, really. Useless parents, all very sad. Was it murder?"

"We reckon so but nothing's certain yet."

McAllister looked slightly puzzled. "You said deaths? More than Scott?"

"I'm afraid so. Two more. I'm sorry to have to tell you that Councillor Mallender was killed yesterday!"

The reaction seemed genuine. "Oh, my God, Margaret! How?"

"Road accident. Hit by a car. Just bad luck, I guess." DI Allsop followed Day's instructions to the letter. DC O'Neil noticed a slight change in McAllister's demeanour. Could it have been relief?

"That's tragic; she supported the school and I know she worked hard for people in Somersgill," replied McAllister.

"You're right, and if that wasn't bad enough, we've just heard that another person linked to the school was killed in a car crash in Hull last night. You remember the Ofsted Inspector, Mrs Davenport?"

There was a distinct pause after Allsop's lie. "Yes, I do remember her, I think she was called Mary?"

Something in McAllister's expression confirmed that relief was in there somewhere.

"I'm terribly sorry to be the bearer of such bad news but we really need your help. Can I get you a glass of water before we continue?" DI Allsop was acting out sympathetic care.

"No, I'll be fine. What a terrible coincidence, though; four people linked to one school in just a couple of days. On second thoughts, I will have a drink. May I get something for you two gentlemen?"

"Some water would be good," said O'Neil, realising a few seconds break would provide time to write some notes.

Ms McAllister returned with three glasses of water on a neat little tray. She placed it on the coffee table, sat in the armchair and smoothed down her skirt before looking up and smiling at the two detectives. "Now, gentlemen, how can I help?"

"Thank you. Did you have access to the school diary, the one that Mr Carmichael kept on his desk?" asked DI Allsop.

"Of course, I put a lot of entries in it; details of meetings – things like that. Why do you ask?"

Allsop ignored the question. "Did you ever see any peculiar entries, for example, sequences of letters and numbers that you didn't understand?"

"Yes. George had his own form of shorthand – his normal handwriting was painstakingly precise."

"More than mere shorthand, Ms McAllister; there was a code – a code detailing his many sexual conquests!"

There was a long pause as a whole variety of confused expressions flickered across the teacher's face.

"You seem surprised?" continued Allsop.

McAllister coughed. "I am surprised. I knew he was a terrible flirt, of course, but I didn't really know much about that side of his personality."

"No? Okay, would you take a look at this, please?" Allsop carefully removed a folded piece of A4 from his pocket and handed it to McAllister. She studied it intently but made no comment.

"Does it make any sense to you, at all?" asked Allsop.

A rather relieved woman looked up and said, "No, should it?" There was no 'VM' anywhere in the thirty-six lines of code.

"Do you do crosswords?"

"Avidly!"

"Look at the lines of code. They give the date, time, venue and score for each of his sexual encounters. The initials were a puzzle at first but then we worked it out. They're the second letters of the first and second names of his willing or unwilling partners." DI Allsop was now looking much less friendly. "If you look down at the grouping for July two years ago, you'll see 'ac', does that mean anything to you?"

"They could refer to a million other women!" McAllister protested, but it was obvious her heart wasn't in it.

"Correct me if I'm wrong, but I understand you're gay and in a long-term, stable relationship?"

McAllister reached over to the sideboard and pulled back a framed photo to hand to DI Allsop. "There you are, Inspector. Meet my partner, Pauline."

Allsop studied the picture. Two attractive, middle-aged women seated on a bench with a background of some lovely, wild countryside were smiling at each other.

The mutual affection in the beautifully composed picture was obvious.

"Lake District, summer holidays, two years ago," commented McAllister.

"It's a glorious photo. Where is Pauline now; I'm sure you could do with her support?"

"Oh, she works away a lot, I'm not expecting her back until Friday. She doesn't even know what's happened yet."

"What's her job, if you don't mind me asking?"

"Trucker. Owner driver. Long distance, quite often into Europe. I've tried to persuade her to get a more settled job but she loves the travel and adventure as much as she loves me." There was just a hint of bitterness in McAllister's tone.

"What's Pauline's second name?" asked O'Neil.

"Scanlan – Pauline Scanlan. Why?"

And then the room fell silent.

McAllister's eyes had been firmly fixed on the carpet for two full minutes before DI Allsop hinted to O'Neil that he should phone the boss. The DC was grateful for the opportunity to get outside.

Day answered almost immediately.

"Something fishy here, sir," said O'Neil. "Nervous reaction when we pointed out the significance of 'ac' and, to top it all, the girlfriend's an 'ac' too. As soon as she realised that, she went into some kind of stupor." He looked through the lounge window. "She's still not moving or saying anything by the look of it."

"Sounds like you've both been doing some good work, Dom. The 'ac' isn't damning, there'll be thousands of them, but your observations are increasing suspicions all round. Give her a few more minutes in the hope of a confession or other revelation then make her a cuppa and ask her to go through the list to see if she can identify anyone else, particularly the teachers. My guess is that, when she recovers from the shock, she'll want to be super-helpful. Note the names of any new suggestions and when she stalls, invite her to Beetwell Street to have a chat with me. Don't let her out of your sight, I don't want any more road accidents."

"Consider it done, boss!" DC O'Neil put his phone into his pocket and returned to the interview.

Chapter Twenty

CRIMINAL ACTIVITY - Two Weeks Earlier

Janice Rhodes had seen Gary Petersen walking past her house in Somersgill even before she'd known he'd been released.
How had he found her; she'd lived here for years with a new name? But there he was - he'd stopped immediately outside and looked up and down for thirty seconds before moving on.
Janice began to shiver; she'd just about got her emotions under control since that bastard Carmichael seduced her – and now this! Was her ex-husband biding his time – would he come back for her in the middle of the night? She knew what she had to do. Her son, Sami must be protected at all costs. She phoned her mother, explained the situation and asked if she'd pick up the boy at the end of school. Minutes after she put down the phone, her brother called. Preston was now twenty-two and had developed somewhat since Peterson had last seen him. Preston hadn't worked particularly hard at school but he had worked very hard in the gym. Where his sister was tall and slim, Preston was tall and wide. This young man worked as a bouncer outside Chesterfield pubs – not an easy job by any standard. Luckily, this was to be his night off and he offered to come around and spend the night at his sister's place. Brother and sister were close – very close.
By 10:30 the last of the daylight had gone and there was a predictable knock on her front door. A simple plan was put into operation before she slipped the bolt.
"Hello, bitch!" hissed Petersen as he pushed past Janice.

As he entered the house, a voice from behind said, "Hello, twat!" and everything went very dark for Petersen.

When he woke up a short time later, his arms and legs were secured to a kitchen chair with cable-ties.

Petersen struggled and cursed the brother and sister who were calmly studying him from the other side of a Formica table. Eventually he realised that aggression was not moving his situation forward and relaxed. "My, you've grown, Preston! Bid lad now," he said scornfully.

"Yeah, and you've shrunk, Gary. Eight years of prison food, eh?" replied Preston.

"I could still take you!" hissed Petersen – but all those present suspected that wasn't true.

Janice Rhodes had decided exactly what she wanted and, although he didn't know it yet, Gary Petersen was going to help her get it. "What do you want, Gary?" she asked.

"To see my son!"

"Why? You mean nothing to him."

"I have rights!" Gary exclaimed.

Preston stepped around the table and slapped Gary across the face. His lip split and blood trickled down his chin.

"I'm going to tell you about your rights, you twat! Me and Jan have been talking and, if you help her out with a little project she's got planned, you might just get to see Sami when it's all sorted." Preston thought he had made himself clear.

"Fuck off – I'll see him on my terms!"

That response earned him a much harder backhand slap. "Listen, you pathetic little fucker," hissed Preston, "you're going to do exactly as you're told, cos' if you don't I'm going to beat the shit out of you! And, if at any time you lay a finger on Janice, I'm going to bring my mate, Gord round and we're going to kill you. I repeat - kill you very, very slowly. Gord likes that kind of thing!" The sincerity in Preston's words was obvious even to Gary.

Janice re-entered the conversation in a placatory tone. "Listen Gary. Someone has hurt me," she snivelled. "Raped me!" she began to sob. "The police won't do anything. If you help me get my own back maybe everything could be the same between us? Perhaps we could be together, you and me and Sami?"

"Happy families, Gary – how do you feel about that? Better than the alternative, eh? Janice is still a looker, isn't she? And your boy's a bright kid – better that you deserve – but it's all on offer – think about it!" offered Preston.

Petersen thought about it. First thing he needed was to be untied and the best way to achieve that was to agree. He had no intention of getting involved in any plan.

"There's money in it, too. The bloke's rich – we're going to give him a beating and take all his cash. Two for the price of one - what do you think about that, Gary?" suggested Janice.

That was more like it. "Okay, now I'm interested. What do I have to do?"

"Nothing yet. You have to piss off and keep a low profile. Behave yourself and come back here when she tells you. Keep in touch by phone. Don't give Janice any hassle." There was serious menace in Preston's tone.

Ten minutes later, Gary was back out on the street. 'Great,' he thought, 'Getting paid for something I'd enjoy doing anyway.'

Preston tailed him for half-an-hour to make sure he was leaving the area. The young man was not entirely happy; he'd wanted to do for Carmichael himself but Janice had persuaded him against it. 'This way,' he thought, 'Janice will get her revenge and I'll not have to be involved! We'll both be in the clear!'

Seated alone in her kitchen, Janice Rhodes was also smiling. 'Great stuff,' she thought, 'now Gary's turned up, I'll be able to do the job without getting Preston involved. I'll be rid of Gary and Carmichael in one go!' She sat back and put her hands behind her head as she thought about the wonderful future she would share with her brother.

REVENGE NIGHT

George Carmichael was slightly annoyed. If some interfering bitch hadn't made that phone call earlier, his plan to leave his wife during the school summer holiday would probably have gone smoothly.

Angie was alright – physically – young, good looking and she'd had a great body too – until she'd deliberately snared him with a pregnancy. Trouble was, she thought she'd made it rich by marrying the headteacher but these days moaned continually because they could barely make ends meet.

Now he was stuck in school at nearly midnight on a Sunday. He had played his first 'Get Out of Jail Free' card by calling his ex. Okay, she had gone a bit nutty since the split but Carmichael had convinced himself he could work his old magic and restore a happy family. He missed his girls. Although he loved every child in his care, his own two were obviously very special to him. Strange then, that he would do anything to protect and nurture young girls but on reaching their eighteenth birthdays they immediately became prey. And it wasn't just the lookers – when his sexual needs were running high any female in the right age bracket would do. In his own twisted mind though, this was an honourable thing; he had never forced himself upon a woman because he had never needed to – he was doing them a service.

His second call had been more rewarding. Melanie Price – the 'Perfect Ten' – was coming to see him. Melanie – beautiful, talented and rich – all his problems would be solved! Pity she hadn't invited him to her house, that would definitely have been best but she was coming to him and, soon thereafter, she would be seduced once more. Confident he now knew where he would be spending the night, George Carmichael settled down to wait.

The gentle tap on the outer door came much sooner than he had expected but, hey, Melanie was a rally driver; she moved fast. It didn't occur to him that there'd been no sound of a car. It wasn't his brain that was doing the thinking.

He placed his hand on the inner handle and whispered, "Melanie?"

It was a puzzling ten seconds before a response came.

"Yes."

Definitely a female voice, he thought, but it didn't sound like Melanie. Had she got a cold – but she'd sounded fine on the phone. But what George Carmichael's ego needed was a quick fix from a beautiful woman and that blunted his doubts. He turned the key - and hell arrived!

The brief glimpse of a hideous mask, a strange hiss and then fire. Fire in his eyes, nose and mouth; he staggered backwards, screaming.

The punch in his face was almost a relief and the bliss of unconsciousness overwhelmed him.

He'd no idea how long he'd been out before the hideous pain in his eyes dragged him back to reality. He blinked and blinked but it didn't seem to help. He tried to lift a hand to rub his tortured eyes but found he couldn't.

He was still in the office but something was very, very wrong. Through stinging tears, he could just make out the shapes of three or four blurred figures in front of him. Despite the pain and confusion, he also registered that at least one more was behind him rifling through cupboards and drawers.

Apart from blinking, he remained perfectly still, taking stock. He realised he was naked and was strapped into his own swivel chair, Something was hanging around his neck but he couldn't twist sufficiently to see what it was. He could move his feet a little but his arms were paralysed.

As his vision began to clear, the nightmare took shape. Donald Trump, Darth Vader and Freddy Kruger were staring back at him. Was there another behind them?

Suddenly, a series of flashes blinded him once more; the bastards were taking photos of him!

Then a wonderful realisation struck him. Being a fan of American TV detective dramas told him that attackers wearing disguises didn't intend to kill; they were here to humiliate him. He knew he could talk his way out of any humiliation and he almost sighed with relief.

Through an enormously sore throat he managed to say, "What is it you want?"

"Revenge!" said Donald Trump.

A woman – even better thought Carmichael – women don't kill, at least not in this way. "What have I done to deserve this?" he asked with a tiny bit of bravado in his voice.

"You humiliate women. You seduce them and abandon them," said Freddy Kruger.

Carmichael made no reply. The tears were still burning his cheeks but he was beginning to see more clearly.

Despite the anonymous grey boiler suits, it was obvious at least three of the figures before him were female. The odds on his survival were improving. Humiliation was way better than the alternative.

The seed of optimism in George Carmichael's brain disappeared in a split second when the figure from behind came into view. It was a man – and he wasn't wearing a mask! When Gary Petersen was angry, he needed no mask to make him look scary.

EARLIER

When Gary Petersen was summoned to his ex-wife's home in Somersgill that Sunday afternoon, he was a man on a mission.

He'd already resolved to go ahead with the plan just to get to the money. After that he would take control. He brushed the back of his hand against the hammer stuck inside his belt. With that weapon, he was confident he could handle Preston when the time came and, as for Janice, she was going to get a right seeing to.

Preston opened the door and beckoned him inside. Janice was in the kitchen, looking rather good. There was a steaming mug of tea on the small table and Petersen was invited to sit and take a drink. A plate with a Cornish Pasty and brown sauce was laid in front of him.

"Your favourite, Gary – if I remember correctly?" asked Janice.

Petersen liked this reception – he was being treated with the respect he deserved. He smiled as he chomped into the warm pasty. This was going to be so easy.

"Everything's in place for tonight. We should get a call around nine to tell us if we're on. Then we'll get ready. The real action should start around eleven." Janice was almost shaking with excitement.

"So, what do you need me for?" asked Petersen, spraying pastry flakes. "Why don't you keep all the cash for yourselves?"

"Muscle," replied Janice.

"Why not him, he's got plenty?" scorned Petersen as he pointed towards Preston.

"My brother isn't part of this. He's going to be a long way away with an unbreakable alibi. We have a good plan but even the best plan just might go wrong."

"Such as…?"

"Well, the police might stick around longer than expected…"

"Police? What have they got to do with it?" interrupted a rather less cocky Petersen.

Janice laughed. "Don't worry, they're part of the plan to get Carmichael to come to the school. They won't hang around after a call-out to a school late at night."

"How do you know if Carmichael will stick around?"

"Past record. When his first marriage was on the rocks, we've been told he slept in his office several nights."

"How do you know all this?" Petersen was a psychopath but he wasn't completely stupid; he needed to know that this over-complex plan had a chance of making him some money without undue risk.

"Contacts," stated Janice. "We have contacts who know all about Carmichael and his history. You'll be meeting some of them tonight, but don't expect them to introduce themselves."

"Shit! How many of us are sharing the money?"

"That's the good bit; the money's all yours; our thank you for your help. You can keep anything you find; are you happy with that?" offered Janice.

Petersen thought for a moment. "Yes," he said.

Janice nodded. "Okay, Preston's leaving now. We'll get some rest once he's gone because it's going to be a late night. And Gary, if this all goes to plan, you're going to get your proper reward tomorrow!" The look on Janice's face gave Petersen a strong hint that a real treat would be coming his way.

He wouldn't have been so sure if he'd seen brother and sister part at the back door; the hug and kiss were warm – in the extreme.

At 9pm Janice Rhodes answered the call after the second ring. She listened for ten seconds and then put the mobile down. "It's on," she said. "The wife's gone bonkers – certain to be a massive row!"

The second call came two hours after. Again, Janice listened for a few moments before exclaiming, "It's bloody worked! He's up at the school with the cops!"

"No cops! I'm not getting involved with cops – I'll be back inside for life!"

"I told you, don't worry. We won't be making a move until they've gone. We've got a spotter and she'll let us know when it's safe."

Janice Rhodes and Margaret Mallender knew every inch of Somersgill. They knew that most village streets would be all but deserted at this time on a Sunday but no chances were taken. Each participant's route to the school had been carefully planned and rehearsed.

The message arrived. "We're on – third time lucky!"

The group converged at the school gates precisely on time and, without exchanging words, walked up the drive.

Janice Rhodes turned and looked up at Mallender's window. Although the room was in darkness, she could just make out the white shape of a hand waving them on.

The inside office light was on but the entrance was unlit. Rhodes put her ear to the door and could just make out the sounds of someone shuffling around. She gave her pepper spray a last shake for luck and tried the door handle. It was locked. This wasn't part of the plan but Rhodes improvised; she tapped lightly on the door.

More movement inside and then she felt a slight pressure on the door handle from the other side. She just made out the whispered enquiry. "Melanie?"

'Who the hell is Melanie?' she thought and almost panicked – but Mary Davenport was quicker witted.

"Yes," she responded.

After a few moments they heard the key turn and the door opened a fraction. George Carmichael just had time to register surprise before the pepper spray hit him full in the face. He screamed.

Petersen pushed his way between the women and punched Carmichael hard in the mouth. Silence. Job done. The bloke would be out of it long enough. Rhodes took a bunch of cable ties from her pocket.

-

Now Gary Petersen was really pissed. He'd opened up every drawer and cupboard in the office and all he'd got to show for it was twelve quid in change from an old chocolate tin and twenty-five quid from Carmichael's wallet. Still, the guy was coming to. He didn't know it yet but he was going to tell where all the real money was and give up the pin number for his bank card.

From behind the restrained headteacher, Petersen listened impatiently to a brief conversation before intervening. "Where's the money, twat?" he demanded as he swung the chair around.

The sudden change to an expression of horror on Carmichael's face almost made Petersen laugh – almost.

"Money, what money?" Carmichael's reply came in a sob.

"All the money you keep in school, where is it?"

Carmichael realised his situation was now desperate.
"There's a chocolate…"
"Fuck that – only twelve quid…"
"There's cash in my wallet!"
Petersen snorted. "Twenty fucking five quid. That's no good to me. Where's all the dinner money and stuff?" He put his fist against Carmichael's face.
"Dinner money? There's no dinner money – it's Sunday night. Most of our kids don't bring dinner money anyway – those few that pay bring cheques or bank transfers." Carmichael was praying that a rational explanation might placate this very angry man.
Angry was an understatement. Petersen turned toward Rhodes; she doubled his anger by giving a theatrical 'how was I to know' shrug.
Petersen pressed his hand into Carmichael's unprotected face and gave a hard shove. He'd expected the chair to roll backwards, but it didn't. It began to topple.
Carmichael had a fleeting glance of his office ceiling light before the back of his head hit the corner of the partly open bottom drawer of the filing cabinet – and his light went out – permanently.
It only took a few seconds for Mary Davenport to declare that Carmichael was dead. This was a total catastrophe! Murder! "Out! Everyone out!" she hissed. "Go!" She turned to Petersen as she left. "This is your mess – sort it!"
Petersen was in no mood to sort anything; his emotions were raging. There was panic, fear, hysteria – but rage was winning. He took the hammer from his belt, and began to pummel the face of the deceased.
"You bastard! Thirty-seven quid! You fucker!"
More blows.
"I need your fucking pin!"

More blows.

"You shagged my woman – bastard!"

More blows.

"Now you've fucked me up, too!" And with this statement Gary Petersen realised just how much shit he was in. "Think!" he shouted at himself. He found the office keys on the inside of the outer doors and removed them. He returned and locked the door to the headteacher's inner office before going outside and locking the outer door. He noticed the sports car parked in the playground and briefly considered taking it. Instead, he ran down the drive and closed then locked the main gates as quietly as he could.

"Shit! Shit! Shit!" he repeated silently then, in another flurry of madness, he hurled the bunch of keys far into the playground.

"Gary, this way," he heard whispered from the other side of the road. It was Donald Trump, indicating the first steps of the safest route to her house.

They left just in time. Only seconds later, another figure arrived and rattled the padlock. Puzzled hesitation, followed by a phone call. There was no answer and, after a second try, the woman walked away, shaking her head.

-

Much to Petersen's surprise, his ex-wife didn't scream at him when they arrived in the temporary sanctuary of her house. He was almost disappointed because he'd already decided to give her a good slapping if she made any kind of criticism.

"Don't panic," she stuttered, "I'll phone Margaret, she'll know what to do."

Petersen didn't reply. He'd already begun to appraise the possibilities for his future. Committing a murder while on parole left no room for mercy in any court; he would now do anything to avoid arrest. Anything.

Rhodes picked up the throw-away 'burner' phone and almost fainted with shock when it rang.

"How did it go? Did you get the photos we need?" Margaret Mallender sounded near hysterical with glee.

"It went wrong," Rhodes admitted calmly. "He fell over and hit his head. He's dead! Accident!"

The admission was delivered so bluntly that it took Mallender almost a minute to understand the consequences of what she'd just heard.

Rhodes was waiting for a major outburst – and she got one. "He's dead? You've killed him? Idiots! Oh, God, that means we're all murderers – it'll look like a conspiracy - we're all guilty!"

"Calm down, Margaret, like I said, it was an accident!"

"That doesn't matter, you idiot, we're all done for!"

"Only if we're caught!" Rhodes tried to impose a little calm but Mallender was heading into full panic mode. This wasn't helpful – ideas were needed.

"Christ, what happens if Grimshaw goes to the police?" asked Mallender.

"Oh, come on, he doesn't know it was you. I saw your disguise and it was really good, you looked seventy!"

"The phone! He's got the phone I gave him! If he gets caught, the police will track his calls. I must have been crazy to get mixed up in all this; I must have that phone!"

Rhodes had hoped for calculated planning from the woman who had coordinated the whole event but she realised she'd have to take control. "I think I can arrange that, Margaret. Give me the number and I'll talk to him." She looked across at her ex-husband and studied the grim expression on his face. "Yes, I'm sure I can sort that out, don't worry!"

Councillor Mallender gave over the required information and hung up – not even slightly reassured.

Rhodes smiled and revised her plans for the next day. "Gary," she said with a forced grin, "do you remember the Fallen Oak Clearing and what we got up to one warm summer evening?"

-

After she'd revived his spirits with a glass of brandy, Rhodes set about explaining what must happen. "You know, I'm really glad Carmichael's dead; that's what I'd wanted all along but the others wouldn't go for it. You did me a favour and I'm grateful. The important thing now is to keep you out of trouble but first, we need to tie up a loose end."

Knowing the area well, Janice Rhodes had no difficulty in concocting a plan to deal with Grimshaw and retrieve the incriminating material. If the boy was as gullible as Mallender said he was it was going to be easy. Petersen listened to her plan with interest and he thought some more violence would make him feel good. The world was against him and he needed an outlet for his anger.

"I'm going out in the morning to get the cash I need to entice the boy. After it's all over, that cash will be yours, Gary. Listen, I've been thinking, when this is all sorted, we can be together again, the three of us, a happy family. Tomorrow afternoon you're going to get the reward of all rewards!" She grinned and undid the top two buttons of her shirt to clarify her intentions.

Petersen reached for her but she gently pushed him away. "Later, Gary," she said. "I need you fresh for tomorrow's action – all of it!"

He wanted his reward now and anger flashed across his face but, thinking of a handful of cash, he contained himself – merely dropping into a sulk.

"After your first reward, I'm going to let you have a couple of hundred quid and I want you to disappear for a couple of days. Go to Sheffield, see that old mate of yours. Stay there till the weekend and get yourself noticed. Then come back over here and see your Parole Officer. Tell him you're really sorry – grovel, 'Oh, it won't happen again, sir – it was the stress' – you know the crap. They don't want the nick any more full than it has to be so they'll let you off with a warning. A couple of days later you can come back to me. Think about it – as much sex as you want – anytime you want!"

With many celibate years behind him, Petersen thought seriously about it. Rhodes' plan didn't strike him as particularly good but he liked the end bit. He decided to go along with it because he wasn't bright enough to think of anything better. When he returned as man of the house, though, things would be very different from his ex-wife's imaginings. He would be in charge and she would pay for abandoning him when he needed her most all those years ago.

Oh yes, she would pay all right!

Chapter Twenty-one

1.00pm BRIEFING

"Unfortunately, we still know very little for certain," admitted Day with a strong emphasis on the word 'know'. "We can be fairly confident that Mallender was involved in some significant way but something tells me she wasn't in the office when Carmichael was killed. She had no alibi for the Grimshaw murder but, again, I'm not sure she had the bottle to be directly involved. Davenport is a near cert. for the Mallender hit and run – which couldn't possibly have been an accident and, as far as we know, she hasn't got an alibi for either earlier killing. Anyhow, we're stumped there until she comes round – assuming she does."

Groans filled the room; everyone wanted this particular killer to survive.

"Right ladies, let's have some opinions. How many women would it have taken to overpower and tie up a fit thirty-five-year-old like Carmichael? Mandy?"

"Just me," she said and that quick response got the intended laugh. Now she had everyone's attention, she raised a more serious point. "What makes you think no men were involved?"

"We've no reason to suspect he's been bonking blokes as well, have we?" DC O'Neil's interruption was also intended to generate a laugh – but it didn't.

"Jealous husband, partner? Always worth considering. Would two people be enough?" asked Day.

"With pepper spray, possibly. Three would be safer," offered DI Allsop.

"I agree, Trev. At least three, I reckon. So, assuming Davenport was one, who were the other two, or three, or more?" Day threw it open to his team.

"Janice Rhodes has got to be a candidate; she's admitted having a motive but, beating a man to death, I don't think she's got it in her," offered PC Dawson.

Day nodded his encouragement to the young officer. "You might be right but, remember, we're far from certain the killing was intended. I still think it's at least fifty/fifty unintended."

"Agreed boss, but at least one of them had a lot of pent up rage to do that to someone already dead!" said DC Grainger.

"Definitely! We have to include Rhodes in the 'serious suspects' list. Now, what's this about Ms McAllister and her partner, Trev?" asked Day.

"Really weird. Her reaction to seeing the initials on Carmichael's conquest list was pretty sharp until she got her face under control. When she realised her partner's got the same second initials, that also created a reaction. I'm uneasy about both of them."

"McAllister claimed her partner was abroad at the time of the Carmichael killing, sir – but not according to Border Force," added DC O'Neil.

"Find the partner, Dom. Bring her in, I want a word. Now, there's the conundrum of the ex-wife, Veronica Davison. She's no real alibi for the Carmichael killing and she lied about her whereabouts for the Grimshaw murder so I want to talk to her, too."

"Nutty as a fruitcake," interrupted DS Sharp.

"Maybe so," said Day with the briefest of chuckles. "Let's have Rhodes, McAllister, Davison and Scanlan in first thing tomorrow. We'll have a good go at turning 'em on each other."

It was at that moment the whole case changed. Phil Johnstone entered the room, paper in hand. "I've just left Sarah Jacks, boss; she's been going over Carmichael's bunch of keys with a fine-tooth comb and, bless her, she's found a partial print – and we've got a 90% match!"

A cheer went up. Everyone in the room thought there was a chance they'd get some time off by the weekend.

"Don't tell me," said Day, "it's Petersen, isn't it?"

Instant silence. All eyes were on Phil. He nodded.

Now the whole room erupted in a buzz of discussion but Day only paused for a few seconds. "Pug, put out an alert for Petersen. I know he's already being looked for but I want the full works now. He's a murder suspect – armed and dangerous. Trev, warrant to search the Rhodes' house – thoroughly this time. Mandy and I gave it the once over and he definitely wasn't there but I want to know if he's ever been in the place. Tell SOCO to find me a hair – anything! Mandy, go and get Rhodes – bring her in. We'll leave the others for a while." Day issued a string more instructions and then, with a more confident smile on his face said, "Go to it!"

-

"D. Day? Hilarious! And a Detective Sergeant already – and so young. But Sergeant, what a terrible dereliction of duty – caught fast asleep on a stakeout!"

The splash of icy water on his face had brought Day around pretty quickly but, although he tried to make sense of what he was hearing, a bursting headache was absorbing all his thoughts.

Calm. He had to stay calm.

As the voice droned on, Day began to take stock of his surroundings. He was seated on an old-fashioned bentwood chair facing a desk behind which sat the speaker. Curly ginger thinning hair sat atop a blotchy red face and a pair of truly massive shoulders. Day slumped forward and attempted to put his head in his hands but was immediately pulled back by two pairs of strong hands.

"Listen to the man, copper!" said a voice from behind.

But Day wasn't listening, he was too busy feeding adrenalin into his system. There was a tiny glimmer of optimism; he wasn't tied up – these stupid sods had no idea who they were dealing with.

He was in an office. The walls were mainly glass and it looked down into some kind of warehouse. The warehouse! On the open floor below it was possible to make out the ruins of at least six expensive motors. As he glanced around his immediate surroundings, he counted five enemies in the tiny room.

"So, are you coming back to us, D. Day, it's time we had a proper conversation?" said the man behind the desk. What was the accent? Australian? South African? Day wasn't well travelled enough to work it out.

What an idiot – he'd actually gone to sleep while observing a possible crime scene!

Day had had his suspicions about 'Top Car Spares' for some time. Workers from neighbouring units on the Sheepbridge Industrial Estate had told police that the 'comings and goings' didn't make sense. During the day very little happened except for machining noises from within – in a storage warehouse? Then one chap on a nearby late shift had reported he'd seen high-end cars driven in during the night. No one ever saw them come out. It had been time for DS Day to see for himself. Trouble was, on an industrial estate in late evening, it was very difficult to place an observation vehicle where it wouldn't attract notice. He thought he'd found a good spot but he was wrong – very wrong. He should never have come alone, but cuts in the budget had left Derbyshire Police drastically short of officers. He'd intended just to watch, take a few photos and, if the suspicions proved to be correct, he would be organising a raid to catch them red handed the following evening.

He'd gone to sleep! These devils had obviously crept up on his vehicle and bashed him on the head to give him a deeper rest. How very obliging!

Now he was in the shit. On the positive side, there were only five of them but, against that, he was still pretty dazed. He needed to play for time.

The man behind the desk helped him out by carefully studying the contents of Day's wallet. He'd already thrown the police I.D. on the floor and was now holding up a family photo. "Beautiful family, Mr Day. Attractive wife, lively toddler and a bouncing baby – who, I guess, is the cause of your neglectful tiredness?" He laughed.

"I'm afraid so. Sophie hasn't quite grasped the concept of night time, yet!" The statement had the desired effect – several of the men surrounding Day laughed.

"Ah, Sophie, beautiful name. There is, however, a distinct possibility that Sophie might become an orphan this very night." There was no humour present now. "We have a problem, don't we, Mr Day? Who else knows you've been watching us?"

A choice. The truth was, he'd discussed the suspicions with his immediate boss, DI Halfpenny but she didn't know he was doing a semi-official solo observation tonight. He could lie and tell these thugs that backup was only minutes away – but that happened in movies so they probably wouldn't believe him. Day opted for a suicidal, dangerous third option. "Truth is," he lied, "I had a phone call from one of your neighbours earlier today and decided to pop in for a quick look on my way home."

Nobody in his position would make up such a risky story and a ripple of relief ran through the crowded office.
The man behind the desk sat back and put his hands behind his head. "Paradoxically, Mr Day, your irrational enthusiasm gives us options. I have to say that, at the moment, my preferred option is to lock you in the boot of your car, drive you up to a favourite spot of mine near Ladybower Reservoir and push you in, car and all."
Still playing for time, Day looked around and said, "I'm open to other offers – I don't much like that one." He took great care to put an almost indiscernible tremor in his voice.
The men around him laughed – more darkly this time.
"This is a very profitable business, Mr Day - and I don't want to go to the effort or expense of relocation so, I'll tell you what, you make all police suspicions go away and I'll let you live." He paused for dramatic effect. "Also, the three ladies in your life will not be harmed!" he added. He held up part of an electricity bill he'd retrieved from Day's wallet; home address clearly visible.
A hiss of craziness swept through Day's brain but he was able to channel it into pent-up aggression. He nodded to indicate he was interested.
"So, you'll work with me, then?"
Day nodded again. "My department is so overstretched, I can easily bury any concerns in a pile of paperwork." He hesitated and seemed to change his mind. "If this is going to be a long-term thing, we ought to put it on a more business-like footing. How does five hundred a month sound?"
The man behind the desk smiled at his team. A stroke of luck; the copper in front of him was bent but five

hundred was too much. "It sounds like an invitation to swim in Ladybower to me, Mr Day but, I'll tell you what, if you do make police interest in my business go away, I will send you much more than that when my balance sheet allows it!"

Day put on a show of deep thinking for a full minute before saying, "And my family..."

"Will be perfectly safe," the man behind the desk interrupted. "They won't even know we exist – unless you do something wrong. In the meantime, think positive; book a holiday for next summer – somewhere warm, you'll be able to afford it."

Day smiled. His audience thought he was thinking of the extra income but they were wrong. He was smiling because he thought that his body and state of mind were now ready for the next few seconds of action.

"I'll make this go away for you, Mr...?" and Day stood, walked confidently to the desk and held out his right hand.

The man behind the desk only moved his eyes – towards the fella behind Day's right shoulder. "Throw him out, Dave, but don't mark him!" he smirked.

As Dave moved forward, his face met Day's right elbow coming back very, very fast. Shattered cheekbone – goodnight Dave.

Day knew a good weapon when he saw one and the bentwood chair fitted the bill; light and hard. As he raised it and completed a half turn, his peripheral vision registered a crowbar descending from his right. With a quick twist he managed to snare the weapon in the leg support of the chair, forcing the thug to let go. A swift jab put the metal end of the chair leg into contact with the unbalanced man's throat causing him to collapse in agony.

The other two standing men were dressed as mechanics and they hesitated, realising that this person they were about to fight had serious skills. Day had a split second to realise that the man behind the desk hadn't moved. Strange!

Using the chair like a lion-tamer, Day forced the two men to retreat to the glass wall of the office. One made the mistake of pulling a screwdriver from a pocket and received a slashing blow from a chair leg that ripped skin from cheek and nose. The other man fled out the door and down the steps.

Day turned to face the man behind the desk. From this new angle, Day realised that the man was in a wheelchair – and he was holding an elderly revolver that was pointing directly at Day's face.

The detective threw the chair across the desk and dived for cover. Bullets flew over his head. The giant roller door at the front entrance of the warehouse clanked open and, from his limited position, Day saw more mechanics running away from the sound of the shots. He could also see the wheels of the wheelchair under the desk – and they weren't turning. He was fairly safe where he was, so he settled down to count. He'd clearly heard five shots and was waiting for number six but the guy was patient, apparently waiting for Day to show his face.

Stalemate. Day had no idea if anyone in neighbouring units might have heard the shots and would call the police. Even if they did, it could be an hour before an ARV turned up. For all Day knew, his opponent might have a desk drawer full of spare bullets.

The desk was heavy but desperate men seem to gain strength. Without raising his head above the top, Day began to shove the desk into the man with the intention of trapping him against the back wall. There was a terrible shout of anger and frustration followed by the sixth gunshot. There was a crash as something heavy hit the floor out of his line of sight. Day froze for many seconds before he heard a tiny series of sounds. The gentle drip, drip of blood onto the floor; the man behind the desk had shot himself in the head.

DS Day stood and looked around. He was the only person in the office still capable of movement. He calmly put on a glove, picked up the desk phone and dialled Beetwell Street Police Station.

The car-breaking scam was no more. Within a couple of days, most of the thieves, mechanics and enforcers had been rounded up. It transpired that the boss was terminally ill and had obviously decided that the police intrusion was as good as any time to bow out.

As usual, Day was suspended during an investigation into his conduct but, despite telling the absolute truth, he was exonerated - his usefulness to the police force clearly outweighing his nuisance value.

Chapter Twenty-two

2.30pm

To everyone's surprise Janice Rhodes came willingly with DS Sharp to Beetwell Street Station. In Interview One, she smiled innocently at the two detectives facing her. "How can I help? Have there been developments?" she asked.

"Thank you for coming in, Ms Rhodes. Am I right in thinking you've waived your right to a solicitor?" said Day.

"Why would I need a solicitor, Chief Inspector? Am I being accused of something? Am I under arrest?"

DS Sharp had been instructed to take the lead and she began without any subtlety, hoping to unbalance their interviewee. "In answer to your questions; there have been developments; you're not being accused of anything – yet; and you're not under arrest – yet. Where's Gary Petersen?"

"I've no idea, Detective Sergeant. I've told you that at least twice already. I haven't set eyes on him since he was sent down at the trial."

Rhodes unflustered response confirmed Day's guess that she had been expecting exactly that opening question.

DS Sharp continued. "Two things combine to convince me you're lying, Ms Rhodes. We know you had a motive for wanting to harm Mr Carmichael and we are now certain your ex-husband was involved in the killing. Try as we might, the only link we can find between George Carmichael and Gary Petersen is you."

Day nodded his agreement with Sharp's statement.

Janice Rhodes looked hard into Day's eyes and did a brilliant impersonation of delayed shock. Her expression changed to dismay and she put her left hand up to her mouth. "Oh, my God, what have I done?" she whispered through her fingers. She paused, apparently struggling to control her emotions. She looked around the featureless room and coughed. "Do you have a tissue?" she asked of no one in particular.

Without comment Day took one from his pocket and passed it across the table.

Not amused by the theatricals, Sharp asked, "Just what have you done?"

Another cough. "I wasn't lying when I said I hadn't seen Gary but, you remember, when I told you Carmichael raped me, I said I knew no one would believe me. I had to share it with someone, so I wrote to Gary. I told him what had happened – I can't believe he attacked Mr Carmichael – I guess that makes it sort of my fault?" Rhodes was full of unconvincing remorse.

"Bullshit!" stated Sharp. Although Day was expecting some kind of scathing reply, he still had difficulty suppressing a laugh.

"Absolute bullshit!" repeated Sharp. "You know it's the easiest thing in the world for us to check if Petersen had a letter from you when he was inside?" she lied.

Rhodes looked dismayed and began the next stage of her misinformation strategy. "It seems I've been caught out lying to police officers," she whispered sadly. "I have seen Gary, or rather he came to see me. Fortunately, it was when Preston was visiting and he didn't get inside. You do remember my little brother, don't you Mr Day?" She didn't wait for a reply. "Preston's grown into a very big lad and he hates Gary's guts. Gary calmed down when he saw the size of Preston. I had to think fast and, to get rid of him, I made up a stupid lie. I told Gary that Mr Carmichael had been chasing me for years – even when we were still married. I said that an affair was the reason for our divorce – not his violence or his conviction. He's too thick to work it out and he believed me. I genuinely had no idea it would end up like this! Does that make me guilty of some crime or other? Perhaps I do need a solicitor?"

Day thought Rhodes was getting a little nearer the truth but there was still a long way to go. "There's a subtle difference between telling someone about a crime and encouraging him to exact revenge. You'd better sort that out in your mind and decide for yourself if you need a solicitor."

Rhodes incorrectly concluded that Day had fallen for this latest pack of well-rehearsed lies and relaxed a little.

"Made your mind up?" asked Sharp.

"Of course. I'm certain I didn't encourage him to attack Mr Carmichael, let alone tell him to…" Innocence oozed from a guilty woman.

"So, you're okay to continue without a solicitor?"

"Carry on? More questions? I think I've told you everything I know."

"Ms Rhodes, is Preston involved in this?" asked Day.

Rhodes almost reeled at that question. "No! No! He protected me from Gary, that's all!" Very defensive.

"Phone number and address; we'll need to speak to him."

The information was handed over with more protestations of his total lack of involvement.

Sharp wasn't impressed. "Where's Petersen now?" she demanded.

"I repeat, no idea. He's kept away from me ever since Preston had words."

Sharp knew she was lying. Day knew she was lying and Rhodes knew they both knew she was lying – but there was no evidence and they all knew that!

"Come on, Janice, we all know this was a well-planned attack by at least three people. Even if we believe you weren't present, you must know who planned it all," Day asked.

Rhodes looked down at the table and pondered her options. Then, apparently resigned, at last, to telling the truth, she looked Day in the eye. "When I told Gary about Carmichael, he asked me who could do something about it. I told him that Councillor Mallender was the top governor and he told me to complain to her and get Carmichael the sack. I bottled out but I guess he didn't; he must have gone to her and agreed on that cruel revenge."

A classic plan – incriminate someone who was far too dead to issue a denial. Rhodes sat back in the chair, trying hard to give the impression she had unburdened herself. "May I go now?" she asked.

"You're here voluntarily, Ms Rhodes, so you can leave at any time but, I should remind you that we have a team of detectives searching your home. It would be a good idea not to go and get in their way. They've been instructed not to make a mess." Day was all smiles. "Is Sami still with your mother in Clay Cross?"

"Yes," she replied uncertainly.

"Has your ex threatened him? Is that what's making you lie to us?" Day gave the impression he was primarily concerned for Sami's welfare.

"No," she muttered – but neither detective was convinced.

"Say the word and I can have two burly coppers protecting your son within half an hour. Just say the word!" offered Day.

"Not necessary," said Rhodes. "Gary's never threatened him."

Day needed a break from this complex character. "Okay, he said, "that's enough for now; thanks for your help."

As Rhodes left the room, Sharp looked at Day as though he was crazy. "What on earth are you thinking, boss?"

"Something very fishy here, Mandy. She's still lying of course. I'm wondering if Petersen is making threats against young Sami but I'm balancing that against my certainty that she's involved in the murders – and probably at quite a high level. What I don't get is that, if Petersen's pulling her strings in some way, why is she making him look guilty? But she's definitely the only link between Petersen and Carmichael so, if we find evidence that Petersen's stayed in her house, we'll arrest her before the day is out. Now, it's a big ask but I want every empty property in Somersgill searching asap. If he is intimidating Rhodes and making her spill all this nonsense, he must be somewhere nearby. Dom and Mr Dawson are to check out Preston; I suspect he'll have a convincing alibi – tell them not to let up until they're absolutely certain he's not involved in either of the first two attacks. Also, send Andy and Ms Sindhu to check that Sami's okay and his Gran hasn't been threatened – tell them to make sure they actually see the boy."

DS Sharp wrote furiously in her own version of shorthand.

"Now then, the others," continued Day. "I want to speak to Drew what's-his-name from the telly. If he's still at the Casa, invite him over here – be quite insistent. If he's gone off, track him down, will you? Depending on what he tells us, we'll talk to Carmichael's ex this evening.

Put out an alert for Paula Scanlan's truck. I think I'd like to hear from her before we interview McAllister again. Talk to her yourself, Mandy and tell me what you think. Was it either, neither or both of them that gave in to Carmichael? Don't be your usual subtle self!"

Mandy Sharp's laugh was interrupted by a knock on the door.

"Boss, there's a call from Hull, it's a message from the surgeon who's looking after Davenport. He says there's been some better than expected progress and they want to reassess the possibility of brain damage before the next surgery, so they're going to risk easing her out of the coma tomorrow morning. What do you want to do about it?" Phil Johnstone was having difficulty controlling his excitement.

Day thought for a few moments; it could be a total waste of more than half a day but, on the other hand, a few seconds of clarity might blow the whole case wide open. "I want to be there just in case. Find out the timings as near as they can estimate, please Phil. Then find Dipa Sindhu and tell her to standby for a chauffeuring job."

-

The detailed search of The Rhodes house had revealed absolutely nothing.

"He's definitely not there and there's nothing to suggest he's ever been in the place. It's the cleanest fucking house we've ever been in. We took the u-bends off the bath and all the washbasins and couldn't even find a hair. She must spend half her pay on bleach! OCD gone mad!" The sheer frustration in the techie's report was shared by Day as he received the summary.

"Garden shed?"

"Clean as a whistle; there's less dirt in there than on my kitchen worktops."
"Loft?"
"Bugger all!"
So, where was Gary Petersen? He must be nearby to be pulling Rhodes' strings so effectively, but the search of empty properties was getting nowhere. A threat to the little boy was the most likely method but an interview with his grandma in Clay Cross had produced no hint of intimidation.

6.00pm
Drew Challenger had agreed to accompany officers to Beetwell Street Police Station if they promised to smuggle him inside via the secure car park.
The TV star wriggled uncomfortably in the bleak surroundings of Interview Room 2; he wasn't at all pleased at the prospect of being recognised leaving a police station and had demanded an equally discreet return to his hotel. A little reassurance prompted him to begin an account of the night of the Carmichael killing.
"I arrived as soon as it went dark at around nine thirty. We erm… messed around until eleven then she told me she had to go out. Would you believe it? I mean, fuck, the risks I was taking! Look, you can keep my name out of this, can't you?"
Day gave him an encouraging smile that guaranteed nothing.
"I was furious at first but she promised there would be some serious sex when she returned. So, there I was – bloody babysitting – but fortunately the kids didn't wake up. She was back by one thirty…"
"Didn't that strike you as odd?" asked DS Sharp.

"Very. We'd made this arrangement weeks previously. I was expecting a dusk to dawn session. I'd even hired an ordinary car so the nosey neighbours…"

"How did she seem when she came in?" interrupted Day.

Challenger's face showed he was used to rather more respect than he was currently receiving but he continued. "A little bit shaky, to be honest. She apologised and went straight to the bathroom. I took her a brandy and found she was in the bath. We had a brief discussion about my 'reward' and she told me she didn't feel like it then but she'd make it up to me at the hotel at noonish later the same day. I was pretty cross and buggered off soon after. And, as I've already told you, she wasn't even on time for that! What kind of trouble is she in, Inspector?"

"Chief Inspector!" interjected DS Sharp.

"Enough. Is your relationship serious?" said Day, puzzled by Sharp's vehemence.

"Good heavens, no! She's a cracking looking woman and the sex is ferocious but she is a little bit bonkers, you know. Trouble is, with my profile, escaping from an illicit relationship is a lot trickier than getting into one."

Having confirmed Day's theory that Drew Challenger was a complete arse, the TV 'personality' was dismissed with a stern warning his presence might well be required in the future.

After the interview, Day concluded that it was very likely that Davison was involved in the second killing and it had to have been planned that morning - a last minute attack. The poor dupe Grimshaw had had to die because Carmichael had died and witnesses needed to be eradicated. Day was now convinced that the group that had invaded Carmichael's office that Sunday evening had not intended to kill him but events had spiralled out of control.

Whatever the intentions, Veronica Davison had no alibis for either of these two killings. Her behaviour was going to take some serious explaining.

Chapter Twenty-three
Day's DAY 4

8.00am

The first news of the day cleared Preston Driscoll of involvement in the Carmichael and Grimshaw killings. He'd been at a 'Gentlemen's Club' in Nottingham on the Sunday night with a couple of other bouncers and two off-duty policemen. On Monday lunchtime he'd still been sleeping off his hangover in a copper's flat.

-

DS Sharp and DC Grainger were waiting for Veronica Davison when she returned from dropping off her children at school. The tone of Sharp's invitation to visit the police station left Carmichael's ex in no doubt the game was up.

"I will tell you the truth, sergeant, but only if my solicitor is present. May I call him?" she asked with a sad smile.

10.00am

Day entered Interview Room 1 and Grainger nodded and left. Sharp switched on the recording devices and the two detectives introduced themselves.

The solicitor spoke first. "My client has, against my advice, decided to tell you everything she knows about the sad demise of her ex-husband. Given this, I hope you will treat her with respect and courtesy."

Day made no comment but raised one eyebrow at him. He turned to the client. "The truth, Ms Davison?"

"Of course, Chief Inspector. First, I must assure you that a death was never part of the plan; our little group intended nothing more than a terrible humiliation in return for all the wrongs George had committed. My role was simply that of photographer - although I admit I did help with the cable ties."

Day nodded as Sharp wrote a detailed list of questions she would ask when the time was right.

Davison took the hint and continued. "With George disgraced, I knew I'd have no trouble getting the courts to order him to keep away from the children – permanently! My solicitor was going to have a field day," stated Davison with a glance to her left. The solicitor looked far from comfortable with that.

"Drew had promised to leave his wife for me, so I knew money wasn't going to be a problem. Everything was going to be brilliant – and then that fucking man turned up!"

Once again, Day was astonished just how quickly Davison could turn from calm to vehemence. He slid a picture of Gary Petersen across the table. "Recognise him?"

"That's him! That brute was just after money; he lost his temper and pushed George hard. The chair went over, I guess it caught in the carpet. The crack as he hit his head on the steel cabinet was horrible. As soon as we saw he was dead we all panicked and left. It was that man!" She stabbed the photo with her finger. "It was supposed to be women only; I didn't want him there! I didn't want George dead! Now it's murder! I didn't want this…" Hysteria wasn't far away.

"Actually, Ms Davison, I believe you," Day said calmly.

She looked up from the table and, in a little-girl voice said, "You do? Really?"

Day knew he had the breakthrough. "Yes, really," he said. "But what happens to you in court depends on what you tell us…"

"Anything, everything," she interrupted. Self-preservation was firmly in charge.

"Then it's going to be simple. I'm prepared to accept your ex-husband's death was not intended but I must have a list of all the other people in the office when he died."

Davison held her breath and stared hard at Day. She pointed to the photograph once more. "Apart from him, I've no idea!"

The response seemed so genuine, Sharp and Day just turned and stared at each other. Even Davison's solicitor seemed flabbergasted.

Day was the first to recover. "Explain!" he demanded.

"We met for the first time at the school gates. We'd all been instructed to wear masks and gloves. She told us not to identify ourselves… that we'd reveal ourselves only when the photos appeared on the internet."

"Who's 'she'?"

"Margaret, the Chair of Governors, she organised it. She gave me my mask. She told me there were at least a dozen women who wanted to be involved."

"And you don't know any of their names?" Day desperately wanted to disbelieve this story but, the trouble was, his detective's brain said it was true.

"No. I was just the photographer." She hesitated. "The woman with the Donald Trump mask brought the pepper spray and him, I think." Davison jabbed the photo of Petersen with such vehemence, Day was surprised she didn't break her finger.

"How many of you were in the office when Mr Carmichael was attacked?"

"Me, three other women – and him!" Another jab at the photograph.

"Three other women? Definitely women – despite the masks?"

Davison thought for a few seconds and Day could see her reliving the whole dreadful incident.

"Three women," she admitted without conviction. "I was given a Darth Vader mask and there was a Freddy Kruger and a Donald Trump." She hesitated. "Sorry, but I really can't picture the other one." She seemed genuinely puzzled.

"Anything to help us identify them, despite the masks?"

"Donald Trump was tall and slim. As I said, I think she brought the man."

Day and Sharp looked at each other and exchanged thoughts. 'Rhodes?'

"Others?"

"One was my height. She was wearing the Freddy Kruger mask. She brought the sign." Again, Davison stopped to visualise the scene. "She only spoke once and she sounded rather sophisticated; not local."

Sharp's raised eyebrows suggested, 'Davenport?'

Day nodded. "And the third?"

"I didn't take much notice. I think she was wearing a mask, but I didn't recognise the face. Maybe she was the same sort of size but she didn't really participate. I can't remember her saying anything. No, I'm sure she never said a word; she just watched, sort of indifferent - you know."

"Yet you're certain it was female?"

The hesitation caused the two detectives a great deal of consternation. "Mmm, think so…"

"Hair colour?"

"Couldn't see any hair. All the masks covered the heads completely."

"Nothing else?"

"No."

"Okay," said Day, changing the direction of the interview, "let's talk about your appointments of the following day."

Immediately, Davison began to look even more uncomfortable.

"You had to rush off from our interview for an appointment at twelve noon, correct?"

"Yes." That single word conveyed a mountain of anxiety.

"To meet Drew Challenger?"

Day imagined the tiniest flicker of relief in Davison's expression as she nodded.

"But you were late! Where did you go first?" Day knew just how to time a crushing blow.

Veronica Davison broke. Her face disintegrated as she flashed her eyes around the barren room, seeking help from any quarter. Sobs rattled her shoulders. She turned and appealed silently to her solicitor.

He patted the back of her hand. "You don't have to say anything, Veronica." He turned towards Day and half smiled. "I think, Chief Inspector, that I'd like to call this interview to a halt now, at least for the time being."

"No!" said Day with such ferocity that everyone in the room jumped. Then, with surprising calm, he said, "Veronica, tell me where you were between twelve and one-thirty on Monday."

The solicitor looked as though he was going to intervene but he was silenced by another poisonous look from Day.

"Bluebell Wood," she whispered.

"Would you mind repeating that for the tape, please?"

"Bluebell Wood." Only marginally clearer.

'Gotcha!' thought DS Sharp.

"Why did you go to the wood? It wasn't a particularly nice day for a walk?" Day controlled his excitement by adopting a conversational tone.

"I was told to; by a woman."

"No name?"

"How were you contacted?"

"By phone – mobile. The one Margaret Mallender gave me; she said we had to clear up a mess or we were all in the shit."

"Where's the phone now?"

"I threw it away!"

"When, where?"

"In the woods – as soon as I was out of sight of him!" She pointed to the photo yet again.

"Was the call from Mallender?"

"Definitely not."

"Did you recognise the voice?"

"Not really, but it might have been Donald Trump."

"Fair enough. In your own words, tell me what happened when you arrived at the woods. The whole story, please."

Davison took a series of deep breaths and began. "I was late. You made me late, Inspector. There was no one waiting for me. I parked the car and set off towards the Fallen Oak Clearing. I was nearly there when I met this vile object coming the other way." She pointed to the photo of Petersen yet again.

'Brilliant!' thought Day. "Was he alone?" he said.

"No, there was a woman," Davison responded.

This was getting better and better. "Who?"

"I didn't recognise her but she moved like Trump - the pepper spray woman."

"Mask?"

"No. No mask!"

Sharp looked at Day and he nodded. A photograph was extracted from a file and slid across the table.

"Yes, that's her. Definitely."

Day looked up at the CCTV camera and mouthed, 'Get Rhodes'. He knew a cheer would have gone up from the watching detectives and they would be falling over themselves to get to their cars.

"The voice? Could she have been Trump? Think hard - this is unbelievably important."

Davison shrugged. "I don't know. Possibly. The masks could have caused some distortion. Yes, possibly."

"Tell me about the man and woman in the woods. How did they seem?"

"He was furious because I was late. I thought he was going to hit me but she told him to calm down. 'The job was done, she said'. He shouted some more but then the woman told me to go. I didn't need telling twice, I ran for it!"

"What was the man wearing?" asked DS Sharp.

Davison turned and looked at Sharp for the first time in several minutes. "That was weird, really. He was all shiny black. Bin liners and some kind of tape, I think?"

This was all fitting together beautifully.

"Had they killed that poor boy, Inspector?"

"Chief Inspector!" snapped Sharp.

Day ignored Davison's question and Sharp's outburst. "Right, Ms Davison, I'm going to allow you a break. After you've had a coffee a couple of my officers will continue the interview. I want you to tell them every detail you remember about the school office and the trip to the woods."

The solicitor intervened. "Are you intending to arrest my client, Chief Inspector?"

"You bet I am. I'll decide what for later in the day. She's not going anywhere for quite a while. During your break I suggest you make arrangements for someone to pick up her kids from school."

Day had a moment of terrible sadness when he thought of his own girls. How would they react to the sudden loss of both parents?

In the corridor outside, Day made half a dozen phone calls before he spoke to DS Sharp. "I'm not going to Hull; I'm sending Trev instead – we'll see how he copes with Ms Sindhu's driving! As soon as the lads turn up with Rhodes, I'll charge her with Grimshaw's murder then leave her to fester for an hour. If she asks for a solicitor, so much the better, it'll give Trev some time to see if Davenport's come around enough to add names. You take over the Davison interview, Mandy. I'm leaning towards believing her about not knowing who the others were for certain but she must have some ideas. Persuade her to remember anything that will help with identification; size, weight, accent, anything. I've told Phil to drop everything except trying to get into Councillor Mallender's throw-away phone and laptop; there must be some contacts there. Pug's going to her flat to have another look at any paperwork he can find – that'll be a fun job. I'm going to grab a coffee and then I'll have a chat with McAllister and partner while Rhodes is sweating; I'm betting at least one of 'em knows what went off."

Feeling very positive, both detectives headed for the offices above to give out further instructions to their delighted colleagues.

The euphoria didn't last long. Dom O'Neil's phone call spoilt everyone's morning. "It's Rhodes, sir. She's scarpered. No sign of her!"

Day was not known for swearing but poor Dom got it in the neck. "Who the fuck was watching the house, I'll have his guts for garters!" But Day knew the dangers of long sessions of 'stake out' – no one would get into serious bother.

"It was Kamil, sir. He swears he's been wide awake all night, sir. Her car's still there. He says…"

Day didn't let him finish. "Have you been inside?"

"Yes, sir. We broke in as soon as we realised no one was going to answer the door. We searched the house, she's definitely not there. There's a smear of blood on the kitchen table that definitely wasn't there yesterday."
Day was almost relieved Petersen hadn't been there. DCs O'Neil and Malysz could look after themselves but this particular villain was obviously still a proper psycho. "Damn it," he said. "Petersen's been for her! I wouldn't be surprised if we find her dead in a ditch! Send the blood off for testing. Check the wardrobes – see if she's packed for a trip, just in case." Day hung up and phoned Communications. Two minutes later a car was speeding on its way to Janice Rhodes' mum's house. The boy was a prime target and must be protected.
Ten minutes after that Day got the call he had been dreading; Rhodes' mother and son were not in.
"Does she have her own car?" demanded Day.
"Next door neighbour says so, sir," replied PC Rouse. "It's not here; I've got Coms. getting the reg. Do you want me to go inside, neighbour's got a key?"
"Just the two of you?"
"Yes, sir."
"No wait, there's a slight chance Petersen might be in there and we know what he's like! ARV's on the way."
"Okay, sir – call you back when we've gained entry."
Half an hour later every police officer in the country was looking for four missing persons. Possibly three hostages and one extremely dangerous criminal?
Superintendent Halfpenny decided a TV appeal should be made on the six o'clock news.

-

"Hi Trev. Anything?" Day wasn't in the mood for conversation.

"She's half-awake boss, but not saying much. Lot of mumbling but nothing concrete except 'sorry' was repeated several times."

"Bit bloody late for that! Stick around as long as you think fit. Your call. Obviously let me know asap if she implicates anyone."

"Sure will. Doc says she should get more lucid as the day goes on so I'll give it a couple more hours. It'll take me that long to get over Sindhu's driving!" DI Allsop laughed.

Day joined in. "How long did it take?"

"Seventy-five miles door to door in just over an hour! Blue lights all the way. Bloody hell!" That was pushing the rules but, at last, they both had a smile to brighten a day that was going rapidly downhill.

11.00am

Valerie McAllister, George Carmichael's Deputy, was not so self-assured now she was in the police station.

DCI Day challenged her about the initials in Carmichael's diary and, almost without hesitation, she burst into a detailed account of a disintegrating relationship.

"I told you before that George was very supportive when I came out. We weren't expecting any serious bother but he said he would squash any nasty talk he heard in school. 'You're a great teacher, Val – your private life's your own business,' he told me. But then he insisted that he meet my partner, so I arranged for Pauline to pick me up from school one evening. We had a cup of tea in his office and, unbelievably, he flirted terribly with both of us - but mainly Pauline; it was almost like a challenge for him – seduce a lesbian! Pauline couldn't stop talking about him for days afterwards; she seemed obsessed. I knew she'd had male lovers in the distant past but I'd been completely confident she was committed to me – until then."

McAllister was on the verge of tears so Day gave her a break and sent for tea. This appeared to convince her that the senior detective was on her side and she continued.

"Whenever Pauline wasn't away, she would offer to drive me to school; I know now that was just so she could take a look at George. You've heard how charming and good-looking he was Inspector; I was concerned Pauline had become his target and she was going to let him take her."

Day was grateful DS Sharp wasn't in the room – an interruption wouldn't have helped at that moment.

"And what did happen? Was the 'ac' in the diary Pauline?" asked Day.

"I really don't know. I hope not."

"Was the suspicion drastic enough to make you think of removing the opposition – even to the point of murder?" Day expected an emotional denial but what he got was anger.

"Don't be ridiculous! Murder? Me? I couldn't hurt a fly! I thought I was here because you suspected Pauline, not me! Christ!"

"I'm totally open-minded, Ms McAllister. How's your relationship now?"

Calm was almost restored. "Everything was sort of back to normal... well, until last weekend. Pauline told me she was off to Germany but we now know she didn't go, don't we Inspector? Is that the only lie she's told me, you're the detective?"

"Could Pauline Scanlan commit murder?"

Day's question was so brutal that McAllister was crushed into silence. Eventually she shook her head. "Not the Pauline I know," she muttered.

Day had heard enough for the time being. The other half of the gay partnership was waiting next door with DS Sharp.

Pauline Scanlan was also very unhappy. She'd been brought up from a Derby distribution centre where her truck was being loaded for an international delivery. This was costing her money.

As soon as DCI Day had introduced himself, Scanlan went on the offensive. "What's going on? Why am I here? Where's Val?

"Your partner is in the room next door; she's being very helpful. We hope you'll be the same." Day put on his very best calming manner. "We're investigating the murder of George Carmichael and we believe that you might have had an interest in him. Am I right?"

Scanlan's laugh couldn't have been more humourless. "Why would you think that? You know I'm gay, right?"

"Yes, but Ms McAllister told us you were visiting school fairly regularly for no apparent reason. Was it to meet up with Carmichael?"

"Ah, now I get it, Mr Day – you're one of those macho blokes who thinks any lesbian can be turned by an attractive man, aren't you?"

Day gave a wry smile and shook his head. "Not at all, Ms Scanlan. It was Mr Carmichael's attempts at seduction I'm investigating – not any alleged submission."

"Well, he could attempt seduction for all he was worth with me and he would get precisely nowhere. Oh yes, he was pretty enough – pretty creepy – and he was after Val! That made him someone to watch – not to lust after!" The anger was obviously genuine.

"Are you telling me that you found him to be a threat to your relationship?" asked Day quietly.

"Yes. He was a pompous, arrogant bastard – a bit like you, Inspector!"

"Chief Inspector!" hissed DS Sharp. Ms Scanlan would never know just how close she came to a good slapping at that moment.

Day ignored the insult. "You realise you've just admitted a motive for murder?" He watched carefully as the statement hit home. "Let's try and make sense of your alibis, shall we? Your partner had been told you were in Germany last Sunday evening. We all know that wasn't true, don't we? Where were you?"

For the first time Scanlan realised she had to defend herself. "I stayed overnight in London – in my truck. I had a short distance job to do for a regular client. All my appointments can be confirmed."

"Why lie to your partner, then?" Day asked.

"The London visit had two purposes. I was planning a surprise for her – a weekend down there with a show thrown in. I can show you the tickets if you like. I thought she might be in danger of giving in to Carmichael and I wanted her away from home and work so we could talk through our future – if we have a future?"

The explanation seemed genuine enough to Day. "So, you thought Valerie was having an affair with Carmichael at the same time she thought you were!"

All the colour dropped from Scanlan's face and she began to slowly shake her head. "Bloody hell," she whispered, "is that it?" She raised her eyes to the ceiling. "What a pair of idiots!"

Day shrugged. "It looks that way to me, Ms Scanlan – but it still gives you both motives for murder. From what you say, you've got a good alibi but Ms McAllister hasn't. Perhaps she wanted Carmichael dead because she believed he was attempting to seduce you – maybe even succeeding!"

Scanlan looked devastated and continued to shake her head slowly from side to side. Eventually, she whimpered, "It's impossible, Val couldn't do such a thing."

"But you could?" challenged Day.

She hesitated as if seriously considering Day's suggestion. "If he was trying to take Val away from me… yes, I believe I could, Chief Inspector - but I do have a solid alibi."

"Okay," he said, "we'll check it out. This interview's over."

-

"Neither of them, then?" asked Sharp. The two detectives were seated in Day's office, drinking tea hot enough to wash away the disappointment.

"No, reckon not," replied Day before lapsing into deep thought.

"So, they both thought the other one was having it away with Carmichael?"

Day arrived back at the present. "Having it away wouldn't be my choice of expression, Mandy – a bit too twentieth-century for me – but yes, you're right. Extreme good looks and a callous nature turned our Mr Carmichael into a very destructive force."

It wasn't one of Mandy Sharp's regular phrases and she'd no idea why it had slipped out until she realised that 'having it away' was exactly what she wanted to do with the man across the desk. He was the complete opposite of George Carmichael; no vanity whatsoever and an almost innocent kindness – for a copper!

Day studied his Detective Sergeant's face. 'There she goes again,' he thought. 'One pair of suspects eliminated and already planning the next part of the investigation. She's a good 'un!'

12.00noon

Day and Sharp were in his office looking through the list of decodes from Carmichael's three diaries when Phil Johnstone knocked on the door.

"Boss, Rhodes' mum's car's been spotted!" Phil had a smile like Christmas morning.

"Fabu-bloody-lous!" shouted Day, in a second rare swearing moment. "Where?"

"Top of Walton, near the Blue Stoops; parked on a drive on Foljambe Avenue. I've got the layout on satellite if you want to look?"

Day knew the area fairly well and immediately ordered cars to be despatched to either end of the street.

As they walked towards Phil's workstation, Day asked, "Who reported it, Phil?"

"One of our eagle-eyed response car drivers!"

"Genius, I'll buy him a pint!"

"Her."

"Okay then, two pints." They both laughed – this could be progress? "She still there?"

"Yes. She told me she's as far away as she can be – trying not to be too obvious."

"Good lass. Name?"

"PC Hopkinson. Dawn."

"Put me through, will you?" Day studied the bird's-eye view of the detached house on the desktop as Phil pressed buttons. Large house in an affluent area. Long drive. Garden backing onto other residential properties. Not great for a hostage siege.

Phil passed Day the phone.

"Sir!" came an excited young voice.

"Ms Hopkinson, can you still see Mrs Driscoll's Nissan?"

"Yes sir, it's not moved since I noticed it."

"Can people in the house see you?"

"Yes, if they really looked. I'm a good hundred metres away, so not too obvious."

"Good. I owe you a beer. Stay put, a lot of your colleagues will be arriving in minutes."

"Could I have a glass of red instead, please sir?" The question sounded so earnest that Day burst out laughing.

"A bottle!" he said. "If the car moves before reinforcements arrive, report who's in it and I'll decide if you should try to follow, understand?"

"Sir!"

"Phil, get Mandy, Dom and Andy down to the car park. Find the nearest ARV and order them to the Blue Stoops car park. Tell the Super what's happening – I don't know if she'll be happy she won't have to go on the telly!"

The top end of Foljambe Avenue was cordoned off by the time Day and his team arrived at the other end. DS Sharp's Mondeo slid in behind PC Hopkinson's response car and Day took in the scene. No sign of life around the target house – was it a hostage situation; could Petersen be inside? They needed to find out quickly; Day was picturing that vicious devil holding a knife to a little boy's throat.

As Day climbed out of the car, he heard an argument behind him. A delivery driver was arguing with the officer who was blocking the lower end of Foljambe Avenue where it joined Greenways. Day had an idea – two birds with one stone. He walked back to the scene of the confrontation and flashed his ID at the irate driver. "I need to borrow your van," he said politely.

"Fuck off!" replied the driver in the opposite tone.

Day turned to the officer. "Mr Collingwood, if this man uses bad language again, arrest him."

"It would be my pleasure, sir," replied the constable, trying hard not to smile.

Day waved to his colleagues and DS Sharp skilfully reversed her car towards the van. "You three get in the back," said Day as he opened up and removed a large parcel. "I'm going to knock on the door to see who answers. If it's Petersen, I'll yell – come running!"

O'Neil, Grainger and Sharp all immediately volunteered for the role of delivery driver even though they knew their boss was by far the best qualified to deal with an evil sod like Petersen. Day wouldn't ask any of his team to do something he wasn't prepared to do himself. "You don't look anything like a delivery driver, Mandy," said Day to break the tension.

'Wow! Has he noticed I'm female at last?' she thought. She said, "Neither do you in that suit!" Anything to put him off taking risks.

"You're right." He took off his jacket and handed it to O'Neil before waving a finger at the van driver. "When this is all over, I'm going to phone your boss and describe how polite and helpful you've been. Now, lend me your sweatshirt."

The driver hesitated for a split second then, realising he was surrounded by five coppers, decided to comply with good grace.

Day didn't consider himself a particularly good driver but he managed to manoeuvre the van across the top of the drive, blocking off the parked Nissan's escape route. He took the parcel from the passenger seat, walked down the drive and knocked on the door. Nothing. He knocked again. Nothing. He opened the letter box and yelled, "DHL. Delivery for Mr Branston. Come on, it's heavy!"

He heard footsteps inside and tensed himself to use the parcel as a weapon.

The door was opened by a woman of about sixty. "You've got the wrong house, there's no Mr Branson here," she said with a tremor.

Day put two and two together. "Oh, sorry love," he said loudly. Then he whispered, "Mrs Driscoll?"

She nodded.

"Is Petersen here?" he whispered again.

"No," she replied.

"Your daughter and grandson?"

Suddenly, there was a burst of movement and Janice Rhodes emerged from a rear doorway. "Oh, Inspector, it's you! Thank God, we thought Gary had found us! Let him in, mum – he's the kind policeman I told you about."

Day raised one eyebrow and turned to look at the three detectives marching up the drive. He didn't swear, but his expression needed no interpretation. 'What the fuck?'

-

"Bloody hell, Derek, that was crazy – what were you thinking?" Detective Superintendent Halfpenny was not happy.

His actions didn't match his own definition of 'crazy', but he knew when not to argue. "Sorry, ma'am. It seemed like a good idea at the time." DCI Day occasionally had a rather casual relationship with police procedures but it was quite a while since he'd been on the receiving end of this kind of earache.

"I know we've had disastrous budget cuts but we've still got the resources to deal with situations like that properly! What if Petersen had been there and come at you with a knife?"

"I'd have broken his arm, ma'am." Said without even a trace of bravado.

"What if he'd had a gun?"

"Both arms?"

"Very funny! What if he'd shot you through the door – you wouldn't be laughing then, would you? You're not Jack fucking Reacher – you're a senior police officer – you're supposed to use restraint and brains!"

"Sorry ma'am."

"Listen Derek, I'm retiring in two years and, as yet, I haven't had to perform an address at one of my officer's line-of-duty funerals; I don't want to start now! Clear?"

"Yes ma'am."

"Who would you want to knock on your front door to tell Jess she was a widow?" She hesitated. "Me or your mate, Sharp, perhaps?"

That hit home. "Sorry, ma'am, I'll think it through more carefully next time."

"If there is a next time! Now, what exactly is going off with Janice bloody Rhodes?" The dressing down was over and Dsupt Halfpenny indicated that Day should sit down.

"You've got me, there. She says they were hiding from Petersen in that house. Her mum cleans for the old couple who live there and they're away on some cruise or other – so she's got a key to feed the goldfish! They claimed it would be a good place to hide for a few days until we catch him."

"How did Rhodes get away without being spotted?"

"My fault, ma'am. I'd had a good look around the house and garden but hadn't spotted that one of the back-fence panels lifted out easily so I hadn't warned

DC Malysz. Rhodes' mother was waiting for her in the next street and they drove straight up to Walton."

"So, what's her game?"

"She's just told me she's been making up stories because Petersen's been threatening her and the boy. She showed me a load of texts and most were very, very unpleasant. The words 'whore' and 'bitch' appeared frequently and we've got what amounts to a confession because he's told her she's going to get what Carmichael got. He'd also sent a photo of Sami playing outside his Gran's house."

"Is his phone still on?"

"Not at the moment, but Phil's got her mobile and he's waiting for the next abusive message to come through. When it does, we'll have a chance to get him."

"So, is Ms Rhodes another victim here?"

Day sighed. "No. Davison's already fingered her and Petersen for the Grimshaw murder. I haven't tackled her with that yet but I'll guarantee she'll claim Petersen coerced her into helping him. She ought to get a degree from RADA; you can have my pension if she's not as guilty as sin!"

"Better get on and prove it, then. I'd hate to see you hard up in your old age!"

2.00pm

Janice Rhodes was now accompanied by a solicitor but, despite his advice, was more than willing to talk.

DS Sharp went through the formality of arresting her for the murder of Scott Grimshaw. When the words 'anything you do say…' were uttered, the floodgates opened.

"He said he'd make me watch while he killed Sami! I really thought he meant it. I had to do what he told me. What happened in the school office was all him. We had no intention of killing Carmichael even though you already know I hated his guts. Showing him up for the bastard he was would have been good enough for me – we were going to splash him all over the internet!"

"Steady on," soothed Day. "Relax a little and describe what happened in the office on Sunday night."

Rhodes took a breath. Her solicitor whispered something in her ear but she shook her head and began again. "We knocked on the door and, when he came to open it, Gary squirted him with an aerosol can then hit him really hard. While he was dazed, we took his clothes off and tied him to his chair. Gary started to look for money."

That sounded plausible so far. "Who was with you?" asked Day.

Rhodes looked puzzled for a moment. "There was me and two… no, three other women and Gary."

"Names?" demanded Sharp, pencil poised.

"Don't know, we were told not to introduce ourselves!"

"By?"

"Councillor Mallender – it was all her idea, well – her and Gary! She gave me an old phone with four numbers in contacts. She said 'no names'."

"Where's that phone now?"

"I smashed it and threw it in the river!"

Day knew that there would be a lousy job for someone if he decided that phone was vital for the prosecution. "You were all wearing masks?" he asked.

"Yes, except Gary. The councillor didn't get him one for some reason."

The plausibility took a dip. There was something very wrong about this scenario but Day wanted her to continue so threw in an easy question. "What was your mask?"

"Donald Trump!" she replied without hesitation.

"And the other three?"
"Three? Yes. Darth Vader from Star Wars then Freddy something from that horror film, I think." Rhodes stopped and looked confused.
"The fourth woman?"
"I'm struggling with that. She didn't do or say anything. I really don't know why she was there…"
"Margaret Mallender?"
"No, I saw the councillor looking from her window as we went up the school drive."
Sharp was getting impatient. "Number four – what mask? Tall? Short? Fat? Thin?"
"Like a creepy, wizened old woman, I think? Ordinary sort of size."
Why were both women who had been interviewed about the assault in the school office so vague about the fourth woman? Could there be more threats lurking?
"Who killed Carmichael?" asked Day without preamble.
"Gary!" No hesitation this time.
"How?"
"He lost his temper 'cos there was no money and pushed the chair back real hard; it toppled over and Carmichael's head hit the filing cabinet with a right crack." Her voice softened. "I'm not sure Gary meant to kill him."
Day sat back in his chair and in the quietest voice imaginable said. "Neither am I – but he did mean to kill Scott Grimshaw, didn't he, Janice?"
"I… I…" Rhodes stuttered then turned to her solicitor in apparent desperation.
"We know you were there Janice. The only thing we don't know is who struck the fatal blow – you or Gary? Who was it, Janice?"

"How could you think I would do such a thing?" she stammered. "Gary made me go with him. I was bait. It's partly my fault, though – I could have shouted to the boy to run but Gary said he would kill Sami if we didn't do for the boy! I just stood there and let Gary creep up behind him and smash him with a hammer!" Torrents of tears followed. Day thought of RADA again and called off the interview.

Chapter Twenty-four

3.00pm
DCI Day and DS Sharp retired to Day's office and sent for the rest of the team. "So, we know three out of the four women. We know Petersen killed Carmichael - perhaps even unintentionally. We'll be lucky to get anything better than manslaughter on that. Mallender was the organiser but she's obviously beyond our reach and Davenport might be on the way to join her any time now. Grimshaw wasn't in on the conspiracy, he was just a mug. I'm 90% convinced that Petersen killed him – with intent this time but I wouldn't trust anything Janice Rhodes says." Day paused for breath and the others waited expectantly. "Two priorities: find Petersen and identify the fourth woman. At a push, I'm prepared to believe Rhodes and Davison that they don't know her but they need pumping for any detail that might send us in the right direction."

Jobs were allocated and detectives left to continue interviews. Day's mobile rang.

"Boss, it's Trev. Davenport's getting more lucid and the doc allowed me five minutes. She's admitted killing Mallender and being there when Carmichael died. She claims they had no intention of killing him, though – it was meant to be a humiliation with a photoshoot until a bad-tempered bloke showed up. Seems genuinely remorseful – every other word is still sorry."

"Bit late for that but it more or less confirms everything we know. Did she say anything about the other women?"

"Yes. She called them Donald Trump and Darth Vader – masks I guess - but she claimed she had no idea who they really were."

"What about the other one?"

"Another? She didn't mention anyone else. I'll go back in and see if the doctor will give me more time."

"Other witnesses said four women altogether but we're having difficulty pinning down a description of number four; I'm beginning to wonder if she actually exists. Anything else?"

"Absolutely – the best is yet to come – we've recovered two mobiles. One from her handbag and another from under the car seat. Sindhu's got them now and she's pretty handy with tech. Shall we have a look or bring them back for Phil to work his magic?"

"I'm guessing the one from under the seat will be old or cheap. Tell Sindhu to check it for call records and contacts. Tell her not to push it if it's protected in any way. Send any revelations to Phil immediately."

"Will do!"

There was so much excitement in DI Allsop's tone, Day was struggling not to laugh. "Good work, Trev. Be your persuasive best. Cheers."

Just two bits to clear up and Day was confident they'd find the missing links within a matter of hours. He needed a break and headed home for a hot meal and a shower. Spending time with Jess always lifted his spirits and they planned a trip to Meadowhall on his next day off – those new suits wouldn't wait much longer! He asked Alice and Sophie about their day at school and gave both a big hug. On his way back into the station he called at the Tesco petrol station and bought a decent bottle of Aussie shiraz for PC Hopkinson.

Feeling refreshed didn't last too long. There was a message from DI Allsop, who was now on his way back – once again trusting his life to Dipa Sindhu's awesome driving skill. He had been allowed another couple of minutes with Mary Davenport but she had insisted that only three women, plus the unwanted man, had entered the headteacher's office at Somersgill Primary School. Allsop put the error down to Davenport's condition; the former Ofsted Inspector was still critically ill. More surgery on her brain injury was imminent.

Day pondered the question – none of the witnesses could give a detailed description of woman number four. He knew that in cases of extreme trauma memories blurred; was this additional evidence that no murder had been intended? Could this put the whole prosecution in jeopardy?

Then came a much more positive development. A breathless Phil Johnstone appeared in Day's office with the message that Gary Petersen had switched on his mobile. A brief ungrammatical text to his ex-wife stated simply, 'your dead, bitch', but the idiot had then left it switched on! Phil had little trouble locating the source; it appeared to be on the M1 near Nottingham, travelling south. Cars were despatched to the area; as soon as the vehicle stopped, they should have sufficient information to find him.

An hour in an interview room with Petersen would be all Day needed to find out if there really was a woman number four. Problem solved. Case closed.

-

DI Allsop and PC Sindhu arrived back alive and unharmed. Davenport's two phones were handed in to Phil Johnstone who immediately set to work on the cheap 'throw-away'. Much to his surprise, there was minimal security and only seconds later he was able to begin tracking down the four numbers in 'contacts'. All were switched off. The first phone was easy to find; having been picked up in Margaret Mallender's flat, it was now in an evidence locker upstairs, awaiting decoding.

No luck with the other three and the call records were of limited use. All four phones had been used only a handful of times and most calls were to one of the other three. The exceptions were identified as Carmichael's home number at 9pm on the Sunday and a mystery number that had been called twice, once by Mallender on Sunday and once by an unknown person on Monday morning. Day immediately guessed that Scott Grimshaw had been on the receiving end of both those calls.

But DCI Day was confused. Four phones? That couldn't be right! If there were four women in Carmichael's office and Petersen was heavily involved from the planning stage onwards, there should be at least six throw-away phones – not counting Scott Grimshaw's!

When Day and Sharp marked the times from the call records onto their crime timeline, they were able to begin to make a little more sense of the conspiracy.

"We now know Mallender's number and this indicates the other three phones all received two calls from it on Sunday night. If we believe Rhodes, she received a call from Mallender on Monday morning, so that identifies her burner." Day was thinking aloud.

"If!" stated Sharp.

"True. She's still only telling us a fraction of what she knows. But if that is Rhodes' phone she really is in it up to her neck because it's her number that directed Davison to the woods for the Grimshaw murder and told Davenport to silence Mallender! Trouble is, her defence is bound to be built around Petersen using her phone."

"We need that phone, boss!" said Sharp. "Do you think she really threw it in the river?"

"Your guess is as good as mine, but you and Andy can have another go at her. See if she'll give you an exact location - but I fear it will be a waste of time and effort."

"If it still had prints it could prove she was the ringleader and get her on a murder charge," suggested Sharp.

Day shrugged. "True, but I'm not happy even with that. It's clear to me that Mallender was the instigator but, after the accidental killing, she lost her bottle. Then I reckon Rhodes took over and took the lead in the clean-up operation. We'll have no difficulty convincing the CPS to charge Davenport with the murder of Mallender, she's as good as confessed to Trev Allsop, but the others will end up being accused of manslaughter. There's no proof Rhodes persuaded Davenport to get Mallender. Even for the Grimshaw murder, Rhodes will say she was threatened into being there. A good lawyer will be able to sow doubt in any jury's mind. We need that phone but, even more, we need Petersen!"

4.30pm

The unmarked police car following Gary Petersen's phone signal had been ordered to hang back until overwhelming force could be assembled. By the time that happened, the truck had pulled off the M1 and, within a couple of miles had arrived at an industrial estate outside Northampton. No one else had been visible inside the cab so the police waited for the driver to climb down. The watching officers saw him lock the truck and begin to walk towards a nearby building. He was silently intercepted before he made it halfway and escorted round a corner. Once out of sight of his truck the questions began.

Where was your last stop? Tibshelf Services.

Did you pick up a hitchhiker? No – it's against company rules.

Did you check the back before you set off? No.

By the time this brief interrogation was completed the truck was surrounded by armed police officers. A sergeant silently examined the contents of the cab with a powerful torch. Satisfied it was empty, he retreated to the line held by his colleagues and yelled, "Armed Police! Gary Petersen, come out with your hands above your head!"

Nothing! The command was repeated twice more. Nothing.

Two officers approached the rear of the vehicle. While one held his riot shield over the heads of them both, his colleague began to unfasten the straps. There was neither sound nor movement within the truck. More straps were loosened and one officer bravely stuck his helmeted head inside. A quick inspection with a powerful torch revealed no immediate danger and so more of the truck's cargo area was exposed. Six officers climbed aboard and began a methodical search. A mobile phone was found almost immediately but that was it – no sign of Gary Petersen. The crafty sod had deliberately sent the police on a wild goose chase!

Day received the report with dismay. Petersen wasn't well known for being smart but he'd certainly fooled a whole lot of police officers this time.

For the second time, Day went through the pile of search reports on his desk. Every known contact of Petersen's had been tracked down and interviewed. Likely hideouts in the Somersgill area had been minutely examined. Even now, squads of officers were moving on to investigate possible locations in New Whittington, Eckington and beyond. Where could he be?

"He really doesn't have the brains to avoid a search as intense as this," Day said to his team. "And, as far as we know, he has no resources or money to buy help. The Petersen I remember wasn't even bright enough to send a text then put his phone on a long-distance lorry. It's time to look from another angle. Let's suppose he's dead? What if the conspirators killed him for botching the intended Carmichael humiliation? A group of women might have been able to mount a surprise attack – it wouldn't ever occur to his ego that a bunch of women could overpower him."

Day didn't notice the snort from DS Sharp.

"Where could he be? How about Rhodes' back garden? Let's take a look, shall we?" Day looked at every face in the room, hoping someone would come up with a better suggestion.

There were no offers.

"Okay, boss," said Pug Davis, "I'll withdraw Search Team B and send them over to do some gardening straight away." When DCI Day had a theory, however bizarre, everyone took it seriously.

Chapter Twenty-five
ANOTHER CRIME

In the bathroom of her house, Janice Rhodes helped Gary Petersen remove the bin liner and tape. "Take all your clothes off, everything goes in the wash," she said as she stuffed the protective gear in a carrier bag. "Get in the bath and I'll join you when I've seen to these. Your reward's only minutes away, now!" She gathered up the carrier and her ex-husband's clothes and left the room.

Petersen was pissed off and decided he wasn't taking any more orders - but the excitement of beating Grimshaw to death had tired him out so a hot bath wouldn't do any harm. When that woman came back, she was going to get a right seeing to…

He slipped into the hot water and imagined, in detail, what he would be doing in the next few minutes. He heard movement on the stairs and Janice Rhodes reappeared. She was wearing a full-length white dressing gown which she had taken great care not to fasten properly - so the flash of pubic hair concentrated Petersen's mind wonderfully. He hadn't seen a naked woman, in the flesh, for the best part of ten years and he was going to make up for that now. Still in her mid-thirties, Janice could be a very, very attractive young woman when she made an effort – and that was precisely what she was doing now.

She allowed the dressing gown to drift away. Before it hit the floor, she swept it up very gracefully and threw it out the door. "Room for anyone else in there?" she asked.

Petersen looked her up and down. He nodded and eased himself up into a seated position. With deliberate, sexy slow-motion she lifted up her right foot over into the hot water next to his left knee. He studied every curve. Taking her weight on her left hand, she lifted her other leg into the bath and straddled him.

Her breasts were only inches from his face and he was mesmerised. He touched them and she moaned. Her face went blush pink and that had always turned him on. He grabbed hard and, through the pain, she moaned louder. She felt his erection grow against her thigh and knew the time had come.

Janice Rhodes stretched up and took the scissors she had placed on the vanity unit thirty minutes previously. With a frequently rehearsed sudden movement, she thrust the point into Petersen's left eye. She kept pushing until only the two plastic handles remained visible and the disgusting screaming and wriggling had stopped.

She sat back and pulled the plug before taking down the shower head and running water over herself and the corpse until all trace of blood was gone. She stepped out of the bath and, still naked, left the room. She returned two minutes later, wearing only a pair of rubber gloves and carrying a roll of plastic sheeting and her mobile phone.

The text she sent to Preston said simply, 'Tea at 6, don't be late'. He would know exactly what it meant.

She covered the tiled floor with plastic and struggled for five minutes getting Petersen out of the bath. For some reason she would never understand, Rhodes couldn't bring herself to remove the scissors - but that didn't delay the next stage. She rolled the body into the plastic sheet and applied an excessive amount of parcel tape. There would be no leaks!

She stepped over the body and opened a bottle of bleach – let the deep clean begin. Two hours later she was satisfied with the work and she moved on to phase two. She dressed in the old clothes she reserved for gardening and went down to the shed. After piling all her equipment to one side she was able to access the six screws that held in place a section of removable floor. She carefully lifted out the long panel and exposed four 50cm square paving slabs. Donning gardening gloves, she was able to lift out each paver and stack it against the shed wall. This exposed the sarcophagus she had designed and built for George Carmichael. Made of more 50cm pavers crudely cemented together it would serve as a last resting place for Gary Petersen instead.

Earlier in the year, she had planned to lure Carmichael to her house and murder him - but now she'd had a real bonus – this was way better than a 'buy one, get one free' offer at the supermarket.

Preston arrived in time for tea with Janice and they enjoyed a laugh as they watched TV and ate a tasty meal.

As soon as it went dark, brother and sister checked for nosey neighbours before carrying Petersen's tightly-wrapped body to the shed. All his clothes and protective gear were packed around him. As last gifts to the departed, Rhodes dropped in the throw-away phone given to her by Margaret Mallender and the one she had retrieved from Scott Grimshaw's corpse. The four pavers that served as a lid were replaced.

No words were said over the grave although the 'mourners' did manage a high-five. Ten minutes later they were together in the bath – and no scissors were needed.

The following day Janice would mix some mortar and seal the tomb. The floor panel would be refitted and a tiny spot of mud rubbed into each of the screw heads. By the time all her gardening equipment was returned to its correct position, no visitors would ever know they were standing above a one-man cemetery.

-

The coded text told Preston what to do. He typed the message on Gary's phone and then carefully placed it into the back of a soft-sided truck about to leave Tibshelf Motorway Services on its journey south. He followed the truck for a few miles then turned back onto the M1 north at the A38 junction. Half an hour later he was at home in Hasland getting ready for work. While ever the stupid cops were looking for Petersen, it would be hard for them to pin anything concrete on Janice for the Carmichael killing.

Chapter Twenty-six

6.00pm

The weather had picked up and it was a hot July day in Somersgill. Those few areas of Janice Rhodes' back garden that had obviously been disturbed in the previous few weeks were given the full attention of the search party. Nothing suspicious was found and the perspiring officers were beginning to discuss a visit to the pub.

But the sergeant in charge had an unpopular brainwave. They would have a look under the shed before they called it a day.

Eight burly blokes gathered around and lifted the complete shed off its gravel base and dumped it down on the tiny lawn. The exposed 8 x 10 foundation had a neat line of four small pavers across the centre.

"Hello, hello, hello, what have we here?" said the sergeant in his famous parody of a long-dead comic policeman. "Spade!" he said, in a much more business-like tone.

A couple of vicious blows loosened one slab and it was lifted away to reveal the end of a substantial, plastic-wrapped parcel.

"Step away!" ordered the sergeant. "Dave, phone in and let the DCI know what we've found. Right, you lads, as soon as the big boys arrive, I think we'll disappear to an establishment where you can all buy me a well-earned pint."

Back at Beetwell Street Station, all the detectives changed their minds about going home when they got the call from the search party! A fleet of cars headed for Somersgill.

DCI Day and most of his team watched as the SOCOs painstakingly removed the rest of the 'coffin' lid. The photographer recorded the work from every angle.

"It's got to be a body," uttered DS Sharp just to break the tension.

Doctor Smythe wrinkled his nose. "You are, I fear, quite right, young Sharpy!"

Sharp wasn't amused by the restrained laughter from the other detectives but she felt she had to smile anyway.

Day watched one of the white suits pick up two mobiles and display them to the audience before dropping them in an evidence bag. 'Brilliant,' he thought.

Next out was a black bin liner that appeared to be stuffed with clothes.

"How shall we proceed, Chief Inspector?" asked Doc Smythe in a mock formal tone.

"Lift the bundle out lads. We'll have a quick look at the face before it goes to the mortuary."

The plastic-wrapped body was lifted out onto a clean plastic groundsheet.

Doc Smythe made a show of donning his white suit but eventually he knelt by the body to supervise the extremely gentle removal of the wrapping.

Ten agonising minutes later the SOCO Chief was able to pull back the plastic far enough to give her audience a clear view of the face.

A glance was all it took. "It's Petersen!" stated Day.

The detectives were ready to give a cheer but Day's grim expression cut them off. The evil behind Janice Rhodes' lies was finally revealed.

Doctor Smythe broke the tension. He pointed to the scissors protruding from Petersen's eye and said, "Working out the cause of death's going to be quite a struggle!"

Result! Janice Rhodes was charged with the murder of Gary Petersen later that evening. Veronica Davison gave a statement of intricate detail that she hoped would convince a jury she had had no intention of ever physically harming her ex-husband. A recording of DI Allsop's interviews with Mary Davenport was transcribed and her confession analysed. DCI Day's team of detectives completed as much paperwork as possible before exhaustion set in and they were ordered to get the beers in at the Rose and Crown.

8.00pm
Day had promised to join them later and continued to type his reports. A call from Reception brought him down into the public area of Beetwell Street Police Station where he was met by an angry Preston Driscoll.
"I've come to get Janice," he demanded. "Where is she?"
"I'm sorry to have to tell you this, Preston but your sister's been charged with two murders and some other offences. You won't be able to take her anywhere in the foreseeable future."
"Bullshit!" he shouted – attracting a great deal of attention. "Jan wouldn't hurt a fly; she's lovely… and gentle!"
"Sorry, but it's true. I'm one hundred percent certain your sister has committed murder."
This prompted Preston to poke Day in the chest. "Get her! I need her!" he yelled.
This action caused him to be surrounded by suddenly very interested uniformed officers.
"It's okay lads, he's upset." Day turned to face the confrontation. "Look Preston, you need to leave. Phone

in tomorrow and I'll see if I can arrange for you to visit her."

Preston looked on the verge of tears. "But you don't understand, I really need her."

"Off you go, I'll see what I can do for you – tomorrow." Day gently ushered the young giant towards the door. "It might be a good idea if you went and broke the news to your mother – but perhaps not Sami, eh?"

The see-saw of emotion in Preston's eyes swept back to anger. "You'll pay for this, you twat!" he yelled.

Day had had enough. He turned and looked at the group of uniforms, raised his eyebrows and inclined his head towards the exit. They didn't need another hint; three of them shoved Preston out of the door.

He would see Preston the next day but not socially. Day was convinced the young man was mixed up in his sister's crimes and tomorrow he would prove it.

Day looked at his watch. 'Another hour on the blessed paperwork and then I'll go and have a pint with the gang,' he thought.

-

Jessica, Sophie and Alice Day were seated at their kitchen table drinking hot chocolate when there was a knock on the door.

Jessica crossed the room and pulled a puzzled 'who can this possibly be' face, causing both girls to laugh. She opened the door and, as she always did, smiled.

Two large men in black were standing there.

"Mrs Day?" asked the larger of the pair.

"That's me," she said brightly. "What can I do for you gentl…?"

Gentlemen was an incorrect description. She was punched hard in the face.

It was the rocking of the cold steel floor that brought Jess back to consciousness. She licked blood from her teeth and opened her eyes. Two wide blue eyes stared back at her; it was Alice and she was clearly terrified. Aware that her mother was now awake, the child tried to scream but no sound emerged through the gag across her mouth. Mother and daughter were both securely bound with cable ties and duct tape.

Jess took stock. They were in the back of a van and it was moving. Then real panic set in – where was Sophie? What had they done with Sophie? Jess twisted around. She could see the backs of the two men up front but there was definitely no sign of her younger daughter.

It might have been some comfort to Jess had she known that Sophie was at home in the kitchen. Just before they had left, the two strangers had ripped the duct tape from her mouth and put her mother's phone in her hand.

"Phone your dad and tell him what's happened!" Sophie was a bright little girl; she had no difficulty in obeying the simple instruction.

-

DCI Day put his mobile back in his pocket. All around him, members of his team were gearing up for a seriously lively celebration.

He caught the eye of PC Sindhu and waved her over.

As she approached, the young officer looked into the face of her much-admired leader and saw fear – no, not fear – terror!

She gulped. "Sir?" she said.

"You fit to drive?" he asked, obviously trying to maintain a degree of self-control.

In a reckless attempt at levity, she replied, "Oh, you know me, sir – lightweight – I've only had a half of Golden Bud so far!"

He looked at her blankly. "Take Andy Grainger to my house, will you? Sophie's there alone. Look after her, please. Tell Andy to lock all the doors and windows – keep her safe!"

Sindhu was puzzled and alarmed by this bizarre set of instructions but she did not question them. She nodded, stood up, walked over to Grainger and tapped him on the shoulder. After a brief conversation, Andy put down his pint, glanced across at Day then left the pub.

Outside, there was a brief screech of tyres as Sindhu set off towards Sophie Day.

With his last ounce of self-control, Day wandered over to DI Allsop and handed him £40. "I can't stay, Trev. Buy 'em all a drink on me, will you?"

"You okay, Derek? Feeling a bit rough?"

"Rough, yeah, rough that's it." Day was saved the ordeal of further explanation when his mobile went off in his pocket. "See you tomorrow, Trev," he said and wandered outside.

As soon as he was far enough away from potential eavesdroppers, he answered his phone.

"Mr Day, I have your wife and little girl…"

"I know, Preston. What do you want?"

"Oh, you realised it was me, then? Good. I just want my sister. Bring her to me and you get two for one!" The voice was so calm, so matter-of-fact, it actually increased Day's terror.

He gulped down the phone. "I can't do that, Preston. There's no way I can simply take her from the cells and bring her to you. If there was a way, I'd do it, believe me!"

"You'll have to find a way!" he shrieked. "I need Janice! Life without her wouldn't be worth living. I'll kill myself - but before that, I'll break two pretty necks!" Preston was clearly very unstable.

"Okay, okay, Preston, I'll do it. I'll find a way. Please don't hurt them!"

Preston instantly switched back to calm mode. "That's more like it - very sensible. Get it done! I'll ring this number again in half-an-hour. Give me some good news and there's a chance your two girls will survive the night!" The line went dead.

Day staggered towards his car and opened the door. Any watcher would have assumed he was desperately drunk but not one drop had passed his lips that evening. For a few moments he considered the best way forward but his brain simply couldn't grasp the agony of the situation. He started the engine and set off on the five-minute journey back to Beetwell Street nick. If he'd looked in his mirrors, he'd have noticed another car leave the Rose and Crown and stick close behind him.

When the second call came through, Day was sitting with Janice Rhodes in her cell. He had explained his plans to her and emphasised that she must not let the Custody Sergeant know what was about to happen.

"Have you sorted your problem yet, Inspector?" asked Preston.

"Yes. I'm with your sister right now. Tell us where to go and we'll be there."

"Put her on, I need to know you're not lying!"

"Lying! You've got my wife and daughter – why would I lie?" He handed his mobile to Rhodes.

"Preston, well done my love! Mr Day's told me he's going to bring me to meet you. He did say before he takes me outside, you've got to prove you have his missus and she's all right. Can you put her on?"

Day heard hollow movements and a brief tearing sound followed by a subdued shriek. Then he listened as Preston told Jess to speak.

Jess coughed twice. "Hello love," she said calmly, "we're both safe. You do what you think's best. How's Sophie?" Jess was feeling anything but calm; she knew her husband needed no extra pressure in this terrible situation.

There was sound of more movement and Day realised that the phone had been snatched away before he could answer. "Okay, Preston – what's the deal? Where and when? And tell her Sophie's okay – no thanks to you!"

Preston laughed without humour. "One car, two people – you and Janice. Any sign of other pigs, you won't see your family again. I even smell a helicopter – both dead. Any weapons on show – same result. Two o'clock tomorrow morning drive to the first layby out of town on the Hasland by-pass, do you know it?"

Day replied that he did. Only two minutes from the Police Station at that time of night.

"Wait there until I contact you again and tell you where to go. Needless to say, don't tell anyone else!" The threat in Preston's tone left nothing to the imagination. "Put Janice back on."

Day handed over the phone and stood just outside the cell door. He didn't hear most of the rest of the conversation but Rhodes seemed happy enough with the plans, so Day told her he'd see her later, recovered his phone and ordered the door to be locked. Rhodes smiled brightly. There was no trace of a blush.

-

It had been Andy Grainger's turn to 'save the day'. Arriving at Day's house with Dipa Sindhu, it had been the DC who had listened to seven-year-old Sophie's account of the kidnap. Knowing his DCI as well as he did, Andy knew that there would already be some unofficial, crazy 'superhero' rescue in the planning stage.

After some soul-searching, Andy decided he must inform Detective Superintendent Halfpenny. She was off-duty and it took a full hour to track her down but, after hearing Grainger's assessment of the situation, she reassured him he'd done the right thing.

She put the phone down and thought the scenario through. She knew Day wouldn't be intimidated by a few kidnappers and he'd be arranging to meet them. 'We'll let him think he's doing it on his own because it'll look more convincing that way, but we'll be close by with support,' she thought. But how to do that when they had no idea what the ransom demands were or where the exchange point would be? She phoned Phil Johnstone and ordered him out of the Rose and Crown. Drunk or sober, he'd know how to obtain all the relevant information.

When she had as much information as she needed, the Superintendent issued a string of orders. Four detectives in an unmarked car, an ARV, a Dog Van and a crew bus full of the angriest coppers she could muster were placed on alert.

In Beetwell Street Police Station, Phil Johnstone, now stone cold sober, was ready to coordinate the support - or would it be a rescue mission?

Chapter Twenty-seven
Day's DAY 5

2.00am

There was no rain but clouds largely obscured what little moonlight was around. Day and his passenger arrived at the layby with five minutes to spare but it was another twenty-five minutes before the call came through. During that time several cars had passed them, all except one at high speed. A blue Honda had crawled past and the driver gave them a serious once-over. For a moment Day had almost panicked, thinking it might be a police car but then he realised that the Traffic Squad had no such vehicle. It had to be a spotter for Preston; Day committed its registration to memory.

When it came, the call was brief and the directions and instructions concise. Stainsby Mill car parking area. It helped that Day had parked there only the previous summer when he took Alice and Sophie to a National Trust flour-making exhibition. He visualised the area; why had they chosen it? Not overlooked by dwellings and only two minutes from the M1 were good reasons but it was a single, narrow lane not a car park. A couple of hundred yards of rough tarmac ending in a slightly wider turning area, with another fifty yards of straight muddy track leading off, made it an easy place for the police to block and trap the kidnappers. 'Preston and his mate must be confident they've got all the cards; they know I'm dealing with this alone,' he thought. He started the car. "Ready?" he asked his passenger.

"Yes," she replied without emotion.

Five minutes later the dark outline of a deserted Stainsby Mill appeared in the headlights. As Day turned left into the lane, he saw two sets of dipped headlights on the rise at the far end. He could just make out that one was some kind of van and the other, slightly further away, was a smaller vehicle; he guessed it was the blue Honda. Day pulled up fifty yards short in the turning area. He could see the silhouettes of two bulky figures at the edge of the circle of light. Switching his own lights off, Day stepped out and looked around. A good place for an ambush; the thick foliage to the left would block out any chance of them being seen from the motorway and, even at this hour, the constant traffic noise, combined with the slight breeze rustling the leaves, would drown out any sounds of violence. Day had decided there was going to be violence.

Day deliberately left the driver's door open. The dim interior light illuminated the passenger in the back seat. She had her face down between her straight arms but the top of her close-cropped blonde hair was clearly visible. She appeared to be handcuffed to the head rest of the front passenger seat and there was only limited movement. A flash of the orange dress Janice Rhodes had been wearing when arrested could be seen by anyone with decent eye-sight.

As previously instructed, Day put his arms in the air and did a slow-motion spin. Wearing only trousers and shirt, it was obvious he was unarmed. The manoeuvre gave him the opportunity to look around again and, satisfied no one was behind him, he began to walk towards his enemies.

"Stop there!" commanded Preston when Day was ten yards short. "Why have you parked so far away?"

There were only two men and Day was surprised to note that Preston was the smaller. That wasn't the main problem, though. Day was dismayed to see that both men were wearing some kind of bouncer-style body armour - possibly presenting a difficulty for stage two of the fight to come.

He had no choice but to continue so dangled his set of handcuff keys. "I need to see my wife and daughter are okay before you get Janice!"

"Anybody else know you're here?"

"Absolutely no one," said Day. It was the truth – as far as he knew.

Preston was obviously very agitated, stepping from one foot to the other like a toddler desperate for a pee, but he had enough control to nod his head in the direction of the Transit. Illuminated by the Honda's lights, the big bloke opened the sliding side door of the van and uttered just one word, "Out!"

After much rustling and scraping, two sets of legs appeared. None too gently the big man reached inside and pulled the two females upright. Both had hands bound in front with cable ties and mouths covered with duct tape.

Day felt his anger rise but he concentrated hard on appearing calm. If the three of them were to have any chance of getting out of this mess alive he needed to be completely in control.

"Bring 'em over here, Gord," ordered Preston. "Let him get a good look!"

As the hostages were brought forward, Preston yelled, "Janice, get up here!"

Mother and daughter were pushed in Day's direction. The detective didn't like what he saw; even in intense shadow and partly obscured with strips of tape, their faces bore smears of blood and grey-blue bruises. Jess' dress and Alice's pyjamas were filthy from rolling about in the back of the van. They had been treated with absolute callousness.

Day felt his anger rise but he had to keep craziness at bay.

Preston broke into his thoughts. "What's up with Janice – why isn't she moving?" A very short fuse was evident from Preston's tone. "Have you drugged her, you bastard?"

Control. Day desperately needed all his self-control. "No Preston, I haven't. Nobody has. You have my absolute word, on the lives of my family, that Janice is safe and well. She can't move because she's still handcuffed to the car!"

This profound declaration seemed to calm Preston and he held out his hand. "Keys!" he demanded.

Day handed over the handcuffs key.

"Car keys!"

"In the ignition. Full tank of fuel as you directed." Day knew this was a red-herring. Even Preston wouldn't be stupid enough to use an unmarked police car as a getaway vehicle; he must know they carried trackers.

Preston appeared satisfied and turned to his accomplice. "Sit 'em down, Gord. I'll give you a shout as soon as I've released Janice - then you know what to do."

Day was under no illusions. He was pretty certain that, when the kidnappers made their escape, they planned to leave three bodies in the lane. Not if he could help it.

Gord kicked Jess' legs from under her and then repeated the trick with young Alice. He laughed.

And Day felt his anger rise close to breaking point.

"You too, get down!" Gord demanded of Day.

"No," said Day as calmly as he could manage.

Gord laughed again. He reached inside his vest and pulled out a meat cleaver. "Get down," he repeated and held the cleaver above Jess' head.

Gord didn't realise that this action had altered Day's mindset. The detective's anger dissipated and was replaced by a murderous calm. His world began to turn in slow-motion as he planned every movement of the upcoming ballet. "Please don't hurt her," he blubbered like a helpless child. He was shaking and twisting his head in a show of fear and confusion – which gave him the opportunity to see how close Preston was to the police car – and Janice.

Ten paces. Perfect.

Day staggered towards his ladies and screamed, "I'm so sorry, this is all my fault, forgive me!"

To Gord, he seemed almost in tears. 'What a pussy,' he thought, 'and Prez said this copper was real tough.' As expected, he stepped forward between his two captives.

In the distance, a yell of fury was heard from Preston – and Day knew it was time.

The shout and the detective's wimpish play-acting had distracted Gord for a split second - but it was enough for Day to cover the ground.

Gord didn't even have time to lift the meat cleaver before Day's right fist broke his nose. Four more blows landed within seconds and the big man began to go down. He dropped the meat cleaver and began to fall towards Alice. Day caught his collar and was just able to steer him into a bit of open ground.

"Bastard!" screamed Gord through bloodied teeth but his troubles were far from over. Day took one pace forward and stamped, with all his weight, onto Gord's balls. Time was against Day and no subtlety was warranted.

He turned and saw Preston staggering backwards from a much smaller blonde female figure. Day kicked the meat cleaver towards Jess and set off at a run towards Mandy Sharp.

Earlier that evening, DS Sharp had followed her boss from the pub and nagged him until he'd given her details of the situation. She had then made a massive sacrifice; using a pair of office scissors to hack off her beautiful hair, she gave herself an approximate look of Janice Rhodes. She even took Rhodes' orange dress from storage to complete her 'from a distance' disguise. Of course, the handcuffs weren't locked and, as she heard the shout of Preston's realisation, she climbed out of the car, armed with a taser and an expandable baton, and hissed, tauntingly, "Come on big man, let's see how good you are at fighting girls!"

The taser wires hit Preston square in the chest – right in the centre of his body armour! He reeled backwards but the shock was dissipated by the vest. After a couple of seconds, he recovered and came forward again. He was big and strong and manic! Screaming hysterically, "Where's Janice, you bitch? What have you done with her?" He swung a myriad of blows at his smaller opponent.

Mandy was giving as good as she got, until a lucky strike from Preston's flailing fist knocked the baton out of her hand. She didn't hesitate for a moment – she went at him with a blistering combination of unarmed combat, kicking, scratching and biting.

But Day was still ten strides away when Preston took a mighty swing at the detective. It connected - and brave Mandy Sharp was out of the contest.

Jessica Day had grabbed the meat cleaver and, holding it, blade up, between her feet, she worked the cable ties on her wrists back and forth. Gord was still on the ground but he had stopped screaming and started cursing, giving a clear indication he was only seconds away from returning to the fight.

He got to his knees and made a dazed lunge at her at the precise moment the last of the cable ties snapped. In an instinctive panic, Jess snatched up the meat cleaver and swung it at her assailant's face. It connected just at the side of his right eye causing him to howl in anger. But she had hit him with the blunt back of the blade! Realising she only had seconds to act, Jess grabbed Alice in her arms and, seeking the protection of a large dark field, ran for all she was worth. Still rubbing his painful balls, Gord picked up the cleaver and began to limp after her.

Seeing his trusted DS knocked to the ground, Day continued at full speed before launching himself into a double footed kick at Preston's back. The fearsome blow connected with Preston's kidney and he went down on top of Mandy Sharp. Day was also down, the colossal impact of the drop-kick winding him. He was the first to recover but not quickly enough. He had picked up discarded handcuffs and just managed to secure one of Preston's wrists when the big man twisted and pushed Day to the side. As he rolled across the rough tarmac, the detective landed on Mandy's baton. He completed the roll and picked up the weapon. Without hesitation, he smashed it into Preston's mouth, shattering a half dozen teeth. Fragments went into his throat and the big man began to choke but Day wasn't in the mood for mercy, he had to end this now – his wife and daughter were in imminent danger. As Preston gripped his throat in agony, Day took careful aim with the baton and made a strike. The crack on impact indicated that Preston now had a broken right arm. Good. A quick glance told him that Mandy Sharp was still breathing, so Day turned and ran back up the lane towards the kidnappers' vehicles. To his horror he found no one there! Wife, daughter and attacker had vanished. He could see nothing outside the area of the headlights and all sound was covered by the distant roar of the motorway. He felt panic rising. If Jess had done a runner, she had three choices: had she jumped over the fence into the shambles of fly-tipping; taken the narrow, winding footpath or run into the field of some dark crop or other? It had to be the field! Then a stroke of luck – in the field, the tiniest glint in the distance as a light reflected from a meat cleaver!

Day set off at speed in the direction of that last flash of reflection but he could see virtually nothing. A tiny sound gave him a clue during the briefest gap in motorway traffic and he adjusted direction. Just as hopelessness was about to set in, the field was illuminated by a sweep of car headlights. There they all were, really close, but he saw he wasn't going to make it in time. Although Gord was injured, he was chasing a small woman carrying a nine-year-old girl and he was within seconds of overtaking his pursuit. Day saw the big man lift the cleaver and prepare to swing it at Jess' head. There was no alternative; Day threw his only weapon and the baton bounced off Gord's arm. He didn't drop the cleaver but it was mission accomplished; Gord stopped. He turned and looked at the source of all the pain and humiliation he felt. He grinned; bloody revenge would be sweet.

"Jess, double back, run for the car. Throw Ali inside and check Mandy. Then drive!" yelled Day.

There was no hesitation on Jess' part, she changed the direction of her run and charged towards the unmarked car down the lane. She had a good idea what was about to happen and didn't want her little girl to be a witness to her father's grim retaliation.

But Gord had also changed direction and was heading slowly towards Day. "You're fucked, copper – I'm goin' to cut you in half!"

Neither of the men gave a thought to the bright lights that were now upon them – this was to be a fight to the death.

Day backed off slowly. This was against his natural instinct, but he needed to read his opponent's eyes; with a broken nose, how alert could he be? Day could see more anger than cold concentration. If he was a mate of Preston's there was a good chance he was a bouncer and therefore used to dealing with drunks - but Day wasn't drunk, he was as murderously sober as it was possible to be - and the man who had threatened his family was going to pay. Day knew that his actions this evening would certainly mean dismissal from the job he loved, so he decided it was time to go for broke and give this thug the treatment he deserved.

Continuing his slow reverse, Day waved to encourage his opponent to come forward faster and so go off balance.

"Come here you fucking coward," yelled Gord, his anger rising as he sensed a delay in his revenge. He leapt forward and swung the cleaver in a backhand flat arc right to left, aimed at Day's nose. It was a vicious but unskilled attempt and Day avoided it easily. Gord attempted to regain his balance for a repeat swing, but from closer. It was another schoolboy error and Day saw his chance.

He dived beneath the swing and then jumped up to hit under Gord's chin with the top of his head. It wasn't a hard contact but it didn't have to be; the end of Gord's tongue was neatly severed. The big man fell, screaming and spraying blood. Day followed him down, grabbing the wrist holding the cleaver and steering the blade deep into the soft skin of his opponent's cheek.

Through multiple agonies, Gord yelled more hysterical obscenities, thus giving Day the opportunity to prise open fingers to remove the meat cleaver and throw it into the bushes.

But the detective wasn't finished. His pent-up anger exploded into craziness. This evil bastard had tried to kill Jess and he had to pay more – much more. Day sat on Gord's chest and began to punch the already badly damaged face. Left, right, left, right – this piece of scum would soon look like George Carmichael...

Strong arms grabbed Day from behind. "Sir, sir, stop – you're killing him!"

"That's the fucking idea!" Crazy.

The arms pulled harder. "No, no, no – leave him. We've got him – and the other one. It's over."

Through the fury, Day recognised Andy Grainger's voice but it didn't stop the violence and he continued to try to punch down.

It wasn't until he received a sharp kick in the ribs and heard an equally familiar voice that sense began to return.

"Derek, you idiot, stop that! That's an order!" Detective Superintendent Halfpenny kicked him again.

Derek Day rolled onto the grass and stared at nothing in particular. "How's Jess?" he said. "How's Alice?"

"Both fine, which is more than I can say for their kidnappers. Paramedics on their way." Halfpenny had already returned to her normal, matter-of-fact, calm.

And then another terror leapt into Day's addled brain. "Mandy! How's Mandy?"

"Not so good. Unconscious but breathing. She'll be the medics' number one priority, not the two scumbags," replied Halfpenny.

Day jumped up and took his bearings. Three police cars and a van had arrived since he'd last looked around. In the glare of their lights he could see a couple of officers bent over an inert figure by the unmarked car. He rushed over. As he peered down at her, one swollen eye opened.

"Did we win?" she croaked.

"Yes, Mandy, thanks to you!" he replied.

And the eye closed.

Chapter Twenty-eight

5am

DCI Day stood, perfectly straight, in front of the desk where Detective Superintendent Halfpenny was shuffling papers. Since she had uttered the words, 'come in' no one had spoken.

Without warning, the silence was broken. In a surprisingly mild voice, the Superintendent asked, "Jess and the kids okay?"

"Jess seems alright, ma'am but I think it might be a long job for Alice and Sophie."

"Hmm, shame. Let me know if I can help in any way."

"You already have, ma'am. Angie from Family Liaison arrived just before I left."

"She's good – she'll be a help." Halfpenny picked up a paper. "Not so good for DS Sharp. According to this report from the A&E Consultant, her injuries aren't life threatening but he can't promise they're not life changing."

Day didn't feel able to speak; he should never have agreed to her impersonation of Janice Rhodes. He prayed silently for a full recovery. Selfish really, he knew he'd never forgive himself if Mandy was permanently damaged.

Sensing his mental anguish, Halfpenny changed the subject by pointing her biro at one of Day's bandaged hands. "Painful?"

This interview was becoming more and more surreal. He was convinced he'd been summoned here at this ridiculous time to receive a mighty bollocking – but she was being so pleasant. Was this a good time to resign – jump before the big push? Not yet, he decided.

"Little bit sore. Skin damage on the knuckles mainly, it'll heal."

"Any other aches or pains?"

"Nothing of importance, ma'am."

"Bruises on the ribs giving you any trouble?"

Dangerous territory. "No, ma'am."

Halfpenny stared hard directly into Day's 'let's get in over with' expression. "Well, I was just going to say, if you feel the need to report me to Professional Standards you…"

"Wouldn't dream of it, ma'am," said Day promptly.

"Don't interrupt! I was going to say 'you can go fuck yourself!"

The mood changed. This was more like the meeting Day had expected.

"I'm very, very pissed with you, Derek. You're…"

"Would this be a good time to offer my resignation?"

"That's the second time you've interrupted me in less than ten seconds. Don't!"

"No, ma'am."

"You will not resign! I've already lost one good detective today and I will not lose my best in some act of heroic martyrdom. You will stay and face the music. In a couple of hours our two kidnappers will be seen by their briefs and they'll be falling over themselves to put in complaints of police brutality. We'll be up to our necks in Professional Standards by lunchtime."

Day was looking straight ahead, his face now sombre. "I'll tell the truth and take the consequences, ma'am," he said.

Halfpenny stood up so violently that her chair hurtled back across the room. "You will bloody not! Sit down, man – we haven't got much time. The only thing that's saved us so far is both your victims are finding it difficult to speak!"

The distraction gave Day a millisecond to consider whether George Carmichael would still be alive if he'd had an office carpet equal in quality to the Superintendent's.

She recovered her chair and made quite a show of adjusting a cushion with a picture of a surprised hare. Was it caught in someone's headlights?

"First, you owe DC Grainger a bottle of scotch – a good one, mind. If he hadn't come to me, I wouldn't be in a position to protect you."

Ah, that explained it. "Will do," replied Day. "He likes Dalwhinnie 15."

"So do I and you'll owe me a gallon by the time this is all sorted."

"Yes, ma'am."

"Grainger and I have already agreed that you ordered him to contact me to arrange support for your rescue attempt. Confirm it with him! We planned this whole thing together, right?"

Day could hardly believe his ears; the boss was sticking her neck out way beyond the cause of respect or friendship.

"They'll never believe it, ma'am. PSD'll know you wouldn't allow a couple of officers to go off-piste like that – it's not your style!"

"They will believe it – for two reasons. One, we'll all tell exactly the same story and two – you've cleared up a half-dozen major crimes in less than a week – you'll be the Chief Constable's 'copper of the month'!

Halfpenny pushed her chair back, rather more gently this time, and crossed her legs indicating she was warming to her task. "It was my gamble. I judged that you and DS Sharp could carry out the subterfuge for just long enough for me to come charging in with the cavalry. A tough decision but I thought it was the best chance given the limited preparation time we had."

Day was still whirling from this turn of events. "But the nature of the injuries to Preston and his mate?"

Halfpenny extracted two message slips from her pile of papers; someone had been working hard to keep her informed.

"Gordon Robinson, who incidentally has three previous convictions for assault," she began. "Report from the Royal: broken nose and cheekbone; lump of tongue missing; face as blue as a Smurf – serves the bugger right!" Preston Driscoll: multiple abrasions, broken arm's getting a temporary repair so he can spend most of today in the Dental Hospital. Neither likely to flake."

Halfpenny suddenly looked very puzzled. "Preston and sister are lovers?" she asked.

"Reckon so."

"Weird! Anyway, classic self-defence by an officer who's already seen a colleague disabled! Keep it straight and we'll all get away with it. Keep an eye on young Sharp and, the minute she's compos mentis, tell her what to remember. Now, I want you to go back to your family for a couple of hours – we'll have a full team meeting at ten. I'll be telling them you're taking a week off to support your family and keep an eye on Sharp. I've already sent for Trev Allsop; he doesn't know it yet but he'll be taking charge of the hunt for woman four, the closing interviews and prep for CPS – he's good at that sort of thing. You've done the hard stuff, now you take some time with Jess and the kids – and for heaven's sake buy a new suit! Finally, you are not to do any of that 'must-tell-the-truth' bollocks you're rather prone to. If you tell PSD you lost your temper and went too far, we'll all end up in the shit!"

Day was almost in tears. "I can't thank you enough, ma'am. You're taking a…"

"Bugger off, Derek!" interrupted the Detective Superintendent.

He took the hint but, as he put his hand on the door handle, Halfpenny just had one more thing to say. "Oh, and Derek, if anybody ever did to my family what those two bastards did to yours – I'd slit their fucking throats!"

Chapter Twenty-nine

LATER

True to form, DI Trevor Allsop led Day's team through a week of interviews and cross-referencing with great skill.

Veronica Davison made a detailed, written confession about her involvement in the planned humiliation of her ex-husband but insisted that murder had never been the intention. She continued to express the view that the violent push by Gary Petersen that resulted in Carmichael's death had not been premeditated. DCI Day had been right from the first few moments of the investigation. Davison also helped the investigation enormously when she confirmed she had met Petersen and Janice Rhodes leaving the scene of Scott Grimshaw's murder at the approximate time of death. Her cooperation, and a good barrister, meant she wouldn't serve a custodial sentence.

Janice Rhodes was charged with the murders of Scott Grimshaw, Gary Petersen and Margaret Mallender but would never accept responsibility. First, she blamed her actions on threats from her ex-husband and later from younger brother, Preston who, she claimed, had made her his sex-slave. The judge didn't believe a word she said; it was yet another tragic story of a young woman's mind ruined in an abusive relationship.

Preston Driscoll vehemently denied his involvement in all the crimes until he discovered that his sister had tried to exonerate herself by claiming the whole series of events had been his idea. He explained the family history. Janice had put him to bed after a beating by Petersen and had then climbed in to comfort him. The close contact had been more than a fourteen-year-old boy could cope with and she had foolishly allowed his hands to wander. They had become illicit lovers and actually been happy until the day she told him she'd been raped by George Carmichael. He'd always suspected it had been more consensual than she claimed but he was still furious and agreed to help her achieve revenge. He denied being present when his sister murdered Gary Petersen but admitted helping with the burial. Everything except the kidnap had been her idea, he claimed. Young Preston would be decidedly middle-aged before he left prison.

Gordon Robinson (aka Gord) eventually admitted that he'd helped in the kidnap of Jessica and Alice Day because he'd been bullied by fellow doorman, Preston Driscoll – even though Preston was younger, smaller and slightly less of a twat. He wouldn't survive his prison sentence.

Mary Davenport also claimed there was never any intention to kill George Carmichael but she confessed to the murder of Margaret Mallender. She would never stand trial. Two days after her second major brain operation, she had a massive stroke and died a month later.

DCI Day decided he would not destroy the career of an exceptional young teacher and did not charge or caution Melanie Price. His lecture left her in no doubt what would happen if she crossed his path again. She returned to school and began a surprising relationship.

Somersgill Primary School did not reopen until September. Ms McAllister did an excellent job of Acting Headteacher for a term. The following year she married her long-term partner, Pauline Scanlan. Derek and Jessica Day attended the wedding.

Angie Carmichael gave birth to an astonishingly beautiful baby boy. Six months later she married her childhood sweetheart - after discovering he'd landed a really lucrative job.

The Professional Standards Investigation:
Senior PSD Officers interviewed DSupt Halfpenny and were critical of the haphazard nature of her plan. She stonewalled every line of enquiry, blaming lack of planning time for the problems that emerged.

Did she take responsibility for the injuries suffered by DS Sharp? Of course she did – but the brave young officer had volunteered after having the risks explained – and she was now making a good recovery. PSD concluded that Halfpenny's decisions had not fallen short of the Professional Standards required of senior police officers.

That left only one potential victim.

DCI Day was a detective who valued, above all, honesty. His facial muscles struggled to cope with the telling of lies. He would have lost his house, family and pension within thirty minutes of joining in any professional poker game.

Therefore, the interviews he was subjected to were fairly fraught even though the PSD Officers were relatively sensitive in response to the trauma suffered by Day's family.

They knew his reputation, of course. He was notorious for physical courage and fighting skills – qualities thought by some to be incompatible with twenty-first century policing.

After interviewing the complainants and seeing reports of their injuries, PSD did indeed conclude that DCI Day had been 'over-zealous'.

Day was prepared to accept the reprimand and the potential damage it would do to his career but Halfpenny was having none of it. She produced call logs that proved the time lag between Preston Driscoll's attack on DS Sharp and handcuffs being placed on both kidnappers was only 2 minutes 51 seconds – absolutely insufficient time for any officer, let alone a highly respected DCI, to be involved in premeditated revenge violence.

(What statistics Phil Johnstone couldn't amend with his computer weren't worth considering.)

Eventually, DCI Day would receive a 'no action' letter from PSD. The following day he received an email invitation to tea and biscuits from the Chief Constable. Day knew he had been exonerated when he was offered a second Hobnob.

-

DS Amanda Sharp didn't really understand what was happening in the days following the Stainsby incident because she was in and out of consciousness inside Chesterfield Royal Hospital.

In a rare lucid moment, she made the mistake of looking in a mirror. She was far more concerned about her hair than her concussion and numerous other injuries. As her condition steadily improved, she began to receive plenty of visitors, some more welcome than others. DCI Day came regularly and described how her actions had helped to save his family. Her head injury had left several gaps in her memory of the night of the kidnap but Day's recounts of the events gradually filled in the blanks - until she had clear recall of the makeshift plans they'd discussed with Detective Superintendent Halfpenny.

She was also interviewed extensively by officers from Derbyshire Police Professional Standards Department. They indicated that the two kidnappers had complained about their rough handling at the time of arrest. Unsurprisingly, Mandy didn't give a shit.

The heroine DS didn't tell any lies to PSD Officers.

Coincidentally, Sharp's memory of the actual events returned almost immediately the investigation was concluded. She didn't feel the need to call PSD and ask if she could revise her statements.

After two weeks Mandy was assured by her consultant that all her injuries would eventually heal and there was no reason she shouldn't eventually return to duty – if? It was a big 'if' – some police officers never returned to duty after life-threatening injuries.

DCI Day had brought flowers every day as he checked on his colleague's progress but, on the day before the planned discharge, it was Mrs Day who appeared.

"It hardly seems adequate, but I've come to say thank you for saving my daughter's life – and mine, of course," said Jess.

Mandy smiled, nodded and failed in her attempt not to look embarrassed. "How are you all?" she asked. "Girls recovering?"

"They're not too bad. Awkward questions and occasional nightmares. It'll take a while, but I'm sure they'll be fine, eventually."

There was an awkward silence.

"Your hair looks a bugger!" said Jess and both women laughed.

"Your husband says he's going to treat me to a session with the hairdresser of my choice as soon as I get out of here!"

"Make it an expensive one!" And they both laughed again.

The mood changed. "He won't talk about it. I know so little. Tell me what happened, Mandy."

The detective began her story with undue modesty. "Simple really. We were in the Rose and Crown having a celebration drink and I saw he'd had a phone call. It was obviously very bad news. I saw him speak to a few folks and then he left. When I saw the expression on his face, I just had to do something so I followed him and he drove back to the station. I tackled him and, at first, he told me to bugger off, but I can be pretty persistent and eventually he told me about your kidnap and the demand. I suggested impersonating the delightful Ms Rhodes and after twenty or thirty refusals, he agreed. So, I snipped off my lovely..."

"You love him, don't you?" interrupted Jess.

Mandy flinched and took a deep breath before she looked Jess in the eye and counted to ten. "Is it so obvious?" she whispered.

Jess looked down at her knees while she considered her response. There was an agony of silence. Suddenly, she raised her gaze to meet Mandy's. "You know I'll fight you every inch of the way for him, don't you?" There was no mistaking the ice in that statement.

Much to Jess' surprise, Mandy burst out laughing. It was clear that the laughter was painful so it was a full minute before Mandy regained her composure. "Mrs Jessica Day – you've no bloody idea, have you?" Mandy laughed again. "Oh, I know I'm just about equal to you in the good looks stakes – well, apart from the black eye, of course – but don't you realise your husband only sees you? Even if I wanted to, I couldn't come between the two of you. I'm one of his detectives, a team member. Oh, he knows I'm good at my job but, to be honest, I'm not sure he's even noticed I'm a woman! I hope he sees me as a friend but there's no contest here; he belongs to you, simple as that."

Realisation dawned slowly. Of course it was true. Jess nodded and a tear ran down her cheek. "That must be agony for you. How long?"

"Pretty much since the day I first met him."

"How can you bear it?"

"It's life. Sometimes it's hard. We just have to get on with it. One day I'll be a happily unmarried Detective Superintendent. That's my future; you can't win 'em all!" The half-smile said as much as the words.

Jess placed her hand on Mandy's wrist. "You're a good person. He's lucky to have you protecting his back."

Horror crossed Mandy's face. "Don't tell him what I've said; I'd die!"

Jess forced a painful grin and put a finger to her lips.

To cover her embarrassment, Mandy laughed again. "Do you know, I'm quite relieved to have been able to tell someone; I actually feel a bit better. But, hey, if you ever kick him out, all bets are off!"

Jess smiled and stood up. She stretched over the bed and kissed Mandy next to her rapidly fading black eye. As she turned to leave the ward, she said to herself, "Not gonna happen."

-

The identity of the mysterious fourth woman had been the sole topic of conversation in Somersgill over the summer months; everyone had a theory.

Only one man thought he really knew the truth. The fourth woman might just have been Josephine Riley. Miss Riley had been a teacher at Somersgill Primary for 37 years. One day in 1956, she had gone to the staffroom complaining of feeling unwell. Colleagues had found her twenty minutes later seated bolt upright in her favourite chair with a wry smile on her face - quite dead. The verdict had been natural causes – the old lady had worked herself to death. To this day, Pete Barker occasionally thought he saw her wandering around school when he was locking up after dark.

The Caretaker shared his theory with DCI Day - but no arrests were made.

By this time, Day was too busy. A young soldier, recently returned from duty in Afghanistan, had been found dead in Chesterfield - and his comrade was missing.
Several groups were claiming responsibility and the town was soon full of teams of investigators and journalists. These newcomers thought Day would be out of his depth – but they were all wrong.

Our Detective Chief Inspector was soon to be embroiled in the case of 'Two Dead Heroes'.

The End

If you can't wait for 'Two Dead Heroes' (2020) you could try reading the 'TREBIAN TRILOGY' written by Ian a couple of years ago – under the name George Ian Stuart.
'Trool's Rules', 'Cruel Trool' and 'Trool's Fools' are comedy thrillers about the end of the World!
So, if you like stories about the human struggle to survive against all the odds - and eccentric aliens who are trying to help them (with very mixed results), this trilogy might be for you.
Sorry – strictly adults only. (Contains violence, sex and laughter – sometimes even on the same page.)

Lightning Source UK Ltd.
Milton Keynes UK
UKHW010740051021
391704UK00004B/559